A YOUNG ADULT FANTASY

SEVENTH DIMENSION
BOOK 5

THE
PRESCIENCE

LORILYN ROBERTS

A YOUNG ADULT FANTASY

SEVENTH DIMENSION
BOOK 5

THE PRESCIENCE

LORILYN ROBERTS

To Sylvia
a dear friend and soul sister

"Time is an illusion until God's appointed time."

— LORILYN ROBERTS

INTRODUCTION

A spiritual kingdom lies all about us, enclosing us, embracing us, altogether within reach of our inner selves, waiting for us to recognize it. God Himself is here waiting our response to His Presence. This eternal world will come alive to us the moment we begin to reckon upon its reality.

— A. W. TOZER, *THE PURSUIT OF GOD*

The Seventh Dimension
Multi-Award-Winning Series continues in
The Prescience
A Young Adult Fantasy
Book 5

Seventh Dimension – The Prescience, A Young Adult Fantasy, is the fifth book in the *Seventh Dimension Series* that combines contemporary, historical, and fantasy elements into a Christian "coming-of-age" story.

When bombs fall on Jerusalem, Shale and Daniel rescue an orphan and return to the first century. Amid supernatural tribulation, they attempt to unravel the mysterious disappearance of Daniel's father and the goal of the New World Order. When multiple realities collide, God reveals once again time is an illusion until the appointed times.

CHAPTER 1

A LOUD EXPLOSION shook the ground as dust blew in my face.

"Run!" Daniel shouted.

Blinding light lit up the night sky. If only these were celebratory fireworks, but they weren't.

I stared. My feet felt as if they were entombed in concrete. This couldn't be happening—not now.

Daniel pulled on my hand. Seconds ticked away as I imagined my body being blown to bits. Sirens faded in and out as swishing knives cut through the air. Distant rumbles and alarms sounded as transformers blew across the city. I felt something burning and slapped my arm.

"Ashes," Daniel exclaimed.

I wiped off the soot. How could this be? My ears rang from the constant dinning. Were those people I saw in the distance? They looked more like zombies.

I couldn't believe what was happening. One minute we were celebrating our first kiss, and the next we were running for our lives. I brushed back my dark brown hair with my fingers as another missile whizzed by and the grass sizzled underneath our feet. Minutes later, Daniel found an enclosure that reminded me of a bus stop.

I struggled to catch my breath. "We're going to die."

Daniel reassured me. "We're in a bomb shelter."

For the uninitiated, I never dreamed I would need one. We didn't have such things in America.

"You're shaking," Daniel said. He wrapped his arms around my waist. I didn't want to think I'd taken my last breath. A thousand thoughts replaced that one. Was my mother still alive? When I returned from time traveling to the first century four years earlier, I never told her where I went. She would've taken me to that psychologist who wrote that report, and the wretched principal would have expelled me.

Why couldn't this attack have waited a few days? Jesus told us to marry, but we had just returned to Jerusalem.

Daniel whispered in my ear, "I love you, Shale."

I broke into sobs as a dog barked. I touched Daniel's shoulder. "Did you hear it?"

Unperturbed by my unusual gift—after all he had his own—Daniel's eyes met mine. "What did he say?"

Now the sirens drowned him out. I stepped toward the shelter entrance, but Daniel blocked me.

"I'm not going to let you rescue that dog."

"The dog needs help for an injured child."

Daniel stared. "No, can't be."

"We must go." I said.

Daniel shook his head. "You stay here and let me check."

"You don't understand dog talk. I must go."

Daniel hesitated. "Let's hope he keeps barking. Watch your step for landmines."

Light flickered from fires burning in the distance, and shadowy embers floated down on us.

The dog barked again.

"What is he saying?" Daniel asked.

I interpreted, "Hurry."

Straight ahead, a four-legged creature stood in the shadows. He reminded me of my dog friend, Much-Afraid, who guided me back in time. This black and white furry animal appeared to be part Border Collie, and he wagged his tail as we approached.

Another bomb screeched by, and the boom nearly broke my eardrums. The dog backed up a few steps and lowered his head. Two bodies lay on the ground, and a small child was stroking a woman.

"Mommy."

I knelt beside the child. "Thank God, she's alive."

"Her mother and father aren't," the dog said. "She has no one. God sent me to find a rescuer."

My vocal cords went dry as numbness filled my throat.

"I must go rescue others. Take care of Shira," the dog said.

"Wait." I reached over and touched the dog's head, focusing on his crusty eyes. "What do you mean?"

"You are the ones God called."

"I understand animal speak, but I don't know this poor child. What was her name again?"

"Shira," the dog replied.

I tried to pick the child up, but she clung to her dead mother.

"Others need my help," the dog said, and he took off into the darkness.

Daniel walked around the bodies and searched the pockets of her father. "We need to find relatives."

He shook his head. "Nothing, not even a cellphone, and I don't see a purse."

"Her name is Shira," I whispered.

I stroked the child's back and spoke in my best Hebrew. "Sweetie, come with me. Your mother and father are sleeping."

The child turned and focused her scared eyes on mine. I tried once more to pick her up, and this time she let me. She was small and light —and couldn't be more than three.

"Let's get out of here," Daniel said.

"Where should we go?"

"Jacob's. He can help us find her relatives."

When should I tell Daniel she didn't have any living relatives?

CHAPTER 2

S OON NUMBNESS CREPT up my arms. Even though Shira was light, I wasn't used to carrying a small child.

Daniel offered to take her, but she clung to me.

We walked past shards of glass and exploded fragments on the ground. The inferno was growing, and too many dead people lay on the ground. I couldn't keep up with Daniel. "How much farther?"

He adjusted our backpacks he'd slung over his shoulders. "Not much."

I sighed.

The missiles had stopped, but smoke burned my eyes. Sheets of flame were still visible in the distance.

Daniel pulled out his iPhone. "Let me see if I can reach my brother."

I started to call my mother, but my cell hadn't worked since I left America. How long would the EMP attack in the United States keep communications down in the West?

I leaned against a stone pillar beside the road littered with debris and switched Shira to my other side. Jumping from one thought to another, I couldn't focus. Even though I knew time was an illusion, how long had we been gone? Could it be more than a few weeks?

Daniel interrupted my musings. "I can't call or text."

"Did the camera work?"

"Yes, I took a photo of her parents. That should help us to locate relatives," Daniel said.

I sat on a nearby bench and ran my fingers through Shira's curly, brown hair. Besides the soot on her angelic face and the singed edge of her light-colored jumper, she was untouched.

"How old do you think she is?" Daniel asked.

The little girl held up three fingers.

Daniel cocked his head. "I spoke in English. She understands English."

"Don't Israelis understand English?"

"Not that young. Kids learn English in elementary school. Her parents might be American or British."

"She understands Hebrew also," I added.

"God must have sent us—or you to rescue her. What else did the dog tell you?"

Shira's eyes were closed, but I knew she wasn't asleep. "Shhh. I'll tell you later. Let's get to Jacob's first."

As Daniel led us through Jerusalem, I shielded my eyes. The few who were alive wandered. Frozen cars sat motionless on the roads.

"Why, God?" I asked in my heart. I remembered what Jesus said when he lamented over Zion. "Jerusalem, Jerusalem, you who kill the prophets and stone those sent to you, how often I have longed to gather your children together, as a hen gathers her chicks under her wings, and you were not willing."

The nearly full moon rose higher in the sky as we approached the Old City. Intermittent flames offered a reprieve from the darkness. Despite the damage, the ancient bulwark was a stark reminder Jerusalem would survive because God willed it.

A wedding now seemed farfetched. I sighed. Shira must have fallen asleep because she felt like a bulky package in my arms.

"Daniel, can you carry her?"

I handed her to him, and the words of the dog haunted me. How could I broach what the animal said with Daniel?

I moved in closer. "I didn't want to say this when Shira was awake, but the dog told me she has no other family."

Daniel slowed down. "She must have somebody. We could do a DNA test."

I didn't think of that. "Yes, we could. I'm telling you what the dog said. He also said God chose us to take care of her. For how long, I don't know."

"She's so young."

I could sense his concern—how could we provide for the needs of a three-year-old? We had just turned eighteen and weren't married. What did we know about parenting a child barely out of diapers?

More smoke blew in my face, and another round of sirens pierced the silence. I wanted to pretend I was asleep and wake up to a different reality. "Do you remember how to get to the underground bunker?"

"Yes. However, will we be able to get through at this time of night?"

Stores closed hours earlier. We passed the Old City Jaffa Gate and the Muslim and Armenian quarters, and I followed Daniel down the stairs.

The Old City was spared during the attack although much cleanup remained. Endless steps and dark corridors brought us to the bunker door. No one could imagine behind the steel barrier was a secret command center and stargate to the seventh dimension.

Two watchmen stood at attention. I wasn't sure if that was good or bad, but at least somebody was here. Shira woke up, and Daniel passed her to me.

The guards, dressed in Israeli fatigues, held menacing guns and blocked us from entering. Daniel spoke in Hebrew. "I'm looking for my brother, Jacob Sperling."

CHAPTER 3

"SHIRA, GO BACK to sleep," I whispered. "Jesus is here."
What danger could we pose with a small child? The guards eyed Shira and lowered their guns.

Daniel and the uniformed men conversed in Hebrew. Because they spoke with heavy accents, I wasn't sharp enough to catch most of it. My year and a half of Hebrew earned me an "A" but didn't make me conversant with Israelis.

The taller man motioned for us to follow. He punched a code into the keypad of the heavy steel door, and after a few seconds, the door opened.

The ominous shadows that flickered over the walls from the emergency lighting felt cold and calculating—walls that were an illusion. I expected bright floodlights to illuminate the vestibule and to see the command center humming with computers connected to cameras in strategic locations around Jerusalem, but no one was here.

The uniformed officer pushed open a hidden door on the opposite side. As we entered, a cool breeze poured in, probably from an air conditioning vent. The guard said nothing, and I found the silence unnerving.

We passed through a narrow hallway, and my anxiety increased. I'd never remember how to get back to the front if something went wrong. I reached for Daniel's arm. He shot me a reassuring glance.

The guard flipped a light switch as we entered an unmarked door. "Jacob will be here shortly," he said and left.

I tried to relax.

"The guards are all business," Daniel said. "They have their orders. Even when they know we're one of them, they won't deviate."

I held Shira close to me. "What did the guard say? You talked so fast."

"When you told Shira Jesus was here, their demeanor changed. Up until then, I don't think they believed I was Jacob's brother. They thought we were spies."

"Oh." I glanced around the room. A black leather sofa filled up one wall with matching chairs on each side. Three photographs above the sofa highlighted historical Jewish landmarks—the Temple Mount, Masada, and a third location I didn't recognize. I pointed to it. "Where is that?"

Daniel eased closer to the photo. "That's Petra, in Jordan, also known as Bozrah in the book of Isaiah." I edged over to see.

Off to the side of the room was a small kitchenette and bathroom. A well-used tea kettle sat on the kitchen counter. White plastic cups and an assortment of herbal teas filled a straw container. A square refrigerator took up the rest of the counter space.

We both noticed the open Bible on the coffee table, and Daniel picked it up. "Someone underlined Ezekiel 38:14-16: 'On that day when my people Israel dwell safely, will you not know it? Then you will come from your place out of the far north, you and many peoples with you, all of them riding on horses, a great company and a mighty army. You will come up against my people Israel like a cloud to cover the land. It will be in the latter days that I will bring you against my land, so that the nations may know me when I am hallowed in you, O Gog, before their eyes.'"

I let the words sink in. "This must be a prayer room."

I stepped back from the table and sat on the sofa. Shira readjusted herself in my lap, clutching my shirt. "Whoever was in here must have believed Israel was facing the Ezekiel 38-39 war."

Daniel sat beside me.

I glanced at the closed door. "Are you sure your brother is coming?"

"I hope." Daniel leaned back and nodded off.

Suddenly, a crazy thought swirled in my head. "Daniel, what if we went back to the seventh dimension?"

He opened his eyes. "Back from where we came?"

"No, not Shambhala. The seventh dimension, where we met, in the first century."

Daniel shook his head. "Why would you want to go back in time?"

"Well, it would be safer than here. We could get married in front of our friends in the seventh dimension, and it would give us time to figure out what's going on. We're trapped. I can't go back to America. You don't want to return to your family." I added quickly, "Your mother doesn't need to be burdened with us, especially with Shira."

My words hung in the air. I wasn't even sure I wanted to do what I was proposing.

Daniel ran his fingers through his hair and stared at the ceiling. "How does that help me to find my father, or to be a witness in the last days as one of the one hundred forty-four thousand Jewish evangelists?"

I tapped my finger. "It's the spiritual dimension where we met Jesus. Since we're facing spiritual questions, maybe we should return there to find answers."

Daniel leaned forward. "I don't know. God sent you to the seventh dimension, but I think the evil one sent me there. However, I'd sure like to know who Nidal is."

Before he could finish, the door opened. I remembered the first time I met Jacob in the first century. He was sweeping the floor at the inn.

Daniel stood, and the two brothers embraced. I understood just enough Hebrew to hear Daniel explain to his brother about our trip to Nepal and what he discovered about their father.

After a few minutes, Jacob held up a square black bag in one hand and pointed at me with the other. "Do you need any first-aid? I brought some emergency supplies."

I ran my eyes over Shira's small body, relieved that I didn't see anything needing attention. "No, but I could use a towel to wash off the soot and dirt."

No sooner did I speak than Jacob produced one from the kitchen. He even took the time to soak it with warm water.

As I wiped her down with the warm cloth, Daniel explained to Jacob her story and showed him the photograph.

Jacob shook his head. "I don't know her parents. Thousands have died in this latest attack. It would be difficult to find any living relatives in this chaos—most likely the Gog-Magog War."

He leaned back. Lines covered his forehead, and his sunken eyes were less brilliant than a few weeks earlier, but he was as mentally sharp as ever.

"Ezekiel says it will take seven months to bury the dead," Jacob said. "Who knows how many have died. A lot has happened. The Antichrist will soon rise to power."

"Antichrist?" I repeated.

"I know who it is," Jacob said. "However, the world doesn't, not yet."

Could he see into the future? My curiosity was piqued. "Who is he?"

"You wouldn't recognize his name."

I bit my nail. "What do mean?"

"If he's who I think he is, he's supernatural or close to being supernatural. Like the Nephilim, in a way, but…"

"But what?" I asked.

"You know who the Nephilim were?"

I nodded. "The fallen angels came down to earth and took women as wives. Their godless offspring were known as the Nephilim. They were half human and half demonic."

"That correct," Jacob said. "The Bible says Nimrod became a great one, a Nephilim, and built the Tower of Babel, leading the first rebellion against God. Suppose scientists excavated his tomb and extracted DNA from it?"

That sounded far-fetched. "Scientists discovered Nimrod's tomb?" I asked.

"In Iraq in 2003, during the Gulf War."

Questions popped into my head.

Jacob explained. "Suppose scientists mixed the DNAs? You could create a race of Nephilim or supernatural beings. Remember what Jesus said? As it was in the days of Noah, so shall it be in the days of the Son of Man."

"Do you think he was referring to the Nephilim?" Daniel asked.

Jacob shrugged. "There is nothing to indicate he wasn't. In the beginning, the earth dwellers won't recognize this world leader as evil. Perhaps he's human and then his DNA changes for some reason. Those who would know him to be the Antichrist when it's clearer will probably no longer be here, just as I may not be here when you return."

How many of those underlings did we witness in Shambhala? All those tortured souls in Hades—I could never forget their faces.

As Daniel and Jacob talked, my mind wandered. I longed to see my mother and my best friend, Rachel. "Can we call the United States?"

"Not easily," Jacob said. "The EMP wiped out U.S. communications. Iran was further along in their missile testing than anyone realized. U.S. efforts have focused on rebuilding the military infrastructure. I imagine it will be several weeks to months before the government restores private communications."

My heart sunk. "That's a long time."

"Is the stargate working?" Daniel asked.

Jacob nodded. "Why?"

"What if we went back to the first century? I could talk to Nidal. He must know something."

"Your best source of information is recovering from his injuries," Jacob said.

"Who is Nidal?" I asked.

"Daniel saved his life," Jacob said. "He's from this time, sent to the first century probably by the Illuminati."

Daniel asked his brother, "What do you think we should do?"

"Go where God leads you since time is short. Some things can only be understood spiritually, so prayer is essential."

Daniel glanced at me. "Maybe Shale is right. We don't have many options here, and once Nidal leaves the inn, we may never find him again."

"Do you want to pray?" Jacob asked.

"Yes, let's pray," Daniel said.

We bowed our heads and joined hands as Daniel prayed first. "Dear heavenly Father, help us to discern your will. Please give us wisdom and make it clear what we should do."

Jacob followed with prayer, and I prayed last. "Dear Jesus, please show us what you want us to do with Shira."

Jacob finished with words to a familiar song, "They Will Know We Are Christians by Our Love."

Once our voices stopped, a brief silence followed. Daniel turned to me. "Any thoughts?"

I bit my lip. "I'm trusting you. It's a big decision."

Daniel nodded.

"You're fortunate you were able to rescue Nidal," Jacob said. "This might be your only opportunity to speak with him."

Daniel steepled his fingers. "We can return here as soon as we talk to him. The more I think about it, the more I want to know what he knows. I think this is what God wants us to do."

CHAPTER 4

I PATTED SHIRA on the back. "We must take her."

Jacob nodded. "I need to tell you that time travel is more dangerous now than before."

"Why is that?" I asked.

"The separation between the physical and spiritual worlds is breaking down as Satan and his minions gain more power in the latter days."

Daniel leaned forward. "Did you send me to the seventh dimension the first time?"

Jacob shook his head. "You were transported back in time from Hurva Square—the synagogue. I believe the Illuminati sent you to get Shale's scrolls. That's why they sent Nidal—he was the backup plan if they were unable to get them through you.

"Remember, they want to establish a one-world government that controls every aspect of people's lives. To make that happen, they must take away people's freedom and destroy all references to Yeshua in historical antiquities and literature."

Jacob waved his hand dismissively. "Occult power is limited. Even if the New World Order burns every Bible, beheads every Christian, and takes over every country, they can't succeed."

"Amen," I said.

Jacob pointed his finger at his brother. "You were never meant to enter the seventh dimension at the inn. That's where God's portal connects. God intercepted their stargate. You don't remember anything unusual before you arrived?"

Daniel closed his eyes. "No, but I do remember I received a cut on my forehead that I couldn't explain. Doctor Luke treated it."

Jacob stroked his chin. "I'm certain God intercepted the CERN stargate. Otherwise, scientists would have transported you to the gates of hell."

Surprise crossed Daniel's face. "What?"

"During the time of Jesus, the gates of hell were at the base of Mount Hermon in Caesarea Philippi. Now it's known as the Golan Heights."

Daniel and I sat in silence. What else did Jacob know that we didn't know?

"Are you familiar with Freemasonry?" Jacob asked.

Daniel rubbed his tired eyes. "Not that much."

Jacob tilted his head. "The location of the stargate is at 33 degrees latitude and 35 degrees longitude."

"What does that have to do with everything else?" Daniel asked.

I remembered what my mother said about my father being a Freemason. "Thirty-three is an important number for Freemasons in their initiation rites."

Before the thought escaped me, I added. "I remember my father suggested the Illuminati sent Daniel back in time to retrieve my scrolls. I'd almost forgotten about that because when he said it, I didn't believe him."

Jacob reassured Daniel. "God diverted you to the inn. I truly believe that."

"What is your gift?" I asked Jacob.

"I know things I have no way of knowing." He turned his eyes toward Daniel. "How do you think your room was paid for when you arrived at the inn the first time?"

"I thought the ventriloquist paid for it," Daniel said.

Jacob shook his head. "It's like us to interpret evil for good. Satan gives us enough of the truth or a strand of goodness that we believe we can trust his emissaries."

Daniel's eyes fell. "I figured it out eventually, but not without regret."

"It took a while for you to believe. The ventriloquist tried to thwart God's plans. The prayers of the saints protected you."

"Jacob," I said, "your prayers bear much fruit. Please pray for my mother. I miss her so much." Tears filled my eyes. "I don't think she's a believer."

Jacob's face softened. "This little one is safe because of you. Keep your thoughts on God's miracles."

I sighed. I needed to remember that.

"When you arrive at the inn, two rooms will be available," Jacob said. "Get as much information from Nidal as you can. We need names, like who sent him back in time? Ask him about Tariq. I don't think he's Nidal's brother as the Illuminati wants us to believe. Of course, the New World Order will eventually send someone to the first century to bring both men back. When they learn you're there, they may come after you, too."

"Have you been to the inn recently?" I asked.

"Things have been too unsettled here. It's about the oil. Always has been."

"How do you know?" I asked.

"The four horsemen of the apocalypse indicate it. The black horse represents oil. Yes, we know it also stands for famine in this instance, but I believe it's also about oil. Russia and Turkey wanted to run a pipeline through Syria. Isn't it amazing how they mended their broken friendship so they could collaborate?"

"The war of Gog and Magog," Daniel said.

Jacob nodded. "I think so. The tribulation is coming. Some wonder why the rapture hasn't happened, but I believe God has pushed the pause button."

"Why?" I asked.

"He's allowing more Jews and Muslims to come to faith in Yeshua. Muslims are having dreams and visions."

Silence filled the air as heaviness weighed on me. I wanted Jesus to come back now.

Jacob's reassuring voice helped me to refocus. "Remember, the seventh dimension is a spiritual world. We need God's power to counter demonic forces. We're dealing with people who have occult knowledge and will stop at nothing. They'll win for a while, but we know who ultimately wins."

With that warning, Jacob stood. We left the small prayer room and followed Jacob through a long, dark corridor to the stargate hidden in the complex.

CHAPTER 5

WHEN WE ARRIVED, a night sentry stood at the door, and Jacob cleared us through security. Computer equipment hummed in the background as a hologram bathed the inside of the cave. Luminous rocks covered the sides of the opening.

"How many people have come through here?" Daniel asked.

"Since we learned about this stargate—thousands, including many of the one hundred forty-four thousand Jewish evangelists. We've sent people all over the world."

Jacob slid a wall back that revealed a bank of computers. He turned up the hologram power as he spoke. "The scientists at CERN have been opening stargates in strategic locations that are portals to other dimensions. Every time they open a new one, they release antimatter, also known as dark matter, into our physical world. Whatever Nidal tells you could be important."

Jacob focused on his brother. "Because you saved his life, I think he'll talk. I don't know how many secrets he knows. Nidal may be a pawn in a bigger chess match, but he came through their gateway, so he must have contacts."

I remembered when Much-Afraid came to me at the King David

Hotel before Jacob transported her back to America. "How much time has passed since we were last here?"

"About a month," Jacob said, "but it probably seems longer. Not long enough to fix the power grid in North America."

Jacob took two wooden chairs from a side closet and placed them inside the cave opening. "Are you ready?"

"I think so," I replied, although I couldn't believe I was doing this again—three and a half years later.

He pointed to the chair, and Shira sat in my lap with Daniel beside us. The light bathed us in blues, greens, and yellows, and Shira raised her hand as if to touch it. She had no fear.

"I'll stop by the inn once the crisis here is over," Jacob said. "Godspeed."

Soothing music filled the cave and the heavens as we journeyed into the seventh dimension—but all that serenity evaporated when a voice shouted, "They're mine."

CHAPTER 6

I HELD SHIRA tightly and swallowed my fear so as not to alarm her. Soupy nothingness surrounded us, and the voices mimicked the sounds of Shambhala. I knew a chasm separated us, but it was too close.

Seconds later, a shofar blew, followed by blinding white light. As my eyes adjusted, I made out the images of dazzling angels wielding flaming swords.

God's warring messengers were battling creatures wearing black cloaks and holding scimitars. The eyes of the darkened ones seethed. Even if we died between the worlds of good and evil, we belonged to the King.

A sinister voice spoke to my mind. "You won't escape this time."

I prayed for God to strengthen his warriors, and I watched as they cut through the blackness with flaming swords. The fallen angels fought back, brandishing terrifying weapons no less potent than those of God's army.

I covered Shira's eyes and caught glimpses of Daniel through the shafts of scattered light. Fire dripped from their weapons as lightning flashed across the heavens.

The battle seemed unwinnable. God's holy army, however, would never give up.

Faintly, I heard singing in the celestial sphere.

"Angels," Shira said.

The praises increased, strengthening God's mighty ones. The fighting intensified, and I covered Shira's eyes. I heard the voice I heard in the beginning. "They're mine."

I remembered to whom I belonged. The angels of light fought valiantly. I knew the good angels and the underlings would battle to the death—if it were possible for them to die.

Tears came to my eyes. Every quarrel on earth had its counterpart in the heavens. The divine lights sang with such conviction and power the strength of the fallen ones couldn't last. Some fled behind a veil. Others slunk away in humiliation. There was no choice in the matter— the fallen ones could never win. Everyone must submit to the risen King, even the smallest peon in Hades.

Once the darkness fled, Yeshua's light filled every corner of the expanding universe. A good angel laid his hands on Shira. Her soiled clothes turned into first-century garments, and even our twenty-first-century backpacks were now first century bags. Who was I to think I came up with this idea? God went before us, and soon we arrived at Jacob's Inn.

CHAPTER 7

WE MATERIALIZED UNNOTICED, and memories from the first century returned in dynamic vividness. I didn't feel like I was four years older. I recognized a couple of Dr. Luke's patients lying on mats. Chirping birds reminded me of Worldly Crow who I thought was my feathered friend—until he betrayed me.

Travelers filled the dusty streets. A food cart under some fig trees drew hungry visitors, and the happy voices of children playing nearby caught my attention.

I examined my beige toga and eyed Daniel. "You have a beard."

"I do?" He ran his fingers across his chin.

"We were either gone for a few days, or you grow a beard fast."

Daniel laughed. "I can't grow one that fast."

I reflected. "The last time I came, by way of the garden, I bought something to wear. That's how I met your sister, Martha."

"I remember that," Daniel said. He focused on Shira. "She looks like a different child."

The transformation was remarkable. Shira scooted off my lap and twirled, stroking her white tunic with her hand. Then she pointed to her new sandals, but her new-found joy suddenly evaporated. She frowned. "Mommy."

I squatted in front of her. "Your mommy is in heaven—" I pointed to the sky "—with Jesus."

She looked up, and after a brief hesitation, a smile crossed her lips. "Angels told me they would take care of Mommy."

Daniel's and my eyes met. At her age, how would she even know about angels? I smiled. "She told me she heard angels singing."

"Nothing surprises me anymore," Daniel said.

A voice shouted Daniel's name.

We peered through the shaded doorway. As the man entered the sunlight, he vaguely looked familiar.

Daniel opened his arms. "Ami."

As he approached, an older man with a cane followed. Daniel and the two men spoke excitedly as their eyes focused on Shira and me. I sighed—too much explaining to do.

Daniel introduced me. "Shale, this is Ami and his brother, Levi. And this is my betrothed, Shale, and Shira. She is staying with us for a while."

The men did a slight bow.

"Ami and Levi were good friends when I stayed here before."

I smiled. "Glad to meet you."

An awkward moment followed. Did I miss an important protocol? Or maybe I was just nervous.

Daniel's gentle eyes reassured me. "Let's check in and see what we can find out."

Levi waved his cane. "Come visit us when you're settled. Much has happened in Jerusalem that I want to discuss with you."

Shira tugged at my tunic. I could tell she wanted to explore. I didn't want her to walk around alone, especially here, and I needed to hear what they discussed.

What should Shira call me? Perhaps Auntie would be good since the dog said she didn't have other relatives. "Sweetie, you need to stay with Auntie. We'll go for a walk in a few minutes."

Shira frowned impatiently, venturing to the edge of the porch, obviously disappointed. Children's voices tempted her.

"So what's happened while I've been away?" Daniel asked.

"Oh, many things," Ami replied. "You know about the crucifixion of Yeshua?"

Daniel nodded.

Levi leaned on his cane and whispered. "Somebody stole his body from the tomb. The Roman soldiers have been ruthlessly scouring the countryside looking for him. Hundreds of graves have been dug up. They've questioned his followers, hounded people for clues, and interrogated dozens. Whoever stole the rabbi's body left his clothes in the tomb. Doesn't that seem strange, that they would steal a naked dead body? How unclean is that? A Jew would never do that. I don't even think a Roman would do that."

Ami sighed. "I hoped Yeshua was the long-awaited Messiah."

"Maybe he was the Messiah," Daniel said.

Ami shook his head. "He saved so many others, why couldn't he save himself? I did hear he appeared to five hundred people in Galilee a week ago."

Daniel pointed at himself. "I saw him."

Ami's eyes lit up. "You saw the resurrected Yeshua?"

Daniel nodded.

Renewed hope appeared on Ami's face. "We must talk more."

"Yes," Daniel said. "I have much I want to share with you."

Shira stared longingly at the small group of kids a short distance from the porch. I walked over and whispered to her. "You can go and sit with the children, but I'll be watching you."

Her eyes danced as she ran over to two boys and two girls playing with small pebbles in the grass. One of the girls scooted over to make room. The young girl was a little older than Shira, but none of the children were more than five or six. I turned my focus back to Daniel and his friends.

"The Romans are everywhere," Levi cautioned. "A sense of uneasiness has everyone on edge. The Romans are looking for someone to hold accountable for the debacle."

Levi quipped. "The soldiers got drunk and fell asleep guarding a dead man's tomb. How could someone steal his body? Even moving the stone would have taken superhuman strength."

"Unless he did rise from the dead," Ami countered. "Remember, five hundred people saw him alive. Those are ordinary people, too. Not just his disciples."

Levi spit on the ground. "It's all rumors. Only rumors."

"Five hundred people, Levi. That's a lot of people."

The men went back and forth debating what happened. I noticed an old woman wearing a green dress approaching the circle of children. The hag was almost bald with sunken cheeks and a curved back causing her to be bent forward at the waist. She held black flowers in one hand with a brown bag draped over her shoulder.

When was the last time she ate? I imagined her offering flowers to anyone who pitied her for a few scraps of food or a small coin.

I turned my attention back to the men.

Ami crossed his arms with an air of authority. "I've heard rumors of something happening in Jerusalem during Shavuot. The disciples have been hiding in someone's home. What will become of us, Daniel? Even Doctor Luke has been nervous."

Suddenly Daniel took off, shouting at the top of his voice. "Shira!"

"My God," I screamed.

CHAPTER 8

T HE OLD WOMAN in the green dress was scurrying off, pulling Shira behind her. Daniel reached the would-be kidnapper in seconds and snatched Shira away. Then he punched the wicked crone, and she fell to the ground.

"Get out of here," he shouted.

I'd never seen Daniel show violence toward anyone. Who was this mischievous panhandler? Immediately Roman guards appeared and surrounded us. The old woman lay in a heap.

Daniel handed Shira to me as the guards closed in. Rubberneckers were gathering.

"Call Doctor Luke," someone shouted.

A couple of men ran into Jacob's Inn. No sooner was the request uttered than the shyster sprang to her feet.

One of the guards asked her, "Are you all right, ma'am?"

She picked up her bag, leaving the flowers on the ground. I was surprised they wilted so quickly. How could that be? And when had I ever seen black flowers?

She pointed at Daniel. "You need to arrest that young man. He could have killed me."

Where had I heard that voice?

Bulging eyes and wispy strands of hair made her repulsively ugly, but why would Daniel slug her after he had Shira?

"Do you have anyone who can take you home?" the guard asked.

She shook her head. "I'm alone. I must go." She turned her back on the gathering.

Why did her voice sound familiar? I'd never seen the decrepit woman before, but thank God Shira was safe.

Dr. Luke dashed out of the inn as the guards dragged over the chains to arrest Daniel. The doctor hesitated, and for an instant, I thought he might follow the strange beggar.

Suddenly, one of the guards shouted, "Leper!"

The Roman soldier bolted to his horse, and then the other guard did the same. Within seconds, they fled. Fear silenced the onlookers. No one moved except to back away from Daniel.

I remembered he'd mentioned working at the leper colony. He held up his hands. "I don't have leprosy."

I stared at his hands and didn't see anything unusual—not that I would know what leprosy looked like anyway, but fear filled my heart to see Daniel behave so erratically. "Why did you strike the old woman?"

"The ventriloquist," he uttered.

Then I remembered the recording on Daniel's iPhone. How could I forget that voice? Queasiness flooded my stomach, and I collapsed on the ground.

Dr. Luke ran over to me. "Stay still."

Daniel started to rush over, but Dr. Luke held up his hand.

I did my best to hold back tears. How could so much go wrong so quickly?

Dr. Luke spoke to a friend. "Abbey, can you take care of Shira while I help Shale?"

Abbey took Shira from me, and Dr. Luke helped me to relax and gave me some water.

After a few minutes, I felt better.

"You need food," Dr. Luke said, "and a good night's rest."

I thanked him. "I'm feeling better already."

The doctor turned his attention to Daniel.

Again, my betrothed held up his hands. "I don't have leprosy. The guards were mistaken."

Dr. Luke examined Daniel's extremities. Several anxious seconds passed. "You're right. I don't see any leprosy on you."

I took a deep breath. Could I believe the doctor? "Daniel, can I see?"

He walked over and spread out his hands. I checked them, but I didn't know what to look for. "What should I see if someone has leprosy?"

"You would see skin sores, like pale-colored lumps," Dr. Luke said.

Did God make it appear as if Daniel had leprosy to the Roman soldiers to keep him from being captured? I would never let Shira get more than two feet from me again.

Daniel and Dr. Luke began to talk about other things, and I stood and walked over to Abbey. "Thank you. I feel much better."

The young woman took my hand in hers. "Any time you need me, I live over there. Our daughters are friends now."

Shira was sitting happily beside her child.

Abbey whispered, "I hope that woman doesn't come around again."

I nodded. I took Shira by the hand and returned to Daniel. He wrapped his arm around my waist, squeezing me tightly.

Dr. Luke reassured us. "Shale, strange things have happened in Jerusalem recently, but God is in control. Keep your faith. I sensed an evil spirit in that woman. I hope she doesn't come back."

I nodded.

Dr. Luke gestured with his hand. "I see no leprosy on Daniel."

I brushed my hair back from my eyes to check Daniel's hand and face one more time. The doctor's calm demeanor and kind eyes reassured me. "Thank you, Doctor Luke."

His announcement relieved the borderline panic of the rubberneckers, and the crowd began to disperse. I glanced up the empty road where the ventriloquist disappeared. Good riddance.

CHAPTER 9

W E FOLLOWED DR. LUKE into Jacob's Inn. A large lobby that doubled as a dining hall extended to the right of the check-in counter. The guest rooms were behind the restaurant down an adjoining hallway.

In the dining room, freshly cut flowers decorated the wooden tables. The stone pavement was spotless. Memories of Daniel's brother, Jacob, sweeping the floor returned. I didn't know who he was back then.

"Do you have a room?" Dr. Luke asked.

Daniel nodded. "We should."

"If you have any problems, come get me." Dr. Luke leaned into Daniel. "Stay away from the Romans. Once they make the connection that you're the charioteer who stole those horses and kidnapped that girl—and I know you didn't after talking to Theophilus—they may come after you. They could even find a way to link you to the disappearance of Yeshua's body. Pilate is desperate to find the culprit."

Daniel nodded. "I'll be careful."

We watched as Dr. Luke turned his focus to others, probably patients. A small child tugged on his white toga. I imagined the astute physician dressed as a twenty-first-century surgeon in a white coat and blue scrubs. Why was it doctors had a particular look about them?

Shira lifted her arms for me to hold her as Daniel walked to the counter to speak to the attendant. "I believe we have two rooms reserved—Daniel, son of Aviv, from Jerusalem, and Shale, daughter of Brutus, from Galilee."

The man searched through his list of guests. "Yes, I have a Daniel, son of Aviv, and Shale, daughter of Brutus."

Shira brushed her finger along my lips, and I reached out and kissed her hand.

"Auntie?"

I nodded.

"I need to go potty."

"Can you wait a minute?"

She nodded and clasped her hands around me. I patted her on the back and sighed. They didn't have toilets in the first century, so how was I going to handle this with a child?

Daniel took two large wooden keys from the attendant as the man pointed to the hallway. "Through there. The rooms are next to each other."

"Thank you, sir."

"As Jacob promised," I said. Daniel handed me one of the antiques. Despite being archaic, I remembered they worked quite well.

We found our rooms, and I took Shira to the lavatory. It was the same as before, a trench of sorts, with running water passing through it to take away the waste. I was surprised she didn't question anything, but perhaps she was too young. I'd have to readjust to living like a cavewoman.

When we returned to our room, Daniel was waiting.

"Maybe we should eat," I suggested.

Daniel eyed Shira. "Why don't you and Shira grab a bite, and I'll pay Nidal a visit."

"But I want to come with you." This was too important for me not to be with him—our main reason for coming to the seventh dimension. What did Nidal know? I wanted to hear every word.

Daniel complied, glancing at his hands.

"Why did you work with the lepers?"

"Doctor Luke found it hard to get people to take them food. Yeshua healed all of them. I wouldn't have met Mark and Simon if I hadn't taken them food.

"Besides that, without Simon's concern, I wouldn't have become a believer. He was the one that confronted me with my sin in Caesarea. I wanted fame and money. Mark was the one who found me when I returned to Jerusalem."

I admired Daniel for his desire to help them, but I still didn't like that he was around lepers.

He stood. "Let's get something to eat."

CHAPTER 10

MY APPETITE WAS WHET when the server set lentil stew and barley bread in front of us. We joined hands as Daniel said a quick grace, and I noticed Shira mimicked everything we did—until she dove into the stew with her hands.

I frowned. I was new to this parenting stuff. "Can someone bring us utensils?"

Daniel shrugged. "They forgot to give us something. Let me ask."

A few minutes later, the server brought us spoons. I handed one to Shira.

After eating some of the bread, my mind drifted to Nidal. "Daniel, you and your brother talked about Nidal and getting information from him. Can you tell me more?"

Daniel raised his mug and took a couple of swigs and burped. His cultured refinement seemed to have been left behind in the twenty-first century. I showed my disapproval.

"Sorry," he mumbled.

I leaned forward. "Who is Nidal?"

Daniel relaxed and crossed his arms. "When I took your brother, Nathan, to your father in Caesarea, I asked Brutus for the money he owed me. While there, your father suggested I contact a friend who was looking for a charioteer. I went and introduced myself to him, and he explained to me his team hadn't won in several months because of two new competitors, Nidal and Tariq Naser."

Memories of our time in Nepal filled my mind. "I remember you mentioned the Naser brothers when we were near Mount Everest."

Daniel spoke in almost a whisper. "His best charioteer took too many risks in an attempt to beat the brothers. The horses trampled him."

"That's terrible," I said. I was glad Shira didn't hear.

Daniel sat up and took another piece of bread. "Dominus offered me the job. The downside is it made me equal to slave status in Roman society, but the earnings were substantial."

"How much did Dominus pay you?"

"Once I started winning, I was making in one race what took me three months to earn working for your father. I raced for over a year and made more than enough money for medical school."

Daniel reminisced. "I even dreamed of marrying you and buying you a house."

"What happened to your money? You don't have it now."

"Nidal and Tariq found out where I lived. Probably the ventriloquist told them. They broke into my rented room looking for the scrolls, but they found my money."

I glanced at Shira who was cleaning her plate. The spoon was tossed aside in favor of eating with her fingers again. "How did they know about the scrolls?"

Daniel took a sip of tea. "I noticed at one of the races that Nidal had a tattoo, but it wasn't an ordinary tattoo. There was a strange creature on it, which I recognized as a yeti, the creature we later encountered when we were in Nepal. When I saw the tattoo on Nidal's arm, I made the connection he must be from the future. It wasn't a tattoo from this time period. That prompted me to wonder if he and Tariq were the two men I'd seen in my dreams."

"You dreamed about Nidal and his brother?"

"Yes. I dreamed twice that two men kidnapped my father, and they were holding him hostage in a castle in Nepal. If my dream were true, Tariq and Nidal would be involved in my father's disappearance."

"I remember the email your father sent. I wish we found him."

Daniel nodded. "I know, but remember, Yeshua said he would help me."

Reminiscing, I ran my fingers through my hair. I found it hard to believe Daniel raced chariots when he left Galilee. I lamented I wasn't with him. Instead, I was a prisoner of my stepmother.

Daniel's lips tightened. "I can't remember if I told you, but I almost died in the last race. Cynisca took me to Nidal and Tariq's rented room to tend to my injuries. While there she told me disturbing things involving the ventriloquist."

Daniel looked away. "Sadly, I was blind. God kept me out of the brothels, but I lost God's protection when Simon confronted me, and I refused to repent."

"Who is Cynisca?"

"Cynisca is the charioteer who trained me."

"You mean there are women charioteers?"

Daniel nodded. "Her father was the high-ranking Roman official in charge of the stables."

"Was there anything between the two of you?"

Daniel laughed. "She was attractive. Perhaps if I weren't in love with you, I would have been interested."

I relaxed when I heard that. "What happened after that?"

"Tariq and Nidal coerced Cynisca into finding out where I lived. Or else the ventriloquist told them. They were looking for the scrolls. The ventriloquist knew God wanted me to remain pure as one of the one hundred forty-four thousand evangelists, so she gave Cynisca a potion to seduce me. However, when I almost died, she became spooked. God stopped her from carrying out the ventriloquist's evil scheme."

"I'm glad God was looking out for you. Otherwise, you would've died."

"I know. Cynisca became remorseful and told me the brothers were searching my rented flat. We rushed back, only to find they had been there and left. My money was gone."

I reached across the table and touched Daniel's hand.

Gratefulness crossed his face. "Cynisca was afraid to stay in Caesarea because of the ventriloquist. I suggested she go to Galilee and stay with your father until I could come. I wanted to go to Jerusalem first for Passover."

"What happened after that?"

"Her father must not have seen her handwritten message. The Roman soldiers started looking for me, claiming I stole the horses. When they couldn't find Cynisca, they accused me of murder. I found refuge in the Temple. The Romans are not allowed past the outer Court of the Gentiles, so I stayed within the inner sanctum during Passover week. That's how I witnessed what happened to Yeshua."

I interrupted Daniel. "How did Nidal end up in Dothan at the inn?"

"After I retrieved the scrolls, I traveled to Ein Gedi to hide them among the Dead Sea Scrolls. On the way back to Jerusalem, I came across a man who was lying on the side of the road beaten and left for dead. I stopped to help him, and when I turned the man over, it was Nidal."

I gasped.

"I was staring at the man who robbed me. He couldn't talk. I didn't want to save his life, but I couldn't leave him to die. I heard God speak to me—not audibly, but I knew it was God. 'I forgave you of your sins. Can you not forgive this man of his?'"

"And you did?"

"I asked God to help me do the right thing. I put him on my horse and brought him back here to the inn. Doctor Luke tended to his wounds, and I left him. When I entered the lobby, God opened my eyes. I recognized Jacob for the first time in this era. He told me to walk outside. When I did, I arrived in the garden and met Yeshua."

Daniel's eyes moistened. "Excuse me, but this part is hard for me."

I glanced at Shira and saw she was finished eating.

"Can I have the flower?" she asked.

I handed it to her, and she gently stroked it.

"What happened when you met Jesus?"

Daniel took a deep breath. "Yeshua shared many things with me, assuring me that my father was safe. You pretty much know the rest."

"Do you think Nidal will know you're the one who rescued him?"

Daniel shrugged. "I don't know."

I reached over and touched Daniel's hand again. "Let's hope he knows something about your father."

CHAPTER 11

S HIRA SLID OFF the chair and nudged me. "Auntie, can we go outside?"

I looked at Daniel. "Do you want to go for a walk?"

He smiled. "That sounds good."

Shira ran out to the portico as we trailed her. She hurried down the walkway searching for her new friends from earlier, but they were gone. Her shoulders drooped.

"I bet they'll be back tomorrow," I offered. I noticed the sun was low in the sky. "It's evening and almost time to go to bed."

Daniel reached for my hand. "Shale, you can't let Shira out of your sight—ever."

"I'm sorry, Daniel. I shouldn't have let her go over there. I never dreamed someone would kidnap her."

"It wasn't just someone. It was a demon."

I shuddered. "Do you think she'll come back?"

"You know who she is now. Keep your eyes glued on Shira. Only God knows why she's here, but the demon wants her."

I squeezed Daniel's hand. "I promise it won't happen again."

We walked in silence enjoying the quietness of the evening. My mind drifted. Being responsible for Shira changed Daniel's and my relationship. What would we be doing if Shira wasn't with us?

"Are you speaking to Shira in English or Hebrew?" Daniel asked.

"English."

Daniel shrugged.

"Why?"

"Because I hear you in Hebrew."

"Seems like we had this conversation before. Didn't we?"

"Strange," Daniel said. "The seventh dimension is different in some ways, but not in others."

"Maybe language is the same here. Perhaps the confounding of language was only necessary for our dimension to prevent dictators from assuming global power—like Nimrod."

Daniel raised his eyebrow. "And Hitler, Stalin, Mussolini, Pol Pot, Kim Jon-Un, Alexander the Great, Napoleon, and now the Antichrist."

"I wish your brother told us who he was."

"We'll find out soon enough."

I watched as Shira probed flowers and rocks and whatever caught her attention.

Daniel pointed ahead. "You know where that road leads?"

I shook my head. "No. Where?"

"It goes to the leper colony, about thirty minutes on foot from here."

"Was it depressing?"

"Leprosy is like living death in the first century. Everyone dies. However, Yeshua healed Simon and nine others in the colony."

I glanced at Daniel's face, still fearful I might see something. "You didn't worry about catching it?"

"Not really. It takes a lot of exposure. I mean, I don't think it's that easy to catch."

I leaned into Daniel gently. "I don't think I would have risked it."

Daniel hugged me at the waist. "God didn't call you to risk it. He doesn't call you to do something unless he gives you the strength to do it."

I admired Daniel's wisdom. The sun dipped on the horizon. "Perhaps we should head back."

Daniel nodded. "Let's wait till the morning to visit Nidal. I should pray, and you can put Shira to bed and have some time to yourself."

I pressed Daniel's hand. "I want to be there when you speak to him."

"In the morning after breakfast."

I nodded. "Sounds good."

"Ca-ca. Shale."

I would recognize that crow a hundred years from now, even if he hadn't said my name. "Did you hear that?"

"The Crow?" Daniel asked.

Worldly Crow took to the air as we passed, and he landed nearby in a woody tree. He gazed at me with high intensity. "Shale Snyder, you've grown into a young lady. How old are you now?"

I wanted to pretend I didn't know what he said to me. Anger welled up as I remembered how gullible I was.

"Ca-ca, Ca-ca. Shale, only a couple of months have gone by since I saw you last. Do you have that horrible aging disease to grow old so quickly?"

How rude. Dr. Luke didn't seem to notice any difference. Did I look that different? Or was he taunting me to get me upset?

"I'm quite well, thank you, Worldly Crow. I'm not ill, and you should mind your own business."

He cocked his head. "You'll be an old lady in no time."

I picked up and rock and threw it at the annoying bird. "Go away, hear me?"

Of course, I was a lousy shot and missed him by several feet, but he got the message. He fluttered his wings and took off in a huff.

"What was that about?" Daniel asked. "Throwing a rock at a bird."

"Not any bird—he insulted me."

Daniel frowned. "Are you going to let a crow upset you? What kind of example are you setting for Shira throwing rocks at birds?"

"She didn't see me."

The light-hearted walk had been fritted away by my reaction. I immediately regretted it.

"Maybe it's time to head back," Daniel said.

I called for Shira, and she hurried along after us.

Back at the inn, Daniel walked us to our room. We stood at the door for a minute as I found it hard to say goodnight. Daniel's room was next to ours, but I longed to share the same place. If we got married, everything would be less complicated. Even being in a room alone together was not acceptable in first-century society.

"Daniel?"

"Yes," he replied.

Shira ran into the room and sat on the bed. She was already falling asleep. I peered into Daniel's eyes. "When do you think we can get married? Then we wouldn't have to have separate rooms."

Daniel hesitated. "I don't know. I haven't thought about it since we arrived. So many things…"

I dropped my eyes, embarrassed by my frankness. "I understand. I thought about how much easier things would be."

Daniel leaned over and kissed me. "We'll know when it's the right time."

I nodded. "Good night." I closed the door and locked it. Leaning against the doorframe, I could still feel his lips pressing mine.

"Auntie, are you okay?"

I chuckled. "Yes, sweetheart. I thought you were asleep."

I forced myself to put Daniel out of my mind. Maybe there was something in my bag Shira could wear. I opened it expecting to find my twenty-first-century clothes. To my surprise, I discovered first-century robes. I sifted through the pack to see if anything would fit Shira. At the bottom was a small tunic. I helped her to put it on and then noticed the water bucket next to the door. "Here, let's wash your feet."

Shira bounced over to me and sat, pointing her toes.

I poured the water over them and gently massaged her feet. It didn't take long, and then I tucked her into bed. She closed her eyes before I could say her prayers. I whispered, "Please help us, Lord. Daniel and I need you more than ever."

Then I washed myself off with a soft washcloth. Too tired to pray another word, I fell asleep on the bed next to Shira's.

CHAPTER 12

S HIRA'S SCREAMS SHATTERED the stillness. I jumped up as the horror of her kidnapping exploded in my mind, but it was dark, and I couldn't see.

With an unsteady hand, I lit the oil lamp. As the light flickered, I skirted next to Shira. Relieved, I saw her small frame half covered by the blanket.

Was the door locked? I checked twice. Then I went back to her, hovering over her like a mother hen. She seemed to be in a trance.

"Shira, wake up. Auntie is here."

Her eyes moved around the room, but she kept crying. I shook her gently. Was she awake or asleep?

"Auntie is here, Shira." I took her in my arms, but she seemed unaware of anything. She lashed out at me. What did I know about taking care of a three-year-old?

"Oh, God, what should I do?" I climbed into her bed and cuddled up beside her. I sang the first song that came into my mind.

"Jesus loves me, this I know,
  For the Bible tells me so.

Little ones to him belong,
They are weak, but he is strong.

Yes, Jesus loves me,
    Yes, Jesus loves me.
    Yes, Jesus love me,
    For the Bible tells me so."

Shira calmed down, and her breathing returned to normal. I gently wiped away the tears on her cheeks. She soon dozed off, although she never appeared to have awakened.

When I was sure she was all right, I climbed back into my bed and pulled the covers over me. I wasn't sure if I should stay awake.

"You didn't pray," a voice inside my head accused me.

"Singing is praying," I murmured. Nevertheless, I prayed. "Dear God, please help me with Shira. Help Daniel when he meets Nidal. Please keep the evil one from us."

Peace came over me, and I drifted off to sleep.

CHAPTER 13

THE NEXT MORNING, I heard a knock. Shira was still asleep, so I scooted off the bed and hurried to the door. "Daniel?"

"Have you eaten?"

I rubbed my eyes. "What time is it?"

"I don't know. Haven't seen any clocks around here."

"Not funny," I said under my breath. "No. Give us a few minutes. I'll meet you in the dining hall."

Daniel's footsteps clicked away as Shira called me. "Auntie?"

I turned and smiled, trying to appear more cheery than I felt. "Sweetheart, let's get dressed so we can get something to eat. Do you need to go potty?"

She nodded, stretching out her thin arms. Did she remember anything from the night before? I would ask Daniel about what happened.

We entered the lobby a short time later, and Daniel sat next to an open window talking with Dr. Luke. Patrons filled the dining hall, and friendly voices created a family-like atmosphere. A gentle breeze whipped the window curtain back and forth as the sweet smell of rose oil and cloves drifted through the room. The two men stood as I approached, and Daniel hugged me warmly. "I hope you slept well."

I nodded. "Feeling much better today."

"I'm delighted to hear the good news about you and Daniel," Dr. Luke said.

I glanced at Daniel. Did he mean our engagement?

Dr. Luke's eyes focused on Shira. "And how old are you, Princess?"

She held up three fingers. "Three."

"What a big girl you, are," he praised her.

Of course, that delighted her, and she showed off her sandals to the doctor. "See my new shoes."

The doctor chuckled. "You're a princess."

The server brought us bread and figs, and we made small talk. At last, Dr. Luke stood. "We can get that taken care of, Daniel, but I wanted to talk to you first."

My ears perked up.

"After I visit, I'll get back with you," Daniel replied.

Dr. Luke said goodbye.

Once Shira was eating, I asked Daniel, "Get what taken care of?"

Daniel placed his hand on mine. "Love you."

I smiled, trying not to be impatient.

Daniel leaned over the table. "How is my princess this morning?"

Shira's eyes lit up, but she kept eating.

"She woke up in the middle of the night, Daniel." I mouthed, "screaming."

"At what?"

I shrugged. "I don't know. It was like Shira was still asleep, but I couldn't awaken her."

Daniel ran his fingers through his hair. "I think they call them night terrors."

I put my spoon down and took a sip of water. "What's that?"

"When I was at the Family and Youth Treatment Center, I heard about it. It happens when someone is traumatized. A person wakes up in an altered state of reality."

"I sang 'Jesus Loves Me.' Eventually, she settled down and went back to sleep. It was like she was awake, but she wasn't. She didn't seem to recognize me."

I leaned into Daniel and whispered, "You don't think she has a demon, do you?"

Daniel shook his head. "It's a psychological phenomenon. You're paranoid because of the ventriloquist."

I relaxed until I noticed I should have brushed Shira's hair before we came to the dining hall. I sighed. This parenting stuff was hard.

I shifted my focus back to Daniel. "So what was Doctor Luke referring to?"

"He said Nidal has recovered from his injuries. He asked me if I knew his immediate family. Of course, I told him I didn't."

"Anything else?"

"He said Nidal was reluctant to talk but was grateful to be alive. He also said he was anxious to meet the person who saved his life. Nidal doesn't have any recollection of me bringing him to the inn."

"What did Doctor Luke mean when he said he could get 'that taken care of'?"

"Nidal asked the doctor if he could remove something from his lower right arm. Doctor Luke said when he examined it, although he hadn't seen it before, it reminded him of the Urim and Thummin on the Ephod of the High Priest. They no longer exist, even in this century, but the Talmud refers to them."

"What's that?"

"Doctor Luke said they disappeared in the post-exilic period."

"Daniel, can you explain to me what you mean, Urim and what?"

Daniel took a sip of tea. "The Ephod was what the High Priest wore, and the Urim and Thummin were on the breastplate of the garment. They were like oracles of the High Priest. He used them to make predictions."

"That sounds creepy, but it wasn't underneath the High Priest's skin?"

"No. The doctor said it reminded him of that. More concerning to me is what it is and why Nidal wants it removed."

"Why didn't Doctor Luke remove it?"

"He said he wanted to talk to me first. He mentioned that Nidal was a little odd, and because of everything that's happened—with the death of Yeshua, his missing body, and then his appearances to hundreds after his resurrection—he had concerns."

"The Urim and Thummin haven't been seen for hundreds of years, and to have something similar on a man's wrist…"

"Could it be something like that?"

Daniel lifted his tea and took another sip. "Not if he's from our time. I suppose he could be from the first century, but that would destroy our hypothesis."

I nodded.

"However, if you were Doctor Luke and saw something embedded in someone's skin, you'd be a little curious. I mean, Nidal certainly isn't a High Priest, but Doctor Luke is relating it to something he's heard of."

"So—you're going to let Doctor Luke remove it?"

"After we meet with Nidal. I want to see it first."

I glanced at Shira. Could she sit still long enough for me to eavesdrop on the conversation between them? Daniel must have been reading my mind.

"Are you planning on bringing her?"

"If she causes too much of a disturbance, I'll take her out. But I want to hear at least a part of what Nidal says. I might pick up on something important."

"Are you ready?"

I nodded. I took another rose off the table and handed it to Shira. "For my princess."

She smiled.

I draped my arm around her shoulder and whispered in her ear. "Daniel needs to talk to someone, and I need you to be quiet for a few minutes. Can you do that for me, be very quiet?"

Shira nodded.

As we stood to leave, Ami and Levi entered the dining hall. Ami led with Levi following, using his cane.

Ami waved. "Daniel, do you have a minute?" He pointed to the table. "Sit. I want to talk with you."

I leaned Shira against my body as we sat in the chairs again. Ami was long-winded, and I feared this might take a while. I sighed, hiding my impatience.

Ami grinned. "How are you, ma'am?"

"I'm fine. Thank you." I sensed Ami would have preferred for me to leave so he could discuss business with Daniel.

"What's on your mind, Ami?" Daniel asked.

Ami squinted, looking down the hallway toward the inn rooms. Then he peered around the lobby. Levi leaned his cane against the chair after sitting beside his brother.

Please, Lord, I prayed, let this not be a long conversation. Shira was antsy propped up against my thigh. I stroked her on the back.

"That fellow, Nidal," Ami said, "is the most religious man I've ever seen. Those Followers of the Way are pretty devout, but Nidal is more religious than any of them."

Daniel eyed Ami curiously. "What makes you say that?"

"Or maybe he's one of those hypocrites, like the Pharisees, who pretend to be devout but wants to be admired by men."

Daniel shook his head. "Tell me more. What do you mean?"

Ami laughed. "Now that he's well, he's coming out on the portico. I've been counting, and he comes to the patio five times every day. He places a mat underneath him, faces the same direction, and bows, chanting strange words. He prays at dawn, noon, midafternoon, sunset, and at night."

"You don't know what he says?" Daniel asked.

"Elah, Elah, that's all I can catch. Why would he be talking about an oak or turpentine tree in his prayers?"

Daniel and I exchanged glances. Could Ami be hearing Nidal saying Allah?

Daniel shook Ami's hand. "Thank you, Ami. You've been helpful."

Ami was pleased with himself.

Levi interrupted. "Nidal needs to leave the inn before the Romans show up. They are likely to arrest him. The claims of Yeshua's resurrection are going to lead to the deaths of many Jews. The Romans will kill us. We live in uncertain times. Make him leave, Daniel. Send him away. Now."

I could feel the tension rising around the table, and my temperature rose by about ten degrees.

Daniel stood. "We are fixing to meet with Nidal now. Thanks for your concern, Levi."

I reached for Shira's hand. Was Nidal a Muslim?

CHAPTER 14

D ANIEL MUTTERED UNDER his breath, "I'll be back in a minute." As he turned to leave, I caught a glimpse of his face. I wished I could read his mind, but I knew. Daniel hurried out of the dining hall.

I wanted to run to Nidal's room and confront him myself. Now we knew Nidal was from the future but was he involved in the kidnapping of Daniel's father?

Levi tapped his cane. "You can't trust anyone around here except Doctor Luke. That was a kind thing Daniel did, rescuing that young man, but there is something strange about that him. Why you can't even trust women anymore. That old hag yesterday nearly took your little girl."

I clung tighter to Shira afraid Levi might be scaring her.

"We need God to come and save us from the Romans." The man shook his head. "And I thought Yeshua might have been our redeemer."

Ami interjected. "Levi, it wouldn't have mattered what Yeshua did. You would have doubted him anyway, and Daniel will figure things out. God has never abandoned us."

Levi leaned over to me. "Don't trust anyone, you hear me? That old woman…"

I cut Levi off. "I think I should go check on my beloved," I said softly.

Levi tapped his cane again. "Nidal speaks an unknown language, and I've been around a long time. Strange man, he is."

I did a slight bow to the brothers and took Shira's hand. "Let's go find Daniel."

We walked down the hallway to Daniel's room, and I knocked on his door.

Daniel opened it, and I followed him in as he sat on the bed. Shira chose the wrong time to be needy, running to him and lifting her arms to be held. Daniel placed her in his lap.

I crossed my arms in front of me. "At least we know your hunch was right. There weren't any Muslims in the first century."

Daniel nodded. "Are you ready?"

"I think so. Are you?"

Daniel's eyes flitted about the room. "Let's hope he knows something."

We walked to the end of the hall. As Daniel started to knock, I leaned into him. He tapped the door, but no one answered. He hit a little louder, but we still didn't hear any noise from the room.

"Is he in there?" I asked.

We heard footsteps and someone unlocking the door from the other side. The man cracked it open, and his eyes focused on Daniel. Unexpectedly, he shut the door in our face.

Daniel knocked again. "Nidal, can we come in?"

Silence followed.

"Nidal," Daniel said through the closed door, "I'm the one who rescued you and brought you here."

The man cracked the door, surprise covering his face and now embarrassed by his rudeness. He gave Shira and me a quick glance.

"You saved my life? I mistook you for someone else." Nidal left the door ajar and walked over to the window. "You rescued me?" he repeated. "I didn't know who did it."

"Can we come in?" Daniel asked.

Nidal motioned. "Have a seat." He stared out the window.

An awkward silence followed. I directed Shira to the chair and sat at the table with her in my lap. The door was left open. I wished Daniel would close it.

A small bandage covered the left side of Nidal's head. Other than that, he appeared to have recovered.

The man wasn't very tall, maybe five-ten, muscular, and younger than I imagined. Perhaps he was in his late twenties. I knew racing chariots required a great deal of strength, but what did he do in the twenty-first century? Did he have those muscles before he arrived?

Nidal finally turned and faced us. He didn't look Middle Eastern as his complexion was darker than most in this area.

Daniel cleared his throat. "How are you feeling?"

"Much better, thank you. I didn't know who rescued me. I didn't remember."

"You were unconscious and badly hurt."

Nidal stared at the floor. "Thank you."

"It was the right thing to do, under the circumstances."

That seemed like a good opening for Nidal to explain things, but would he?

"Do you know who I am?" Nidal asked.

"I raced against you in the chariot races."

"What else do you know about me?"

"You were injured on Robber's Road near Jericho."

Nidal looked away. "Why did you do it?"

I was glad I gave Shira the flower as she played with it at the table.

Daniel ignored the question. "Why did you race?"

Nidal laughed. "Like you, I wanted to make lots of money."

"How much did you lose?" Daniel asked.

Nidal squirmed. "A little, not that much."

Daniel frowned. "Come now. It must have been more than a little."

Nidal didn't respond, and I was surprised at Daniel's directness.

"How much money was stolen from you, Nidal?"

Nidal threw up his hands. "I don't know. All of it."

"All of your winnings?" Daniel asked.

Nidal nodded.

"What a shame."

Nidal didn't respond.

"Did you lose any money besides your winnings?"

Nidal wiped the sweat off his face. I noticed the tattoo on his wrist. "What other money could I have lost?"

Daniel sat on the chair beside me, peering intensely at Nidal. "I know what it's like to have someone steal your winnings. You see, someone broke into my place in Caesarea and stole my money, too."

Nidal's eyes bulged.

Daniel gave Nidal another opportunity to explain himself. When he didn't, I felt Daniel's righteous anger. It was one thing for Nidal to be thankful Daniel saved his life, but it was quite another for him then to lie to him.

Daniel probed deeper. "What if I told you I know you and your brother broke into my apartment and stole my money?"

Nidal turned halfway toward Daniel, his reddened face betraying him, although I wasn't sure if it was because we cornered him or because he was sorry.

Nidal shook his head. "He's not my brother."

"And I hear you are praying five times a day to Allah. Ami told me he saw you on your prayer mat"—Daniel pointed to the mat rolled up in the corner of the room—"and we both know Allah wasn't born until the seventh century."

Nidal stared at Daniel.

"Nidal, I know you're from the future."

CHAPTER 15

N IDAL COVERED HIS face. "You knew, didn't you, and rescued me?"

"I knew you stole my money. Cynisca told me, but who are you? What are you doing here? And do you know anything about my father?"

Nidal sat on the bed, staring at the floor.

I felt the tension rise as Daniel gravitated to Nidal. "Nidal, I know somebody must have sent you here. Do you know anything about my father, Aviv Sperling? He's a businessman."

Nidal twisted his hands. "Yes, you're right. I'm from the future."

Daniel asked a third time. "Do you know anything about my father? He would travel to Syria and other countries to purchase expensive cloths, linens—textiles."

"No, no. Don't know your father or a man by that name."

Daniel's lips tightened. "Are you sure? He's been missing since 2013. He was Jewish, tall, dark brown hair, curly like mine. He spoke Hebrew and Arabic well. We have a family business in Jerusalem."

Nidal shook his head vigorously without looking at either of us. "No, no."

I could sense Daniel's exasperation as he pressed harder for answers. "He purchased some scrolls from an antiquities dealer, scrolls that were sought by the authorities. Someone kidnapped him for the scrolls, and he or others held him against his will in the Himalayan Mountains."

"No, no. Don't know the man."

"Look, I'm not accusing you," Daniel said. "I'm asking if you know him."

Finally Nidal made eye contact. "I'm telling you, I don't know the man. Sorry."

Daniel stood and crossed his hands behind his back. Nidal must know more than he was saying, but how would Daniel find out?

"Who sent you here?" Daniel asked.

Nidal started toward the door. I thought he was leaving, but then he faced the window. "Scientists sent me here. I know about the scrolls, but I don't know anything about your father."

"Tell me about the scrolls."

"At first I was told to find you and thought you would lead me to them, but that didn't happen. Tariq said someone hid them among the Dead Sea Scrolls. I went there, but I couldn't find them."

"Who are you?" Daniel asked.

"I'm a Sherpa from Nepal."

"So there is a Nepali connection," Daniel said.

Nidal ignored Daniel's comment.

"How did you get mixed up with a bunch of scientists if you're a Sherpa?"

Nidal walked back to the bed and sat on the edge. "When I led expeditions up Mount Everest, we started seeing strange creatures in the Himalayans, dozens of them. They used to be very rare, perhaps a legend.

"They were aggressive, not typical wild animals. They were different. Some of them seemed human, but they were deformed and very tall.

"The trekkers reported them to the media, the sightings. Some even took photographs, and they came up to investigate from Switzerland or France. I forgot the name of the organization."

"CERN?" Daniel asked.

"Yeah, that's it. The scientists wanted to see what was happening at the top of the world. They said they opened a portal, and apparently, one of the stargates they opened was near Mount Everest. The creatures were coming in through the portal."

"The yeti?" Daniel asked.

"Yes," Nidal replied. "The yeti."

"Like that tattoo on your arm?"

Nidal rubbed the tattoo with his fingers, as if in an attempt to wipe it off, but then gave up, dropping his hand. I noticed a small stone in one of the eyes of the tattooed creature.

Nidal added, "I got very nervous and went to see an old shaman in Deurali."

I glanced at Daniel. We went to that area when we were in Nepal, but I couldn't remember the name of the shaman.

"I sought out the gods to understand. One night, I heard the voice of Shiva. He told me that Allah was the answer. I should become Muslim. Some Muslims lived in the area, and I went to see them. They told me I should make the pilgrimage to Mecca and see what Allah told me."

"What happened after that?" Daniel asked.

"I went on the pilgrimage."

"You did the Haj?"

"Yes."

"Who told you about the scrolls?"

Fear filled Nidal's eyes, and he clammed up. "I don't know any more than I've told you."

Seconds passed. Why didn't Daniel read Nidal's mind? What a perfect time to use the gift God gave him.

"When did you make the Haj?"

Nidal shrugged. "It's hard to say. I've been here a while."

"How did you know to look for me?"

Nidal glanced away. "I've told you everything I know. Tariq said they were following you. I think they even sent you back to get the scrolls because your name was on them."

"And my father's name," Daniel said, "that you claim you don't know."

"I don't recognize your father's name. I never saw the scrolls."

"You went to my apartment in Caesarea to get them, didn't you?" Daniel asked.

Nidal looked up at Daniel. "Yes."

"And found my winnings and stole them."

Nidal nodded. "I'm sorry. I truly am."

Both men remained silent for a moment.

Nidal interrupted the silence. "Look, I don't even want to go back. I want to stay here." He thrust his arm forward. "Can you get Doctor Luke to remove the stone?"

Daniel studied it more closely. I was too far away to see.

"It's a tattoo of a yeti," Daniel said.

"The eye in the yeti is what I want removed."

The word "eye" caught my attention. I set Shira on the chair, but she started to get up. "Wait here," I whispered.

I edged over beside Daniel to see. The creature had one eye, a red stone. I hadn't seen anything like it in a tattoo before.

Daniel ran his finger over it. "Who put it there?"

"They said I needed it to return, and since I don't want to go back, I want it removed."

"What door did you come through?"

"Mount Hermon. There's a portal there."

"Where did you enter the portal?"

"The Shiva Temple in Kathmandu."

"The one destroyed in the earthquake?" Daniel asked.

"It was destroyed?" Nidal seemed unaware. "I've been here for so long...so I couldn't go back anyway."

Daniel glanced at me before returning his gaze to Nidal. I didn't have the gift of mind reading, but if I were to guess, I'd say Daniel had the same thought as me—what would happen once Dr. Luke removed it?

"You still want Doctor Luke to remove it even though you won't be able to return?"

"Yes."

"The stone is what allows you to return?"

Nidal nodded.

"You don't have a family you left behind?"

"Never married."

"One last thing," Daniel said. "You said Tariq isn't your brother. Who is he?"

"I didn't know him before I came here. The scientists sent him from a different location, and we met up."

"What do you know about him?"

"Nothing," Nidal said.

"Nothing at all? You must know something."

"He's powerful, has superhuman strength."

"Anything else?"

Nidal shook his head. "Not really, except we parted ways."

"What happened?"

"Nothing. We just went our separate ways."

Daniel stood. "Let me see if Doctor Luke is still here." He opened the door, and Shira and I followed him.

CHAPTER 16

"**D**ANIEL?"

He was almost to his room but stopped to let Shira and me catch up.

I whispered, "Did you read his mind?"

He held up his finger to his lips. "S-h-h-h-h."

"Sorry, I'm anxious to know."

Daniel checked the hallway in each direction and unlocked the door. Once he shut the door behind us, he walked over and peered out the window.

"You're not thinking he's going to bail on us, are you?"

"I think we need to hurry. Nidal could leave at any moment, and I know he knows more than he's telling. We need to get that mark out of his skin."

I felt faint. Daniel grabbed me. "Are you okay?"

I sucked in a deep breath and sat by the table. "It was the word you used—the mark reminded me of the mark of the beast and disturbing dreams. I worry about my mom."

Daniel waved his hand. "That's not what this is. The mark of the beast is a different thing. I didn't mean to scare you. It's the eye in the yeti, although it's kind of strange the tattoo has only one eye."

I touched Daniel on the arm. "Did you read his mind?"

Daniel sighed. "Believe me, I tried. He knows something about my father, but if he refuses to think about it—I mean, I can't read what someone doesn't think. He's blocking it. He recognizes the name despite what he says."

"You'd think he would be more cooperative after you saved his life."

"If he has something to hide, if he feels his life is in danger—the only way to find out is to spend time with him."

"You know he isn't going to hang around here once that stone is removed. Maybe you should delay removing it. Besides, if it's a tracking device and it's removed, will whoever who is tracking him know it's been removed?"

"I don't think it's a tracking device," Daniel said. "I think the scientists just said that to make him think it was. He's uneducated. There aren't any bar lines on it, and it's nothing like what I've seen in computers. Even animal tracking devices make a beep or blink."

I was unconvinced. "It has to serve some purpose, or why would they have put it underneath Nidal's skin?"

Daniel sat on the bed, and Shira climbed up beside him. "It's probably an I.D. chip, like the mark of the beast, a precursor to the real thing. Perhaps it stores information, Social Security Number, credit card information, stuff like that, but I can't imagine the technology would be so advanced they could track him with a rock that emits nothing."

I bit my lip. Daniel was probably right. "It doesn't light up like the one I saw on Chumana when the UFO's landed at school. That was creepy."

"I need to find Doctor Luke," Daniel said.

"I don't think I should be there with Shira when he removes it. Not after what she's been through. I'll take her outside and let her run around. She needs some exercise anyway."

Daniel wrapped his arm around me as I sat beside him on the bed. "Are you sure you're okay?"

"I'm fine," I reassured him.

He leaned over and kissed me on the cheek. "I love you."

I snuggled up closer. "I love you, too."

"If I spent more time with him, I think I could get him to open up."

"You could encourage him to stay longer," I offered.

Daniel shook his head. "You heard what Levi said. Some people want him to leave. I'm sure he's sensed that already."

Daniel rubbed his eyes. "Even if I asked him to stay a few more days, I'm not sure Doctor Luke wants him hanging around."

I tried to think of something positive. "Find Doctor Luke and let him remove it. We'll figure out something."

I reached over and grabbed Shira's hand. "Want to go for a walk."

"Yes," she said excitedly.

Daniel opened the door, and Shira ran out, skipping down the hall. I placed my finger on his chest. "We'll be back within the hour. Come to my room when it's done, and let me know."

Daniel rubbed his forehead. I could sense the anticipation in his eyes.

"See you in a bit." I took off after Shira, attempting to be more positive than I felt. I mouthed back to Daniel. "I'll be praying."

CHAPTER 17

A SHORT TIME later, we returned to the inn, and I knocked on Daniel's door. When he didn't answer, I assumed he was still with Nidal.

We went to our room, and Shira plopped down on her bed. I opened my Bible, flipping through Psalms, but my heart was too anxious to read

Several minutes later, I heard a tap on the door. I glanced at Shira. Her eyes were closed.

I jumped up. "Daniel?"

"It's me."

I opened the door, putting my finger to my lips. "Shira's asleep."

He showed me a red crystal object.

"That's it?" I whispered.

"That's it."

"What do you think it is?"

"RF computer chip. As I said before, it's probably just to store information, lots of information."

I was still worried. "Could whoever put it underneath his skin want it back?"

Daniel turned the small stone over in his palm. "Anything is possible, but I doubt it. As I said, if it's a tracking device, it would beep or send out a signal. It's as dead as a useless battery."

"Without an antiseptic, it must have hurt."

"Ah, it wasn't a big deal, like removing a splinter."

I motioned Daniel to the chair. "Did you find out anything else?"

Daniel stroked his chin. "The only other thing is what I told you. Doctor Luke thought it might be similar to the Urim and Thummin that the High Priest wore on the ephod over his heart. From time to time, God would give the High Priest a prophetic message. Doctor Luke told Nidal he should pray for wisdom. God might be speaking to him."

Daniel leaned back and clasped his hands behind his neck. "I don't think Nidal took to heart what Doctor Luke said. Besides, the Urim and Thummin were on the ephod, not underneath the High Priest's skin, and we know he's from the future.

"The only thing Nidal cares about is leaving and going back to racing chariots. He wants to win back the money the thief stole"— Daniel's eyes turned to me—"including my money that was stolen from him."

Daniel handed me the red stone, and I inspected the tiny glass bead. Not knowing for sure what it was bothered me. "Maybe we should obliterate it."

"No, I want my brother to examine it. Let's keep it in a safe place."

I reached over and placed it in the small side pocket of my bag. "Did Doctor Luke say anything else?"

"Not really."

"That's it?"

Daniel rubbed his eyes. "Why are you so anxious?"

I crossed my arms. "Is there something you aren't telling me?"

Daniel gripped the edge of the table. "Shale, I'm going to take Nidal to Jerusalem, and I want you and Shira to stay here."

I stared at Daniel. "What?"

"You heard me."

I tapped my foot. "Without us? Absolutely not."

Daniel steepled his fingers. "Think about it. You would be safer here, and I want to visit my mother. Most importantly, I want to witness to Nidal. He's searching for the truth. I mean, he was a Hindu, and now he's a Muslim. If I spent more time and shared Yeshua with him, he might believe. I need to build his trust. Then he might open up about my father."

"Can't you read his mind?"

"I did," Daniel replied. "I told you, it doesn't work that way."

I glanced at Shira. She looked peaceful as she lay on her bed, like an angel. I knew Daniel didn't want to haul around a three-year-old. I didn't want to be left behind. I already felt vulnerable. I didn't know anything about raising a child, and one of my main reasons for coming back to the first century was to get married. I imagined celebrating with friends and how happy we would be. Now Daniel didn't even want to be with me. "I want to go with you. You know how good Shira is. She'll be fine."

Daniel shook his head. "I think Nidal will be more willing to talk if it's just us."

I persisted. "What about your mother? Why do you want to visit her?"

"The last time I saw my mother here, the Romans hauled me away in chains after nearly stripping me naked."

I felt tears in my eyes, tears I couldn't hold back. "How long will you be gone?"

Daniel brushed his hair off his forehead. "A few days maybe, if we can borrow a couple of horses."

A few days seemed like an eternity. How could I make Daniel change his mind? "When do you want to leave?"

Daniel stroked his chin again. "Tomorrow. If we wait, Nidal may go to Caesarea."

I couldn't believe Daniel was comfortable asking me to stay behind. "Have you already discussed this with him?"

"Yeah. I suggested Nidal come with me to Jerusalem. He was open to it. I mean, I saved his life, and he's very thankful for that."

My heart raced. "I don't like this. We've got that demon hanging around. The whole country is on edge."

Daniel took me in his arms. "You'll be fine here, and safe. I asked

Doctor Luke if he could keep an eye on you for a couple of days. You've stayed here alone before. There are many women and mothers at the inn that would be glad to befriend you if needed. You are far away from Jerusalem where it isn't safe."

Daniel sighed. "This might be my last chance to find out about my father. How many more opportunities will God give me?"

"Can we think about it for a couple of days?"

"And let Nidal take off for Caesarea?"

I was out of ideas. I also knew Daniel's mind was made up. "Okay," I said reluctantly, "if it's only a few days."

"I want to take the scroll with me."

"Why? Nidal might steal it."

"If he can't get back, what good is the scroll to him?"

"Why do you want it?"

Daniel smiled. "Well, it's sentimental. I'll feel like you're with me."

"Oh." I rested in his arms. "I still don't like this. How could it make that much difference if we come?"

Daniel rubbed my back. "I want to focus on Nidal without any distraction. Things are more complicated with Shira. We can't travel as quickly. She needs a schedule, predictability, especially as she's still traumatized. That's why she had that night terror. Here she gets home-cooked meals, can take naps in the afternoon—but it's not just because of Shira. It's better if you don't come. Muslim men view women differently."

"What about the Romans?"

Daniel stroked my hair. "They think I have leprosy. Cynisca returned to Caesarea. They won't be looking for me."

I stepped back. "Let me give you the scroll." I pulled it out of the bag and handed it to him. "Did you learn anything else?"

"Nothing that I can think of."

"I guess the least I can do is pray."

Daniel inspected the outside of it.

Feeling defeated, I cast my eyes on the floor.

Daniel reassured me. "I'll take good care of it. I'll talk with Nidal about leaving tomorrow, and I'll also check on the horses."

I puffed out my lower lip hoping to make him feel guilty.

Daniel walked over to the door and blew me a kiss. "I'll be back."

Once he was gone, I shut the door and slid to the floor. Tears filled my eyes. I felt guilty; I resented taking care of Shira. I threw up a prayer. "Help me, Lord, not to be depressed, and help Daniel to find his father."

I forced myself to get up. As I peered out the window, I knew my future would never be as I imagined before we came.

CHAPTER 18

S PRING BUTTERFLIES DANCED outside the window in the budding garden and I spotted the area where the cobra tempted me four years earlier. I closed my eyes and remembered how Daniel was so fearless when he rescued me. Was that the moment I fell in love with him?

I pulled the Opobalamum perfume out of my bag and turned the box over in my hands. Longing filled me—longing to smell it once more. I removed the cap as the perfume filled the room. I imagined wearing it on our wedding day, admiring Daniel's hopeful eyes as he'd watch me walk down the aisle. When would that happen now?

I closed the container and put the box in my bag. Turning to look out the window, I heard Shira's small voice.

"Auntie?"

Shira's eyes were half open, and she sat up and rubbed them. "I'm hungry."

I grabbed the hairbrush on the table and sat beside her.

Shira latched her small hands around my waist. "I love you."

"I love you, too, sweetie. Can I brush your hair, and then we'll get something to eat."

Once I did that, she scurried out of bed and ran to the door.

"Wait, you need your shoes, and I need to find the key."

She grabbed the key for me, and I locked the door behind us.

As we passed Daniel's door, I knocked, but I didn't hear anything.

"Where is Uncle Daniel?" Shira asked.

"He went to meet someone. We'll see him in a bit."

We arrived in the dining hall that was mostly empty, and Shira ran over to a window table so she could peer outside.

"Auntie, I see my friends."

"You said you were hungry. Let's eat first."

The server brought us a light dish of fruits and nuts. Shira stuffed them down too fast and then stood, anxiously waiting for me to finish.

I was glad I wasn't hungry. I sighed. "Let's go," I said, and I followed her through the lobby.

As we stepped outside, I kept one eye glued on Shira and the other eye on the lookout for the ventriloquist. I thought about going into town to get more clothes, but I didn't have the physical energy—or money.

"Ca-ca. Shale, you look sad, my friend."

I glanced up at the top of a palm tree. Worldly Crow had the annoying habit of showing up when I wasn't in a good mood.

"Back so soon?" I asked.

"I never went anywhere. You disappeared for a month."

In my world, four years passed, but in the seventh dimension, only a month. I scolded myself. How could I hold a grudge against a stupid bird? "Have you seen Daniel?"

The bird mocked, "Your lover?"

I stomped my foot. "He's not my lover, Worldly Crow. He's my betrothed."

Worldly Crow tipped his head to the side and crooned. "Yes, I saw him in the last hour."

I ignored his poor attempt at acting. "Where did you see him?"

The bird fluffed his wings and pointed with one of them. "He went down that road to the leper colony."

"The leper colony? You're mistaken. He'd have no reason to go there."

"Just saying."

But the element of doubt was cast. Daniel wouldn't visit there—would he, after everything that happened? I'd reached the limit of my patience. I gestured at the bird, showing my disapproval. "Get away from me, you liar."

The crow uttered a few dirty words. "My name is Worldly Crow." He flew overhead, and I could feel the swish of his wings. Then something hit the ground nearby—a squishy bird dropping. How rude!

Shira was playing with the other children. I wanted to go back inside the inn when I saw two men approaching. Was Worldly Crow right?

Daniel waved.

"Where have you been?" I asked.

Daniel smiled as he drew near. "We took a stroll into town."

I realized then they weren't coming from the direction of the leper colony. Worldly Crow only said that to get me upset.

Dr. Luke greeted me warmly. "Daniel told me about your plans. I hear you and Shira will be staying at the inn for a few days."

"Yes. Is there room?"

"Most certainly. If you need anything, don't be afraid to ask. We want to make your stay as comfortable as possible."

I was thankful for Dr. Luke's kindness. "Thanks."

Dr. Luke bowed slightly. "I will leave you two to enjoy each other." He turned to Daniel. "Can we meet in the dining hall in a bit? I'll bring my scrolls."

"Yes. Sounds good," Daniel replied.

As the doctor walked toward the inn, he stopped to say hello to the children. I took Daniel's hand, and Shira ran ahead of us. "What are you and Doctor Luke going to discuss?"

"First, Doctor Luke is arranging two horses for us to travel to Jerusalem. He gave me some extra coins if we need it. He also asked me to tell him what I know about the crucifixion and resurrection of Jesus."

"Oh, a direct eyewitness account."

"Exactly, with the acumen and accuracy of a top-notch doctor."

We strolled toward the inn, and Shira was waiting for us on the patio.

Daniel squeezed my hand. "We'll leave a little after sunrise. Do you want to say goodbye in the morning?"

I nodded. "Yes. We can pray for safe travel."

"I'd like that."

When we entered the dining room, Dr. Luke was seated at a table. We walked over as the server set fish and biscuits in front of us.

"It's good you are leaving tomorrow," Dr. Luke said. "Otherwise, you'd have a two-day wait to travel."

"Why is that?" I asked.

"Because of Sabbat. You can't travel that far on Sabbat."

"Oh." I smiled warmly. I wanted to look supportive in front of Doctor Luke.

Daniel started the conversation. "Doctor Luke says there has been a lot of unrest in Jerusalem since Yeshua's crucifixion, many clashes between the Romans and the Jews."

"Are you sure it's safe to travel?" I asked.

"We need to pray for God's mercy," Dr. Luke said.

Families began to fill the dining hall for the evening meal. "Perhaps you can make an acquaintance with some of the women here," Daniel suggested.

I wasn't going to change Daniel's mind. Now I wanted him to find out about his father as soon as possible. The sweet aroma of the perfume lingered in my mind.

Dr. Luke said the blessing, adding in a few words for Daniel's safe travel.

After putting a couple of biscuits on his plate, Daniel asked Dr. Luke, "Where do you want me to start?"

Pen in hand, Dr. Luke opened his scroll and studied his notes. "Did the sun really darken for three hours when the soldiers crucified Yeshua?"

"Yes," Daniel said. "Perhaps a rogue planet or large celestial object came between the earth and the sun for three hours, blocking the sun's light. It was too long to be a natural eclipse. It seems strange it happened at the same time Yeshua hung on the cross. With God, it's always about the timing, isn't it?"

Dr. Luke nodded, scribbling down Daniel's words.

My thoughts wandered. I remembered reading about Wormwood in Revelation and the scientists talking about an approaching planet. Could it be the same one, a planet with an orbit that comes close to earth every two thousand years?

After dinner, Daniel walked us to our room. I unlocked the door, not sure whether to invite him in.

Daniel hesitated. "Are you sure you wouldn't rather pray now? Then I wouldn't have to disturb you in the morning."

"Sure. But if I do happen to wake up, I'll see you off again."

We sat at the table holding hands. I prayed that Yeshua would give Daniel wisdom and discernment, and Daniel prayed for Shira and me. When he stood to leave, I wrapped my arms around him. "Godspeed."

He stepped to the door and whispered. "Love you."

CHAPTER 19

I AWOKE IN the middle of the night—freezing. I got up to get more blankets. Insecurity came over me that I hadn't felt in a long time. What if something happened to Daniel? If the rapture occurred, how would I get back to my time? Jacob wouldn't be around to bring me back.

I put another blanket over Shira. My thoughts drifted to home where there was heat, running water, and electricity. I didn't look forward to washing clothes by hand at one of the nearby streams. I sighed. Now was not the time to solve all my problems, when I should be sleeping. I scratched my ankle. The sandals did little to protect my feet, and the dirt from the air made them itch. Even washing them with water brought to our room each day did little to alleviate dryness. Too bad I didn't pack moisturizer.

I climbed into bed and wrapped the blanket around me. I could never adjust to living in this era. How could Nidal want to stay? Of course, guys didn't care about hot showers. My hopes of returning to the first century to have a spectacular wedding were now consumed with single parenting an orphan whom I'd never met until a week ago. I closed my eyes and prayed. "Please Lord, may Nidal reveal everything he knows about Daniel's father."

As I prayed, God revealed possibilities. Maybe Nidal was afraid to tell Daniel, or perhaps he didn't know anything. There was the possibility Daniel could be right—he just needed to build Nidal's trust. Or could there be another reason?

Soon I drifted off, and dreams took over, that state where everything seems real and familiar.

Daniel and I were walking along a white, sandy beach in a faraway place enjoying a tropical paradise. Crystal clear water lapped the pristine shoreline, and Daniel ran into the water and jumped the waves past the breakers. I started to run after him, but I saw someone farther up the beach.

Who was that stranger? Even though she was far away, her presence invaded my space and destroyed my peace.

Daniel called to me, but I ignored him. As she drew closer, I recognized her as the ventriloquist. A smile crossed her lips, revealing several missing teeth. She wasn't a poor beggar. She was a demon, or as my old donkey friend, Baruch, called them—an underling.

Daniel shouted to me. I was too focused on the ventriloquist to listen. Did he not see her? Why didn't he make her leave? Instead, he swam in the opposite direction.

When she was within hearing distance, she announced, "Shale, I come with a warning."

How did she know my name?

She held a pail in her hand, and her long, bony fingers with sharp fingernails looked creepy. I doubted she was looking for shells. She was looking for me. Her sunken cheeks and skin pallor reminded me of death.

"What warning?" I asked.

"Daniel doesn't love, you, Shale."

"Of course he loves me."

The ventriloquist laughed. "If he loved you, he wouldn't leave you. I must tell you the truth. He doesn't want to take on the responsibility of a young child."

She pointed. "Look, Daniel has abandoned you."

I turned to see where he was. His head was barely visible above the waves.

I put my hands on my waist and scowled at her. "I don't believe you. Of course, Daniel loves me."

The ventriloquist held up her hand and swept it through the air, peeling back a divider to another dimension. I was looking into a different universe that paralleled our own.

I was inside a traditional church with pews on each side of a middle aisle. The tinted windows didn't seem right, but I wasn't sure what was wrong with them. I wore a white wedding dress, but there were splatter marks in several places as if red wine was spilled on me.

I didn't like the way I looked, but it was time for me to walk down the aisle. I didn't have another wedding dress to wear even if there was time to change. If I wanted to get married, I'd have to wear this one. How could I wear a dress that wasn't spotless? The music started playing, my cue to make my appearance.

I began walking and managed a forced smile, although deep down I felt humiliated I was wearing a stained white dress. I hoped no one could see my shame. Many people were in the pews, but their faces were blurred.

The music played, and as I walked, I looked straight ahead. The pastor was watching me, but where was Daniel? The officiant didn't seem to realize the groom was missing. No one noticed Daniel wasn't there. I kept walking. When I was within a few feet, I asked the chaplain, "Where is Daniel?"

The preacher didn't hear me. He began to speak as if he were talking to both of us. I looked around the chapel, and all eyes were glued on me.

I dropped the flowers, turned, and ran, tripping over my dress. Once I was outside, I saw a man a short distance away dressed in dazzling white. "Shale."

When he said my name, I recognized him as Jesus. "My Lord," I cried, and collapsed in front of him.

He touched my shoulder and strengthened me. I stood and looked into his eyes.

"Go back. Don't listen to the evil one."

I glanced at the door. Did Jesus really want me to go back? I wanted to ask him where Daniel was, but then he was gone. I went back to the door and was surprised this time to enter a beautiful garden. Many people were in the pews.

A rabbi stood at the front, and Daniel was beside him. As I walked down the aisle, I looked down at my white dress. There were no stains, and Daniel was stunning. And then I noticed my heavenly Father was walking me down the aisle.

A small voice awakened me. "Auntie?"

I opened my eyes, and once they adjusted, I saw through the window curtain that it was daylight. I got up and kissed Shira on the cheek. "Did you sleep well?"

She nodded, pulling herself up. "I'm hungry."

"Let's get something to eat."

On the way to the dining room, I tapped on Daniel's door. When he didn't answer, I assumed he'd left. What was it Jesus said? "Don't listen to the evil one."

CHAPTER 20

THE NEXT DAY after lunch, I had an idea. "Can I have some papyrus paper and ink?" I asked the clerk at the check-in counter.

He handed me a decent supply, and I thanked him. Perhaps Shira could entertain herself drawing pictures, and I could start a new diary.

We returned to our room, and I plopped down on the bed. I set Shira in my lap and wrapped my arms around her small frame.

Downcast eyes reflected back at mine.

"Where is Uncle Daniel?" she asked.

I kissed her on the forehead. "He went to Jerusalem. He'll be back in a couple of days."

Maybe she was picking up on my sadness. The nightmare from the night before still lingered.

Another idea came to me. "Shira, can I tell you a story?"

She scooted up to me, and her eyes widened. "Yes."

I began. "Once upon a time there was a donkey named Baruch. He was a gray donkey with extra-long eyelashes. He was a sad donkey— like you feel sometimes."

"Why was he sad?"

"As you grow up, you must do chores. Baruch didn't like doing chores, so he ran away. He thought if he ran away, he'd be happy. Then no one could tell him what to do."

I glanced at Shira. Her eyes were big and round, hanging onto every word.

I smiled. "The donkey had some terrific friends. They warned him not to go. One was a small white dog with brown spots named Much-Afraid, and another was a pig named Lowly. They tried to get Baruch to change his mind, but the donkey didn't want to listen to his friends. Even Worldly Crow wished to stop him, but Baruch refused to listen.

"So he left his friends and traveled into the wilderness. After he was gone a while, he became hungry and didn't know where he was. He regretted leaving his friends.

"He heard jackals and lions, and it was getting dark. He remembered how well his owners took care of him. He always had fresh straw. Now he was hungry and lost."

Shira tapped me on the arm. "Is he going to be all right?"

I chuckled. "This story has a great ending. Don't worry."

"What happen next?"

"Well, Baruch started crying because he was afraid. Then he heard a sound nearby and became more worried. Suddenly, a sheep appeared.

"The sheep took pity on him. He told Baruch if he would go with him to meet the King, the King could help him to find his way back home."

"Did the donkey go with the sheep?"

"Yes, he did." I peered at Shira. "Would you have gone with the sheep to meet the King?"

"Is he a good King?" Shira asked.

I smiled. "I'll tell you a little secret."

"What's that?"

"The King is Jesus."

"Jesus is a king?"

"Yes. He's King of the garden, the earth, and heaven. In fact, he's King over the whole universe."

"What happened next?"

"Well, after a long time traveling in the wilderness, the sheep brought Baruch to the garden of the King. It was guarded by two angels holding a flaming sword. They wouldn't let Baruch into the garden unless..."

"Unless what?"

"Unless Baruch heard the King say his name."

"Did the donkey hear his name?"

I stroked Shira's hair. "Yes, he did. The donkey entered the garden, and when he did, the King greeted him. Baruch thought the King would be upset with him for having run away, but the King loved him. Baruch made many friends in the garden."

"Did the donkey miss his friends that he left behind?"

"You know what?"

"What?"

"Baruch went back home after he met the King, and he shared everything he learned with his friends."

Shira's eyes grew wide. "You mean with the dog and the pig? I bet they were happy to see their friend again."

"Yes, they were."

I stopped for a moment, thinking about the story when Shira interrupted my thoughts.

"I wish I could go to the garden. That would be so much fun."

"Yes. It's a special place. I met a white rabbit in the garden. I bet Cherios would play with you."

Shira rubbed her foot. "Will I ever see mommy and daddy again?"

I smiled wistfully. "I hope so."

"In the garden?"

"Maybe. You might meet Lowly and Baruch at the stable if we travel to Galilee."

"What about the white dog?"

"Hmmm..." I remembered when I followed Much-Afraid into the woods. I lost her in the garden, but after I arrived in the first century, she showed up the next day. If she came the last time I was here, might she come again? I smiled at Shira. "When Daniel returns, I can ask him to take us to my father's home."

I could see Shira's eyes getting heavy.

"Why don't you climb into bed and take a nap."

Shira hopped over, and I draped the blanket over her. Soon her eyes closed, and I began to think about the red stone in my bag. I couldn't put it out of my mind, even though deep down I wanted to start my new diary.

I pulled the object from my bag and studied it, turning it over in my hand a few times. Nothing about it seemed unusual. It could be just an ordinary stone, perhaps what someone might see in a ring.

I let out a deep breath and placed it on the table. It couldn't be the mark of the beast. According to the book of Revelation, that would be inserted into the right hand or forehead. This object was on Nidal's forearm above his wrist. It was the eye of a yeti tattoo. Besides, the mark of the beast didn't exist when I left.

I glanced at Shira and saw her eyes were open. "You need to close your eyes and go to sleep."

Shira scrunched down on the bed. I put my bag on the floor and started my first diary entry.

I addressed it, "Dear God" this time. I didn't need to worry about Scylla finding it and harassing me, and I didn't need to pretend to be Anne Frank who addressed her diary as, "Dear Kitty."

I wrote a few words, but I didn't know what to write. Soon I felt sleepy, having not slept well the night before. I laid the paper and pen on my chest. I'd rest my eyes for a few moments and think about what I should write.

Soon I drifted off—until I was jolted by a strange voice. When I opened my eyes, a large man stood in the doorway. "Where is Nidal?"

CHAPTER 21

I SCREAMED. I imagined I was dreaming, but I wasn't. I caught Shira out of the corner of my eye, frozen. My paper and pen fell to the floor.

The burglar, in his late twenties or early thirties, wore a white T-shirt, blue jeans, and leather jacket. He was hippy-like with a beard and unkempt brown hair. He lunged at me waving his arms. I ducked to the side, and he crashed into my bed.

He tried to grab me, but I slung the chair at him. He started toward me a third time, and I fell backward. Pain shot up my back.

"Get out!" I shouted. I couldn't get around him to get to Shira. She started to cry.

His eyes were like a wild animal's. "Where is Nidal?"

The monster cornered me. I backed away, but the intruder pressed me against the wall. His breath smelled foul.

"Where's Nidal?"

"He's not here."

The man spit on the floor. "He has to be. I tracked him."

I saw Shira scoot off the bed and run out of the room. She left the door ajar. Thank God she escaped.

I held up my hands to shield my face, and he squeezed my shoulder. Now I was frozen. I'd never seen such icy cold blue eyes. "I told you, he's not here."

Was the man trying to hypnotize me? Those eyes…

"He has to be. The implant was activated."

The implant—was he referring to the chip Dr. Luke removed? "It's on the table," I managed to say.

The intruder loosened his grip and turned. "Where?"

I pulled away. "I…I left it there." But I didn't see it.

Suddenly Jacob appeared in the doorway. His eyes met mine, but his attention quickly turned to the intruder. I saw Shira cowering behind Daniel's brother. The prowler ran out the door, knocking Jacob backward. In a flash, the man was gone. Shira ran up to me.

"I'll be back," Jacob said, as he took off.

I heard him shout. "Grab that man!" Commotion filled the inn. I shut the door and locked it, taking Shira in my arms.

She scrunched up close to me. I wrapped her up in the blanket and rocked her. Now that it was over, tears rolled down her cheeks. "The bad man is gone. You're safe now."

I noticed her right hand was clasped in a tight fist. I opened her fingers gently. To my surprise, she was holding the small computer chip.

"Honey, why did you take this off the table?"

"I wanted to look at it."

"You mustn't take things that aren't yours. That's Auntie's."

"I'm sorry," she said.

Fear gripped me again as I worried the man would be back. We wouldn't be safe staying here. I needed to get rid of the chip.

I continued to rock Shira on the bed when Jacob returned several minutes later. "Did you catch him?"

"Not yet." Jacob glanced around the room. "Where is Nidal?"

"Daniel took him to Jerusalem."

Jacob picked up the chair and sat beside me. "Then why did that guy come here?"

"He was looking for this." I handed him the red stone. "He said it was activated."

Jacob walked over to the window to examine it in the sunlight. "It's a chip of some kind, must be an RF chip. Why do you have it?"

"Doctor Luke removed it from Nidal yesterday."

"Why did Daniel take Nidal to Jerusalem?"

"He wanted to spend time with him. Nidal wouldn't tell Daniel anything, claiming he didn't know anything. I think Daniel wanted to take him to the Temple. He's a Muslim."

Jacob looked surprised. "How do you know that?"

"Because two men here at the inn described him praying five times a day to Allah."

Jacob pointed to the hallway. "Two guards took off after him, but I don't know if they can catch him. Who knows where his stargate is, but I would say Mount Hermon if I had to guess."

"It is Mount Hermon."

"You know for sure it's the CERN stargate?" Jacob asked.

"He told us yesterday."

"Maybe the globalists only have that stargate to the first century. We should send scouts there. As I said, the gates of hell are at the base of Mt. Hermon."

"Nidal doesn't want to return," I said. "That's why he had the chip removed. They can't track his whereabouts without the chip."

"What activated it?" Jacob asked.

I shrugged. "Probably Doctor Luke activated it when he removed it." I changed the subject. "Jacob, we can't stay here. They'll come back."

Jacob cocked his head. "Do you still have the scroll or did he take that?"

I twisted my hands as I held Shira. "Daniel took it with him. You know, I'd given it to that man if I'd had it. I don't care anymore. All I want is for Daniel to find out what happened to your father."

Jacob ran his hand through his hair, reminding me of Daniel. "The Illuminati have two of the three scrolls. You gave one to Scylla. The second one your father sent to the scientists in Geneva for testing. The New World Order only needs the third one."

"Why is it so important to them?"

"They don't want any historical record of Yeshua. We are nearing the start of the seven-year tribulation, and the treaty will soon be signed. The last thing they want is for your scroll to turn up in the news. The authorities are destroying Bibles and historical documents, including Jewish and Christian antiquities. New portals are opening up around the world—even in Antarctica."

"I can't stay here," I repeated.

"I'll post a guard at the door. You are safer here than anywhere else. I need to take this RF chip to be analyzed. Let's give Daniel a day or two to find out what he can."

"Jacob, I don't like staying here without Daniel."

Jacob rubbed his chin. "I know."

"How did you know to come?"

Jacob leaned back. "Remember the first time you came to the inn?"

I nodded.

"I was sweeping the floor because I knew I was supposed to meet someone."

I remembered. That was four years ago.

Jacob steepled his fingers. "I know things without being able to explain it. God told me I needed to come to the inn."

"I'm thankful."

Shira squirmed out of my lap, and I let her down. I watched as she picked up the pen and paper from the floor and placed them on the table.

"Daniel didn't tell me exactly how long he would be gone. He was hoping only a couple of days. I hate not being able to call or text."

Jacob stood to leave. "I'm going to get someone to guard your door." He paused. "Was Daniel going to visit Mother?"

"Yes, he mentioned he was going to see her, too."

"We'll find him if he doesn't return in the next day or two. In the meantime, I'll be praying that Yeshua will keep you safe. Let me see about a guard."

"Thanks, Jacob."

"Make sure you keep the door locked, but I don't think anyone will be back. The intruder didn't find Nidal, the chip, or the scroll, so whoever sent him here will be looking elsewhere."

"Again, thanks for coming."

When Jacob closed the door, I locked it, walked over to the table, and pressed my hands against it. Why did I let Daniel talk me into staying at the inn?

Several minutes later, I heard knocking. "Shale, it's me, Jacob. I want you to meet Matt."

I opened the door, and Jacob made the introductions. His friend was a large black man, and he was dressed in a first-century robe. I extended my hand. "Glad to meet you."

"My pleasure, ma'am."

"Matt will alternate with someone else, as soon as I get a second guard lined up for tomorrow."

I wondered which dimension Matt was from, but Jacob didn't tell me.

Once he left, I heard Matt talking to someone in the hallway, so I surmised he was from this century. I walked over and sat on the bed. I knew what I was going to write now, and I picked up the pen and paper that Shira placed on the table.

CHAPTER 22

F IVE DAYS LATER

WE SAT IN the dining hall finishing up a bowl of lentil soup, fresh figs, and matzo bread. I hadn't seen Jacob since the attack, but the guard kept a vigilant eye. I peered gloomily out the window since we returned from collecting garden rocks. Summer would soon arrive with the hot desert winds and occasional flash flooding. Despite that, I looked forward to the avalanche of summer flowers that would follow.

I knew now why Shira took the computer chip. She wanted to use it to trade with the kids for their colorful pebbles. Yesterday was Shabbat so we couldn't go anywhere. I expected Daniel to return at any time.

Shira scattered several stones around the table. "Can you play with me, Auntie?"

I sighed. "Sure. How do I play?"

"Do you want to be Much-Afraid, Baruch, Lowly, or the sheep?"

"Are we going to the garden?"

"Yes." Shira pointed with her finger. "Here is the garden, and this is the stable."

I started to answer when I heard a woman's voice from the foyer. "Just a minute, sweetie." I stood. "I'll be right back."

Shira nodded, moving a couple of rocks in front of my chair.

The guard edged closer when he saw me scurrying toward the check-in counter. "Is everything all right, ma'am?"

"I heard a voice I recognize is all," I said.

That satisfied him, and he backed away.

I approached the woman.

"It's urgent," the woman said. "I must leave immediately. Could you relay the message to Jacob?"

The attendant handed the woman a parchment. "Daniel Sperling is in this room."

She turned toward the guest rooms, and I stepped in front of her. "Do I know you? I'm Shale, Daniel's betrothed."

The woman's eyes lit up. "Shale! I'm Martha, Daniel's sister."

My heart fluttered. Was something wrong? I fumbled for words to hide my concern. "Yes, you sold me a dress when I arrived a few years ago. You recommended I stay at Jacob's Inn on my way to Galilee."

Martha clasped my hands. "I'm so glad to see you—but I wish it were under different circumstances." Her eyes darted around the lobby. "Is Daniel here?"

"No. He went to Jerusalem with a friend."

"He already left for Jerusalem? He must have known."

I studied her sad face. "Known what?"

Martha's hands trembled in mine. "Mother is very ill. I must go see her right away. I wanted Daniel and Jacob to know."

"Oh, my goodness. I don't think Daniel knows his mother is ill. At least, he didn't tell me. I thought something happened to him."

Martha wrapped her arms around me reassuringly. "I'm so happy to see you. Doctor Luke told me about your betrothal. What a beautiful bride you'll make."

"Thank you."

Martha stepped back and locked her eyes on me. A trace of worry crossed her face. "Shale, maybe we could go together to Jerusalem to see Mother."

I didn't give her a chance to change her mind. "Yes, I want to go with you—as soon as possible."

"Jacob should be able to supply you a horse from the stable."

I shot a glance at Shira. She was still moving pebbles around.

"We have a young child with us. Her parents died unexpectedly in an accident."

"May God give you grace. God takes care of orphans."

I reached for Martha's hand. "I want to introduce you."

Martha followed me to the table, and I touched Shira's shoulder. "Shira, this is Daniel's sister, Aunt Martha."

Martha slid into the chair across from her. "Do you like surprises?"

Shira nodded enthusiastically.

"I have a gift for you." Martha opened her bag and pulled out a small white toga. "I hope it's not too big."

Shira held it up to her chest. "Not too big."

I chuckled. "You will look like a princess."

I glanced at Martha. "Let me see what the procedure is for checking out. Can you wait here with her?"

Shira got up and gave Martha a hug. "Thank you."

I went back to the attendant and explained our plans.

He shuffled some papers in front of him. "Jacob left instructions to make sure you were taken care of. Do you need a horse?"

"Yes, please."

"Give us a few minutes."

I returned to the dining room. "Shira, let's put on your new tunic. Martha, I'm so glad you stopped by. I pray your mother will be healed."

"We must hurry," Martha said. As we went to our room, Martha explained. "Doctor Luke said you and Daniel were taking care of an orphan. I thought she might need something to wear."

"I don't have many clothes for her."

Martha handed me a bag. "I wanted to give you a gift, too."

I glanced down, surprised. "You have a gift for me?"

Martha smiled.

I opened the bag. Gratitude filled my heart when I saw the toga. I leaned forward and hugged her. "Thank you."

Martha beamed.

I glanced around the room. "We probably won't be back here any time soon." I shared with the guard our plans. He offered to accompany us, but I reassured him it wasn't necessary.

"Are we going somewhere, Auntie?" Shira asked.

"Yes, sweetie." I crouched in front of her. "Daniel and Aunt Martha's mother is ill, and we are going to visit her."

That seemed to satisfy her. Daniel was all I could think about. Surely he would have told me if he knew his mother was ill. My other concerns faded as I wondered what he learned from Nidal about his father.

CHAPTER 23

S HIRA AND I WAITED in the lobby while Daniel's sister tidied up the room before leaving. As I peered through the portico, a haze settled outside the doorway, partially obscuring my view. For a brief moment, I imagined the door leading somewhere else. I remembered how God's intervention and the devil's wiles happened at boundaries—between the seventh dimension and our physical world. I squinted, curious, but too afraid to venture outside.

I felt Shira pulling on my arm. "Auntie, I hear singing."

I strained to hear, too, but as soon as she spoke, the haze lifted and sunshine once again beamed through the entrance.

Martha joined us, interrupting my musings. "Have they brought the horses around?"

"Oh, I don't know. Let's go see."

We walked outside, and two horses stood tied to the post outside the inn. Shira's friends were playing nearby, and I felt Shira's hand tugging on mine.

I redirected her attention to the horses. "Look," I pointed. "We're going for a ride."

She leaned on my arm impatiently.

I heard Levi's cane tapping the stones on the porch. I turned and saw him and his brother approaching.

"Stay safe," Levi said. "Jerusalem is extremely dangerous now."

My ankles locked together. That was not what I wanted to hear.

"God will protect you," Ami reassured me. "I'm praying for you."

I brushed my hair back from my face. I hoped I appeared more confident than I felt. "Thank you, Ami."

Dr. Luke strolled out and joined us. "You should easily make it before sundown."

"I'm very familiar with the road," Martha replied. She glanced at me. "It will be nice to have my soon-to-be sister-in-law along—an unexpected surprise."

Dr. Luke tilted his head. "If you feel you need a doctor, please send word. I can come at a moment's notice."

"That's kind of you," Martha said.

Dr. Luke reached into his doctor's bag and handed something to Shira. She turned it over in her hand several times, admiring the wooden object.

Dr. Luke touched his chin. "Mary, the mother of Yeshua, gave that to me a long time ago. Yeshua once was a carpenter."

"What's a carpenter?" Shira asked.

"A carpenter makes things out of wood."

I leaned over to see.

"Is it a bird?" she asked.

Dr. Luke nodded. "It's a dove."

"What do you say, Shira?"

Shira gently stroked the wooden figurine. "Thank you."

A stable attendant walked over. "Are you ready?"

I glanced at the three of us. "I think so."

He escorted us to the horses. With our togas, we would need to ride sideways. Because Martha was a more experienced rider, we decided that Shira should ride with her.

Dothan was on the byway between Jerusalem and Galilee. Perhaps if Daniel and I did make it to Galilee, we would come this way again, but something in my soul told me that was unlikely.

After we left the inn, it didn't take long to reach the outskirts of the small town. Fond memories returned when I traveled this road with Baruch and Cherios. I closed my eyes. When I opened them, Shira and Martha were trotting close beside me.

"We should have no problem reaching Jerusalem before the sun sets," Martha assured me. "We don't want to be on the road after dark."

Shira dozed off for a while but now was awake. Her outstretched hand held the dove over her head. She waved her hand back and forth, pretending the wooden dove could fly.

Shepherds grazed their flocks between the rolling hills. Here and there, beggars lined the road. Discarded cups littered the way, a haunting reminder of the many who died of hunger.

Traders with donkeys burdened with an assortment of provisions passed by us. I didn't see anyone offer food to the beggars. Others pulled carts weighed down with grapes, figs, olives, pomegranates, and grain. Sadly, we did not bring extra food to share. We, like most, had barely enough for ourselves. And without the rains that sometimes never came, there would be no harvest.

I waved reassuringly at Shira.

Martha edged closer to me. "This is the valley between Mount Gerizim and Mount Ebal at Shechem. God appeared to Abraham and Joshua here, reminding them of the blessings and curses of the law."

I watched absent-mindedly as Shira's hand waved the dove through the air. "Is this near where Yeshua spoke to the woman at the well?"

Martha shrugged. "Seems like I heard a story like that, where Yeshua proclaimed he was the Messiah to a Samaritan woman. The Jews took offense to that, you know."

Suddenly, Shira cried out, "I dropped my bird."

Before I could say anything, the dove flew into the sky, transforming itself from a wooden sculpture into a magnificent white bird. Soon it grew into the size of a breathtaking eagle. The bird's mighty wings beat the air as it lifted its body upwards, soaring overhead. He circled against the blue sky in ever-widening circles.

Shira pointed.

Martha gasped.

"I am the bread of life," the transformed dove said. "He that comes to me shall never hunger, and he that believes on me shall never thirst."

The words filled my ears, but Shira and Martha didn't have the gift of animal speak. Soon the eagle flew over the beggars, and as we passed them, I saw their cups overflowing with nourishment.

I pointed. "Look, Shira."

She squealed.

Martha shook her head. "That's impossible. It's almost like the bird —is supernatural."

Then I noticed the vultures leaving—those gathered near the beggars. The eagle flew ahead, beyond Shechem. Shira exclaimed, "I hear singing, Auntie. The angels are singing."

I couldn't hear it, but I was convinced Shira did. I glanced up but didn't see anything.

The shadows became longer as we passed through several small towns before arriving on the outskirts of Jerusalem.

Martha said excitedly, "We're almost home."

When we crested a mountaintop, Jerusalem spread out before us. An impressive wall surrounded the city, and my heart raced. The Temple rose up higher than the walls surrounding it. Its golden columns reflected the reds and yellows of the setting sun. The most beautiful building in America couldn't compare.

I saw hundreds if not thousands of pilgrims descending upon Jerusalem. Music from the flutists reached us as we passed dozens of oxen with gilded horns and olive wreaths. Many travelers even walked to the dusty, overcrowded city on foot.

The eagle again filled the cups of the beggars along the pathway to the gates. I noticed a few travelers offered them handfuls of grapes and figs—unlike in Samaria. I remembered the prejudices in my century— even here it existed. The Jews hated the Samaritans.

I said to Martha, "I didn't expect the city to be so packed. Is it always like this?"

Martha shook her head. "It's because of Shavuot. Many from outside Jerusalem have come to celebrate."

"What is it?" I asked.

"The Feast of Weeks—Shavuot, to celebrate the first fruits from the barley and wheat harvests. It occurs forty-nine days after the first day of Passover and commemorates the giving of the Ten Commandments to Moses."

Shavuot must be the same as Pentecost, the name with which I was more familiar. No wonder everyone was coming to Jerusalem to bring offerings.

Most of the visitors wore traditional clothing like us. Others were dressed in fine linens. Some of the women's baskets, balanced precariously on their heads, were woven together in threads of gold and silver that shone brilliantly in the sun. Others who were poor carried their foodstuff in plain wicker buckets. I caught glimpses of wheat, dates, and olives. I felt naked not having a basket on my head.

As we neared, I saw Roman soldiers in their armored skirts and cuirasses along the wall. They seemed mainly devoted to keeping order. If another riot happened so soon after the crucifixion of Jesus and the mysterious disappearance of his body, I could only imagine the unrest it would ignite—and one more smear on Pontius Pilate's ineptitude as governor.

Fruit carts in the hundreds blocked the crowded gate, slowing things down. The Roman soldiers inspected everything. Once inside the walls, most visitors headed to the Temple, and I caught a glimpse of the Outer Court. The flutists led groups of pilgrims into the Temple Courtyard as the Levites sang, "I will exalt you, Oh, God, for you have saved me and you have not rejoiced in my enemies before me."

We passed the lofty Temple Courtyard and trudged through the Upper City. Contingents of Roman soldiers stood guard on every corner. Their presence reminded the Jews they ruled the world.

The eagle led Martha and I as we worked our way through the crowd. In our dimension, I knew Daniel's mother lived close to the Temple, but did she live in the same area in the seventh dimension?

Suddenly the eagle arced in a large circle overhead. A soft call that sounded like a lament pierced the air. "Commit to the Lord whatever you do, and he will establish your plans." His wings made a sharp whistling sound, and then he disappeared beneath the setting sun.

Shira let out a cry.

I tried to comfort her. "You set the bird free, Shira. Maybe he'll come back."

Tears filled her eyes as she sniffled uncontrollably.

Martha put her arms around her. "We're almost home. Are you hungry?"

Shira nodded, rubbing her red eyes. "My bird was beautiful."

CHAPTER 24

W E APPROACHED SOME yellowed limestone buildings reminiscent of the apartments in the Old City of Jerusalem. Dozens of children played along the cobblestone street. Martha parked her horse in front of a dwelling and dismounted. Then she set Shira on the ground and turned to me. "Do you need any help?"

I shook my head. I slid down as gracefully as I could, and Shira ran up to me. I crouched down to her eye level. "Did you enjoy your horse ride?"

She nodded and dug her head into my chest. Now that we were here, trepidation pierced my heart. Had Daniel heard anything about his father? And could his mother be so sick she might die? As I held Shira close, I whispered, "Can you be very quiet while we're inside?"

"I will, Auntie. Can I play?"

I wasn't going to let her out of my sight after her near kidnapping. "Maybe tomorrow—it's too late today."

She looked disappointed. I lifted her face to mine and kissed her on the cheek. "You must be tired."

She rubbed one of her eyes. "I'm not tired, Auntie."

I held Shira's hand to keep her close.

"Let me go in first," Martha said.

Martha climbed the steep steps and disappeared inside. Shira and I sat on a bench and watched children playing. I felt guilty that I didn't have the energy to introduce her. A couple of minutes passed, and Martha reemerged, waving for us to come.

I patted Shira on the shoulder. "Let's go."

We climbed the steps, and when we entered, the stale air reeked of death. My eyes caught Daniel's as he sat next to his mother, Kitty. If only I could read his mind, but a look of surprise told me he wasn't expecting me.

Nidal sat off to the side by himself. Some other women occupied another corner, and a couple of men stood near Daniel. The darkness of the room added to my depression. I wasn't sure what to do. I took a deep breath and decided to sit with the women.

Kitty's friends acknowledged Shira and me but remained silent. Daniel stood as Martha rushed over and sat in the chair next to their mother.

He came over and sat beside me.

"How is she?" I asked.

Daniel bit his lip. "I don't think she's going to make it. Her condition hasn't changed much in the few days we've been here."

Daniel glanced at Nidal. "I think he's getting impatient."

"Did you know before you came that your mother was so ill?"

Daniel shook his head.

I glanced back at Martha, feeling her pain.

Daniel whispered, "She's saying goodbye."

"Is it that imminent?"

Daniel nodded.

"Do you know what's wrong with her?"

Daniel rubbed his eyes. "Can people die of a broken heart?"

"I don't know."

"She is depressed, has been for a long time. Of course, my father was kidnapped or murdered. But there is something else bothering her. She has yet to say what it is."

"What could it be?" I asked.

Daniel bowed his head. "I know. I read her mind."

At that instant, Martha approached, motioning to Daniel.

"Let's go," Daniel said.

"Are you sure?"

"Bring Shira with you," he said.

Daniel, Martha, Shira, and I gathered around Kitty. She looked half the size of her counterpart in our dimension. She must have lost a lot of weight.

Daniel's mother glanced at Shira and her eyes teared up. "Mari?" she asked. "Is that you?"

I glanced at Daniel.

"I'll explain later," he whispered.

Kitty smiled. "You're beautiful. Come close."

Shira edged closer. For a brief moment, Daniel's mother appeared at peace. Then she closed her eyes. "Daniel, the necklace is on the table."

He walked over and picked it up, fingering it before clasping it in his hand.

Martha leaned over and kissed her mother as Daniel said a Jewish prayer. Then he returned alongside me, and I squeezed his hand. "I'm sorry."

My betrothed held up the necklace in the light from the doorway. I recognized the jewelry from the photo beside his mother's bed. Daniel closed his fingers around it but said nothing. I wished I knew its significance.

Martha came over to us. "She's very feverish, but at least she's resting comfortably now."

Daniel and Martha exchanged a few words, and then Daniel turned to me. "I need to talk to Nidal. He's been very patient. We haven't been able to go to the Temple or even have a conversation since we arrived."

I sighed. That probably meant Daniel still didn't know about his father.

"I'm hungry," Shira said.

I brushed her hair back from her face. "Can you wait a few more minutes, and we'll get something to eat?"

She nodded.

Daniel filled me in on plans. "Tomorrow is Shavuot. In Jewish tradition, it commemorates the giving of the Torah." Daniel turned his eyes to his mother. I hope she doesn't die in the next day. Otherwise, it will delay her burial."

"She might still recover," I offered. "Doctor Luke said he would come if we needed him."

Daniel shook his head. "I don't want to bother the doctor. Only a miracle could keep her alive. The family has a burial plot near the Mount of Olives."

"I'm sorry, Daniel."

He steepled his fingers. "Tomorrow, I want to take Nidal to the Temple. He has agreed to come before he returns to Caesarea."

"Chariot racing?"

"Yes."

I leaned into Daniel. "I want to come with you. Please—let me come with you."

"Martha said she'll stay with Mother tomorrow, or as long as is necessary," Daniel said.

"Perhaps Shira can stay here with her. If Martha is willing, can I go with you?"

"You really want to go?"

"Yes."

He stood. "Let me ask."

Daniel returned a few minutes later. "Martha said she would be happy to look after Shira."

I thanked God. "By the way, Martha brought Shira and me new tunics."

Daniel inspected me more closely. "I didn't think I recognized it."

I changed the subject. "Why did your mother think Shira was Mari, and what is the secret she's hiding?"

Daniel grew quiet. "She never forgave herself for her sin. Her high fever has affected her. She thought Shira was Mari. Guilt consumes her."

Neither of us said anything for a minute. I broke the silence. "You think your mother bore a baby out of wedlock?"

Daniel nodded. "The baby was adopted by Theophilus and his wife."

I stared at the floor. "She never forgave herself, did she?"

Daniel ran his hand through his hair and averted his teary eyes from me.

I tried to make eye contact. "Daniel, with Jesus, there is forgiveness. You must tell her before it's too late." I leaned in closer. "And I don't think Martha believes in Jesus either."

"I did share with Mother that Yeshua is the Messiah, but I don't know if she believed."

I rested my head on Daniel's shoulder. "Daniel, why is it so difficult for Jews to believe Jesus is the Messiah?"

CHAPTER 25

THE NEXT MORNING, I awoke early. Disturbing dreams left me exhausted. I glanced at the ceiling.

In my dream, blood dripped through the rafters, mixed with vapors of smoke. Before the fire reached me, I ran out of the house gasping for air. The sun was black, and the full blood moon ripped the ground in every direction. Mountains shot up where they didn't belong.

I wasn't sure if it was day or night or summer or winter. Time was an illusion, and the seasons were out of kilter. Was it from nuclear fallout or the eruption of Yellowstone? Could there be a solar eclipse and lunar eclipse at the same time?

I rubbed my eyes as I tried to erase the memory. I felt alone— utterly alone. And I was waiting for something, but I couldn't remember what.

The dream faded as I thought about Daniel. I needed to talk to him privately. The mourners the night before made that impossible.

I studied Shira who lay asleep next to me. Her angelic face portrayed a remarkable innocence despite her many heartaches. How happy she would be to stay behind and play while we visited the Temple.

I bowed my head. "Dear heavenly Father, I never knew taking care of a three-year-old could be this exhausting. Help me to be more loving, more patient, and more kind."

A break from my role as surrogate mom would freshen me, and I longed for God to give me time with Daniel.

Soon I heard Martha speaking to Kitty. Thankfully, Daniel's mother survived the night. After a few feeble attempts to pray, I heard knocking on the door and jumped up to open it. I was expecting Daniel at any moment. Blinding sunlight poured into the darkness as the door swung wide.

Daniel hugged me briefly. "Did you sleep well?"

I wrapped my arms around his shoulders. "As well as can be expected." That was the truth, although I wished we were alone so I could elaborate.

Nidal bowed, and I acknowledged him politely.

Daniel must have awakened Shira as I heard her swift footsteps pitter-patter into the kitchen. Soon Martha, holding Shira in her arms, joined us. "Are you ready to leave?" she asked.

Daniel leaned over and kissed Shira on the forehead. "I think so. You look beautiful, Princess."

Shira smiled. "Aunt Martha said I could play today."

Martha stroked Shira's hair. "She'll have a good time while you're gone." She set Shira down. "Daniel, I have something to give to you."

Martha hurried into the kitchen and returned with fruit baskets—" for Shavuot."

Daniel's face lit up. "Thank you." He glanced into the adjoining room. "How is she?"

Martha dropped her eyes. "No change, about the same. I offered her some food, but she wasn't hungry. She wants to sleep."

Daniel wrestled with her response. "I don't want to disturb her."

I grabbed Daniel's hand. "Can I talk to you for a minute, privately?"

Daniel tilted his head. "Sure."

I squatted down in front of Shira. "Sweetie, can you help Aunt Martha in the kitchen?"

Martha smiled, taking her by the hand and leading her off.

Daniel turned to Nidal. "I'm sure Martha has some fresh bread. Help yourself. We'll leave shortly."

Nidal's eyes brightened at the mention of food, and he trailed Martha into the kitchen.

I leaned into Daniel. "I wanted to tell you this yesterday, but I couldn't. You need to know, after you left, a man from the future came to the inn and attacked me."

Daniel's eyes stared at me in disbelief. "Are you serious?"

I pulled him closer. "The man said the computer chip was activated. He was looking for Nidal. When he couldn't find him, he attacked me. Thank God Jacob came. He tried to catch the intruder. When the man got away, he sent a guard. I gave Jacob the chip."

Daniel stroked his chin. "I never would have left you behind if I thought that was even a remote possibility."

I glanced into the kitchen to make sure Nidal wasn't listening and cupped my fingers around Daniel's ear. "Nidal must have known somebody would come looking for the chip. He should have told you. I don't trust him."

Daniel traced me with his eyes. "You weren't hurt, were you? Or Shira?"

I shook my head. "No, just scared."

Daniel pounded his palm with a fist. "I thought I could trust him. Thank God you weren't hurt."

"Daniel, you know Muslims have no respect for Christians or Jews —or women."

"Come on, Shale, that sounds so prejudicial."

"If he truly wanted to repay your kindness, he'd tell you about your father. Has he done that? No. You're too trusting—like your father!"

Daniel stiffened. "You can criticize me, but please don't criticize my father."

A twinge of guilt convicted me. "Sorry."

Neither of us said anything for a moment. I'd made my point, but I wished I'd not mentioned his father.

"Are you sure you want to go?" Daniel asked. "Can you give Nidal the benefit of the doubt?

I bit my lip.

"Forgiveness will go a long ways toward making that happen."

I stared at Daniel. "Forgiveness? You're thinking about forgiveness when we could have died."

"God protected you, right?"

I watched Nidal eat some fruit in the kitchen. "I want to go, but I'm worried. Suppose that interloper comes back? Nidal should have told you about the chip. He must have known."

Daniel grabbed my hand. "I still think we can find out more, but if he thinks we're judging him, he won't tell us anything."

I pulled my hand back and wrapped my arms in front of me.

Daniel peered into my eyes. "If we continue to show him how much we accept him, I think we can win him over. He doesn't understand. Our key to reaching him is Yeshua."

"All right," I said reluctantly.

Daniel hugged me and turned his attention to our bags and fruit baskets. "Can you grab something?"

I nodded.

He walked over and briefly checked on his mother. I kissed Shira, and Nidal joined Daniel at the front door.

Martha and Shira waved. "See you later this evening."

I smiled back.

We walked outside as a gush of wind blew overhead, and a couple of doves scattered to a nearby fig tree. Suddenly the nagging thought of leprosy wouldn't leave me. When we passed through some bright sunlight, I appraised Daniel's face, perhaps too conspicuously.

He frowned. "Do you still think I have leprosy?"

I hated being rebuffed. "Are my thoughts that transparent to you?"

Daniel chuckled. "The evil one will make you doubt, Shale. Don't give him a foothold this day."

Then I heard Worldly Crow cackling from a nearby post. "Ca-ca, ca-ca. What a sucker you are."

I started to pick up a pebble but changed my mind. Why should I give the crow the pleasure of a response? "The Lord rebuke you," I muttered.

CHAPTER 26

THE CROWDED STREETS of the Upper City soon grabbed my attention as every blade of green grass and stone walkway was occupied.

Near the Temple Mount, a long procession of worshippers filled the courtyard. Hundreds of oxen decorated in flowery garlands were loaded down with fruits and grains. Children carried small baskets of figs and dates.

"This reminds me of an American parade," I said.

Daniel waved his hand. "This is the festival of Shavuot, more commonly known to Christians as Pentecost." As we neared the Temple entrance, the breathtaking view overwhelmed me. Thousands of visitors could fit inside the courtyard, not counting the animals. The crowd extended past the city gates and up the hills overlooking Jerusalem.

Daniel headed to the Temple entrance.

"Is it always like this?" I asked.

Daniel squeezed my hand. "Jewish travelers come from everywhere. It's one of the three Jewish pilgrimages."

How could Daniel share anything as significant as Jesus with Nidal here? Wouldn't a quiet place be better? He spoke to Nidal, and I started to ask him to repeat it when the shofar blasted. Singing followed, and the praises of worshippers filled my ears. I caught some of the Hebrew words.

"He brought us to this place and has given us this land, a land flowing with milk and honey; and now, behold, I have brought the first fruits of the land which you, O Lord, have given me."

"Let's make our offering first, and then we'll go to Solomon's Porch," Daniel said.

We waited our turn amongst hundreds of others. The air was cool despite the bright morning sun, and there was plenty of activity around us to fill the boredom of standing in line.

After waiting close to an hour, we made our offering. I'd never seen anything like this in America except at sporting events. Seeing humanity pressed in on all sides to worship was unprecedented. Getting students to attend our prayer meetings and Bible study at school paled in comparison.

Gradually at first, the wind began to stir. Soon it became stronger, but I was distracted by a woman's voice. "Daniel!"

The voice was familiar. Seconds later, I recognized the young girl. Lilly waved her hand as she pressed toward us. I remembered Daniel praying with her in the synagogue over her father. Was she from this time or our future?

Daniel greeted her warmly. "Lilly, this is my betrothed, Shale."

Lilly took my arm and nudged me as she shouted to Daniel. "Follow me. Peter and the disciples are at Solomon's Porch. They have been here all morning praying."

We picked our way through the masses as the wind increased. My anticipation mounted. However, it wasn't a wild wind that blew. It went where it wanted.

"Daniel!" The wind circled over the Temple, descending as a whirl-wind. I saw heaven open, and a voice that sounded like thunderous waters proclaimed, "And it shall come to pass that whoever calls on the name of the Lord shall be saved."

The disciples stood in a semicircle facing the crowd as hundreds gathered around. The Zephyr descended zigzagging through the Temple columns, and tongues of fire alighted upon the disciples and their followers.

Almost immediately, fire transformed them. Words of praise left their lips as hope danced on their faces. A supernatural peace settled over the Temple, and the disciples and others began to speak in tongues.

I heard English. How could that be? I lifted my eyes to heaven and raised my hands in celebration. Quite unexpectedly, I saw the risen Christ bathed in white light sitting on his throne.

Peter shouted for all to hear. "This Jesus has been exalted to the right hand of God, and we receive the Holy Spirit, that which you now see and hear."

Several exclaimed, "I'm hearing you in my own tongue. How can that be?"

The people waved and stared as signs and wonders filled the Temple. Nidal shouted, "I'm hearing the words of Muhammad in Nepali. I've never heard Muhammad speak."

I clasped Daniel's arm, concerned that Nidal thought he was hearing Muhammad and not Jesus, but Daniel reassured me. "Let God speak."

People were talking at once. I caught bits and pieces of several conversations.

"I'm hearing Peter in Arabic," a foreigner exclaimed.

"I'm hearing him in Greek," another shouted.

"Peter can't speak Greek," a woman interrupted. "He's a fisherman from Galilee."

"He's speaking Aramaic," another man said.

"Then why am I hearing him in Parthian?" a visitor asked. "I thought worship in the Temple was only in Hebrew."

The crowd swelled around Solomon's Porch as the winds of fire soared over the heads of eyewitnesses. The tongues alighted on some of the listeners, and they spoke in other languages. The multitude questioned each other. "Are these not Galileans? How is it that we're hearing them in our own tongue?"

A few standing nearby mocked the disciples. "They are full of new wine."

Fear crossed the faces of the Roman guards as they stared into the heavens. Nothing in their plethora of Roman gods could explain this event. Did they consider this was related to the death of Jesus whom they'd crucified seven weeks earlier?

I felt the electricity in the air—a supernatural kind that settled over the Temple environs. We were witnessing the fulfillment of the fourth of God's seven festivals. The next festival to be fulfilled would be the Feast of Trumpets—and my thoughts ran amok contemplating that future event.

The murmurs increased, and I feared a riot might erupt. Then Peter stood on a table and addressed the onlookers. "Men of Judea and those who dwell in Jerusalem, let this be known to you and heed my words.

"For these men and women are not drunk, as you suppose, since it is only the third hour of the day. But this is what was spoken by the prophet Joel: 'It shall come to pass in the last days that I will pour out my spirit on all flesh; your sons and your daughters shall prophesy. Your young men shall see visions, and your old men shall dream dreams.'"

Peter raised his hands and quoted from God's book. "'And on my menservants and on my maidservants, I will pour out my spirit in those days, and they shall prophesy. I will show wonders in heaven above, and signs in the earth beneath; blood and fire and vapor of smoke. The sun shall be turned into darkness, and the moon into blood, before the coming of the great and awesome day of the Lord. And it shall come to pass that whoever calls on the name of the Lord shall be saved.'"

I remembered my dream. The sun turning dark could be a solar eclipse, but what could a red moon mean except something in the atmosphere turning it red—like fire?

Peter explained what happened. "Jesus of Nazareth, the Son of God, seven weeks ago, was put to death by crucifixion. On the third day, he rose from the dead. Even now in heaven, Christ sits on the throne."

Peter said Jesus told them to wait in Jerusalem until he sent the gift of the Holy Spirit. Those present saw that outpouring. He quoted again from the Scriptures. "For David did not ascend into the heavens, but he said, 'The Lord said to my Lord, sit at my right hand, till I make your enemies your footstool.'"

Thousands on the Temple Mount heard Peter's sermon, and many threw up their hands in contrite prayers of repentance. When the people realized the truth of Peter's words, many hearts trembled with fear. Some asked, "What must we do?"

Peter replied, "Repent and be baptized in the name of Jesus Christ for the remission of sins, and you shall receive the gift of the Holy Spirit."

Thousands came forward.

The mikvahs, large baths for ceremonial washing, were set up along the southern walls of the Temple Mount at the base of the double-gate stairs. Lines began to form. I'd never seen a turning to God by so many at one time. I leaned into Daniel. "This is the beginning of the church age."

Daniel smiled. "I know."

I glanced at Nidal who appeared stunned. Daniel draped his arm around his shoulder and spoke in his ear. I turned my attention to the Temple entrance. Some people were dispersing, unmoved by what they saw.

I shook my head in disbelief that anyone could walk away from God's gift of the Holy Spirit. What else could God have done to show his perfect love to a perverse generation that missed his visitation? I remembered the words of Jesus, "For many are called, but few are chosen."

After several minutes of intense discussion, Daniel relayed to me what Nidal said.

"Nidal wants to talk to me, and I can't hear him here. Let's go to another part of the Temple away from the noise."

"Do you think he'll tell you about your father?"

Daniel rubbed the nape of his neck. "If I don't press too hard. He is quite shaken by what we've witnessed."

Daniel led the way. I prayed as we walked that God would work a miracle. Since women weren't allowed in the inner sanctum of the Temple, we stayed in the outer court. Daniel found a small portico, and we sat on some benches inside the columns that buttressed the wall.

CHAPTER 27

"**I** DON'T KNOW where to begin," Nidal said.

Daniel's eyes blazed with such intensity it surprised me. "The beginning is always a good place."

Nidal dropped his face in his hands. "It's too late. I've made too many mistakes."

Did he groan as a man troubled in his spirit? I was skeptical.

"I never want to see the scientists again," Nidal stated. He lifted his reddened eyes, but was it true contriteness or regret because he was caught?

Words gushed forth. "What would they do to me? We didn't complete the mission."

Daniel waved his hands impatiently. "I don't care about that. I want to know about my father, Aviv Sperling."

Nidal rubbed his eyes.

"Is he still alive?"

"The last I heard he was."

"When was that?"

Nidal clasped his forearms and focused on the ground. "I don't know the men who came the first time, but they were connected with scientists. They'd heard about the Yeti from news reports and climbers. Suddenly, the creatures were everywhere."

"The Yeti? You already told me about the Yeti."

"I know," Nidal said. "But remember, they aren't animals, and they aren't human. They're something from another world, maybe something the scientists created in a laboratory."

I touched Daniel's arm, reminding him of what happened when we were in Nepal.

Daniel stood, imploring Nidal again with his hands. "What does that have to do with my father?"

"I'm getting there."

Annoyed, Daniel traipsed a few feet away.

I edged over to my betrothed, concerned that at this most critical moment his impatience would be his undoing. "Daniel, let him talk. Don't rush him. You might find out more that way."

He drew in a long breath. "I want to know what happened, that's all." He clasped my arm. "Thanks."

I was distracted for a moment by the crowd. The earthy smell of animals, carried along by the hot, desert wind, turned my stomach. The Bible told the sanitized version, but if believers could touch the walls of the Temple and see the tongues of fire, how could they not believe?

I dismissed my wanderings and focused on Nidal's story.

"I've been on a quest for the truth," he said. "I grew up as a Hindu. When I heard about Allah, I wanted to be a Muslim. I no longer believed in the Hindu gods. Thousands made it impossible to know them intimately, and I exhausted myself trying to please so many.

"I became interested in Islam when Muslims hired me to lead their expedition to Mount Everest. They prayed five times a day and fasted. Their holy one seemed more real than our thousands. I asked them how I could become a Muslim. They gave me a copy of the Quran."

Nidal fidgeted, tucking his hands under his arms and speaking barely above a whisper. "I went to the local mosque to learn more, and I studied hard. When the scientists came around asking about the Yeti, I told them I became a Muslim. They offered me a deal. They said they would pay for me to make the Haj if I went to Syria to find a businessman. They wanted some scrolls. They said if the scrolls got into the wrong hands, bigger problems than the Yeti could come upon the mountain."

Nidal spoke more intentionally. "I didn't know what I was getting into. Nepal is one of the poorest countries in the world. I was a Sherpa. Every year people die trying to make it to the summit. Now I was given a ticket to a new life."

"What happened next?"

"After I finished the Haj, Tariq met me in Mecca. Tariq knew the location of Aviv in Syria. The scientists tracked him down in Damascus. Then the war started.

"I changed my mind. After spending a couple of days with Tariq, I didn't like him. He said the scientists paid for my trip to Mecca and promised more money when the mission was completed. He threatened to kidnap Mr. Sperling if he didn't give us the scrolls."

"So that information from the police was correct," Daniel stated. "He was kidnapped."

"Alms, alms," a beggar cried as he approached. He tapped his cane to the front and side. I took pity on him, a blind man begging for scraps when he could have received God's Comforter. I reached into my bag and handed him a fig.

The man thanked me and continued on his way.

Nidal waited until the man was a reasonable distance away before continuing. "Aviv, your father, spoke Nepali, which surprised me, although many Jewish families come to Nepal for vacation. He said he didn't have the scrolls. He gave them to someone."

"What happened after that?"

"The war with ISIS in Syria intensified, and travel became dangerous. Despite that, we took Aviv to Nepal to get out of Syria. I promised Aviv we would let him go if he cooperated. I suggested we take him to a shaman. I convinced Tariq a shaman could find out where the scrolls were."

"The shaman claimed Aviv sent the scrolls to Israel. We tried to get permission from the Israeli authorities to get a search warrant. They said any antiquities found in Israel belonged to Israel."

"Wait," Daniel cut in. "You took my father to the shaman. Then what happened?"

"The shaman suggested we take him to Shambhala, to Perlsea Castle, high up in the Himalayan Mountains, where the shaman said he would be unable to escape. Tariq insisted we tie him up, even though I didn't want to."

"What happened after that?"

"Your father refused to tell us more. In reality, his usefulness was done. Tariq lost interest in him at that point and wanted to, in his words, 'eliminate him.' Fortunately, the scientists weren't interested in killing people and had another idea. They wanted us to travel through a stargate and retrieve the scrolls back in history.

"There were several options. First, we could try to find you, but I don't think you were here yet. Something went wrong on their end, so we started chariot racing. I wanted to be a rich man when I returned.

"Or we could search for the scrolls among the Dead Sea Scrolls. The scientists knew where they were hidden. Or we could steal them from Shale, but we didn't know her whereabouts."

"What did you know about me?" I asked.

"That your father was involved with the Illuminati. He was interested in Biblical antiquities, was a world-renowned linguistics expert, and had been involved with the Vatican for years.

"But it also raised suspicions that he created the scrolls, faked them, and then claimed them as authentic. I heard he was deeply in debt and needed money. I never heard how that turned out, but it made getting to the bottom of the scrolls urgent."

Nidal studied me. "No one could explain how you ended up in the first century. You were a mystery but being Brutus' daughter—rumors circulated."

Daniel interrupted. "When I started racing against you, that was your opportunity, wasn't it?"

Nidal nodded. "When you had the accident, we thought that was our chance. Cynisca told us where you lived, but when we went to your apartment, the scrolls weren't there. Then we found your gold."

Daniel ran his hand through his hair. "Makes me wonder if your father was involved, Shale."

I didn't get the connection. "How so?"

"Your father suggested I race chariots. Could he have known Nidal and Tariq were looking for me, already racing chariots, and set this up so they could get the scrolls? We know they are real. Perhaps he wanted to make a profit and was using you to make that happen."

Could it be true? I wondered.

Daniel turned his attention back to Nidal. "As I said, you were too soon. I didn't have Shale's scrolls when I was in Caesarea. And you were one day too soon going to Qumran. I found you unconscious on Robber's Road the day after I hid them on the way back to Jerusalem."

Nidal cast his eyes on the Temple Courtyard.

Daniel began pacing back and forth. "What happened to my father after that?"

"The last time I saw your father was when a scientist met me at Perlsea Castle and took me to the Shiva Temple."

Daniel stopped pacing. "You left my father at the castle?"

"Yes, but I dreamed the great white dog of the north set him free."

"Who is the white dog of the north?"

Nidal's eyes drifted as he reminisced. "Legend says the dog of the north helps the trekkers when they become lost on Everest, or comforts them if they become injured. Sherpas hear the stories. One I know was helped by the dog when he almost died. I dreamed that the white dog of the north rescued your father."

"He couldn't escape on his own?"

Nidal shrugged. "The last day I went to the castle, Tariq wasn't with me. He met me at the Temple. I didn't lock the door. Your father could have escaped."

I put my hand on Daniel's.

"When was this?" Daniel asked.

Nidal thought for a moment. "We left in 2014."

"Before the earthquake," Daniel whispered to me. "Why did you wait until now to tell me this? Why didn't you tell me this back in Dothan?"

Resignation crossed Nidal's face.

A few people walked nearby breaking the spell of the conversation. Again, Nidal waited until they left before saying anything else.

"I'm sorry," he confessed. "I really am." Nidal wiped his eyes with the back of his hand. "You saved my life when you brought me to the inn. If it wasn't for Doctor Luke, I would have died, but I didn't know it was you who rescued me. It's hard for me to understand why you saved my life after I stole your money."

Daniel pressed. "Why didn't you tell me in Dothan about my father?"

"I was afraid. When the scientists find out I've abandoned the mission, I don't know what they'll do. They are opening stargates everywhere. By now other things have probably come through. The Yeti were the first. That's what they said."

"When Doctor Luke removed the chip, did you know what would happen?"

"I knew they could no longer track me. I could stay here and never go back."

"Did you know they would send someone to look for you?"

Nidal shook his head. "No."

"Don't you have family in the twenty-first century? Don't you want to go back?"

Nidal glanced away. "I've had dreams since I've been here, bad dreams. I'm afraid to return. I think the scientists are going to bring about the end of the world. They have opened stargates. At the Shiva Temple and other places, aliens are coming, worse than the Yeti. I know it, and I don't want to be there when they arrive."

CHAPTER 28

I WHISPERED TO Daniel. "Ask him about the dreams."

"What kind of dreams?" Daniel asked.

Perspiration beaded on Nidal's forehead. "I don't want to tell you, except"—Nidal covered his eyes—"maybe it's starting to make sense."

"What is?" Daniel asked.

Nidal wiped his face. "In one dream, I was racing. Heaven peeled away, and a chariot of fire shot through the sky and came alongside me. If I sped up, he sped up. If I slowed down, he slowed down. Four golden cherubim were on both sides of the vehicle. A glowing man sat on a crystal throne riding the wings of the angels.

"I asked the man who he was. He said, 'I sit in the chariot of God. I speak as God, and I am God.' I wanted it to be Muhammad, but I knew it was Jesus.

"Suddenly, lightning bolts flashed across the heavens, and a vast wind spiraled all around me. The chariot flew back into another dimension as the opening through which it appeared sealed. Terror seized my heart. Why didn't I see Muhammad? Why did I see Jesus?

"Darkness blanketed the sky. Electrical particles charged the hair on my arms, and I smelled rotten eggs. From out of the clouds, a UFO zigzagged across the heavens. Then I woke up."

Nidal shuddered. "I keep having this same dream. A UFO is coming to get me. We passed dozens of them when we traveled here through the star-gate. The creatures inside the UFOs—they aren't human. They're aliens."

Daniel cupped his ear to block the background noise as more people and animals filled the Temple Mount. "You mean, when the scientists brought you and Tariq here, you saw UFOs in the tunnel?"

Nidal closed his eyes. "Yes. We traveled through different dimensions."

"Is the real reason you don't want to go back because you're afraid?"

"Yes. It's the truth. Without the computer chip, the scientists can't track me. I've had many dreams. I asked Allah to take away this one dream, but he hasn't. I want to find Jesus—he's the one I saw in the chariot."

"Is Tariq a scientist?" Daniel asked.

Nidal shook his head. "He told me the scientists are using a powerful weapon to open stargates. They are opening portals between our world and another dimension. The tunnel was cold, and I thought we would die of exposure."

Daniel leaned forward. "In one sense, you're right. The scientists are opening portals to another dimension—but it's a spiritual dimension."

"And we're back in time," I added.

Daniel squared his shoulders. "God is the alpha and the omega, the beginning and the end. He's outside of time. Did Tariq tell you anything else about the scientists?"

"He said the scientists worshipped Shiva, the Hindu god of destruction. He said they wanted to deconstruct the universe and recreate the big bang. The facility is based on the Swiss-French border. I asked him why these scrolls were so important. Tariq said the scientists wanted to erase history and rewrite it. They didn't want any historical record of Jesus."

I interjected. "CERN."

"What did you say?" Daniel asked.

The Temple Mount was too noisy. I shouted, "Can we go to another area?"

Daniel motioned to Nidal. "Let's take a walk." He pointed to the Temple. "The Romans destroyed this structure in 70 A.D. Some Jews want to rebuild it. Of course, the Dome of the Rock makes that impossible."

The gold between the Temple stones glistened in the noonday sun. Hundreds stood in line to make their fruit and grain offerings, and merchants set up stands for visitors and travelers. The Temple wasn't just the center of worship. It was also the center for trade and business.

Nidal licked his parched lips. "I heard the disciple speaking in Nepali. I haven't heard that language since I've been here."

"You heard Peter speaking in Nepali?" Daniel asked.

Nidal nodded. "When I heard Peter speak, one thing impressed me."

Daniel studied Nidal's face. "What's that?"

"How much Peter loved Prophet Jesus. He even quoted David, another prophet mentioned in the Quran. I never knew there was a connection between the two prophets."

Would Daniel take advantage of the opening? I wanted to jump in and ask questions, but I knew that would be inappropriate.

However, Daniel wasted no time. "David made many inferences in the Psalms to the coming Messiah."

"Can you give me one?" Nidal asked.

"For example, David said, 'The Lord said to my Lord, sit at my right hand till I make your enemies your footstool.' It's in the Tanakh."

I added, "And Peter said, 'Jesus, who you crucified, was both Lord and Christ.'"

Nidal's eyes turned to me.

"That's right," Daniel said. "That statement is from the New Testament."

Nidal clasped his hands. "I don't understand how Jesus could be both Lord and Christ."

He raised his eyebrow and waved his hand, not waiting for a response from Daniel. "Thousands are in line to be—what was that word Peter used?"

"Baptized," Daniel replied.

Nidal gestured. "All these people don't seem to have a problem with it."

"Three thousand are going to be baptized today," Daniel said.

"That many?" Nidal shook his head. "I don't understand."

The three of us gazed at the new followers of Jesus. What a defining moment in the history of the church, but was it enough to touch Nidal's heart?

The Muslim nervously rubbed his hands. "Let me ask you a different question. Why did Jesus die—if he did die?"

Daniel leaned forward. "Love motivated Jesus. He died for all of us. We deserve death, but Jesus died in our place so we could spend eternity with him."

Nidal looked down and pushed a loose stone aside. "You know, Islam tells us that Jesus didn't die on the cross."

Daniel scooted up closer. "Do you know that no one in history, out of the thousands who were crucified by the Romans, survived the crucifixion?"

"What do you mean?" Nidal asked.

"There isn't a single recorded case of anyone ever crucified by the Romans who came down off the cross alive. Every person who was crucified by the Romans died. Don't you think that if one person, especially someone as controversial as Jesus, managed to survive, it would have been widely known and reported? Plus, think of the eyewitnesses who saw Jesus die. The Scriptures also tell us the Roman guard speared him in the side to make sure he was dead."

Nidal reflected on Daniel's words but remained quiet.

"Crucifixion is torture," Daniel said, "and if by some chance Jesus did survive the crucifixion, do you think he could have made a full recovery based on the crude medical methods of this period?"

"But how can you be sure?"

"As far as I know," Daniel said, "there is very little dispute among most historians that Jesus died on the cross."

"I wish I had a computer. I'd search it on Google, but I have a counterargument."

Daniel brushed his hair back from his forehead. "What's that?"

"I heard an Imam claim that Jesus' body was replaced with the body of Judas."

Daniel shook his head. "That would be impossible. Judas was already dead when Jesus was crucified. The betrayer's entrails spilled out on the ground. That's why the Jews sold the land. His blood defiled it. Besides, dozens of people witnessed Jesus' crucifixion, and Roman guards were present at his crucifixion the entire time.

"They took down Jesus' dead body and gave it to his friends so they could prepare it for burial. They would have declared Jesus dead before they delivered his body to Joseph of Arimathea and the women."

Daniel added, "Believe me when I tell you this. There is no way the Roman soldiers could have removed Jesus from the cross alive, retrieved the body of Judas that was ripped wide open when he hung himself, and then nailed Judas to the cross in place of Jesus. That contradicts the historical record as reported by those who witnessed it. History would have recorded events differently."

"I see what you are saying," Nidal said, "but somehow the Imams make it sound so probable, so certain, that he didn't die. They say it happen supernaturally. Allah did it without anyone knowing, but after hearing what Peter said, I'm not sure what to believe."

Daniel crossed his arms and tilted his head. "People can sound very convincing, but when you study the historical record, when you look at the Scriptures, when you find so many different sources that say the same thing, you have to examine more closely the authenticity of what they say."

That seemed to satisfy Nidal.

Daniel gestured. "Also, if Allah exchanged the body of Jesus for Judas, the body would look different. The Roman guards would have recognized they were taking down a different man than the one they crucified.

"The Roman soldiers handed the body of Jesus to Joseph of Arimathea per order of Pontius Pilate. The mother of Jesus, who was with Joseph, would have recognized that the body the Roman guard handed them wasn't that of her son if it was the body of Judas."

I wasn't sure if Nidal was going to ask any more questions until Daniel asked Nidal one.

"Did you know that all of the disciples were martyred except for one?"

Nidal's eyes brightened. "Muslims also die for their belief in Islam. What makes Christians different?"

Daniel mulled over Nidal's words. "That's true, someone can be sincere and die for what they believe, but even Muslims wouldn't die for a lie. They are only willing to die for something they believe is true. If the disciples knew that Jesus didn't die on the cross, do you think they would have been willing to die?

"Probably not," Nidal replied.

"They were willing to die because they knew Jesus did die on the cross. He also predicted his death. When he died, the disciples remembered Jesus said he would rise again in three days."

"He said that?" Nidal asked.

"He did," Daniel said.

"How could anyone make a claim like that?"

"Only the Messiah could."

CHAPTER 29

NIDAL REMAINED SKEPTICAL. "Christians say Jesus was God's son."

Daniel nodded. "That's true."

"Why would God allow his son to die on the cross?"

"God rescued us, just as we rescued Shira. We risked our lives to save her and have adopted her. Would a loving father not do everything in his power to take care of his child? Would he ever abandon his child on the streets? Or in the twenty-first century, hire an attorney to sue her?"

"Of course not," Nidal said. "No loving father would do any of those things."

Daniel pressed the point further. "If human fathers, who are imperfect, love their children imperfectly, would not a perfect God, who loves perfectly, sacrifice himself on the cross for his children—for you and me, whom he adopted, to the point of death on the cross?"

Nidal swallowed hard. "But how could Jesus be God and his son at the same time?"

Daniel held up his hands. "Nidal, I'm not an expert in these things, and some things are tough to understand. The most learned experts debate these difficult concepts and have for the last two thousand years. But this much I do know. I'm a sinner, and it's only by God's grace I'm saved. That kind of mercy is not free. God can't ignore or excuse sin.

"God is so holy that no one can see him face to face. Only through Jesus can we see God. While our heavenly Father deserves our utmost respect and honor, he doesn't demand our worship. We worship him because he first loved us, and he showed us his love by sending Jesus, his only son, to die in our place on the cross."

Nidal turned away as if to hide his deeper feelings. "I've always longed for more. Hinduism left me empty. I thought Islam would fill me. I wanted to be acceptable to God. That's why I did the Haj, to earn Allah's favor."

"You can't do anything to earn God's favor," Daniel said.

Nidal's eyes narrowed. "Then what can you do if you can't do anything?"

"Jesus did it for you when he died on the cross."

Nidal still seemed unconvinced. I began to see how lies from false teachers had deceived him. Instead of anger at his failings, I pitied him. Here was a man in search of the truth, and perhaps, at last, he found it.

Nidal continued to question. "One of the things that attracted me to Allah is that he's one God. I wanted to worship one God, not many gods as I did as a Hindu."

Daniel answered Nidal's complicated question. "Christians and Jews worship only one God."

"Christians don't worship three different Gods?"

Daniel shook his head. "There is a story in the New Testament where Jesus was approached by one of the scribes. He asked Jesus, 'Which commandment is the most important of all?' Jesus said, 'This is the most important. Hear O Israel, the Lord our God is one Lord.' Jesus also said, 'You shall love the Lord your God with all your heart, with all your soul, with all your strength, and with all your mind.'"

"No wonder Peter spoke so powerfully about Jesus," Nidal said.

Silence filled the distance between us as Nidal reflected on what he'd seen and heard. I prayed that God would close the chasm. I sensed Nidal wanted more in his faith—an intimate relationship with God,

God's unconditional acceptance, and his sacrificial love. Wasn't that a need of everyone, woven into the fabric of our DNA?

Nidal broke the silence. "When the tongues of fire descended upon first the disciples and then on many of the others, their faces shone with joy. I want that joy, too."

"You can have that joy, Nidal. It's free to anyone who believes in Jesus."

Nidal's eyes turned to Peter. Many were still gathered around him and the disciples. "How can I receive the spirit of God that the others have received? Is it too late?"

Daniel replied, "All you have to do is believe Jesus died for your sins."

Nidal shook his head. "I can't. I still can't accept that God would allow his son to die like that."

I whispered to Daniel, "Focus on the works of Jesus. Remember, he said, 'If you don't believe in me, believe in the works I do.'"

Daniel nodded. "That might be helpful." He turned back to Nidal. "One time Jesus said, 'If you don't believe in me, believe in the works I do, as the Father is in me and I'm in the Father.' Do you know what kind of works Jesus did?"

Nidal nodded. "The Quran says Jesus was a great prophet, that he performed miracles, healed the sick, and was a man of peace."

Daniel replied, "That's good. There is also one other thing Jesus did that you may not know. Does the Quran mention anything about Allah forgiving you so you can go to heaven?"

Nidal appeared crestfallen. "The Quran doesn't talk about forgiveness. You have no assurance about making it to heaven. You try to live a good life that will please Allah. Sadly, I think I've failed, and there is nothing I can do about it."

"Do you know what Jesus preached?" Daniel asked.

"No, the Quran just says he was a prophet."

"Jesus said, 'For God so loved the world that he gave his only begotten son, that whoever believes in him should not perish, but have everlasting life.'"

"Christians can be sure they will go to heaven?" Nidal asked.

"Yes, one hundred percent sure."

"It's hard for me to imagine anyone could be a hundred percent certain."

"If you're a Christian, it isn't," Daniel assured him. "God loves you unconditionally."

"If only I could believe," Nidal said, "and understand forgiveness. If only…"

Daniel and I gave Nidal a moment to process this new revelation.

But he shook his head, mumbling to himself. Then he stood and edged away from us. He raised his hands in the air, still saying stuff I couldn't hear. I sensed he was having an emotional crisis right in front of our eyes.

I reached for Daniel's hand. As Daniel's eyes met mine, a faint smile crossed his lips. "Thank you," he whispered.

Nidal turned back to us, appearing more agitated than before. Deep lines dug into his forehead, and he rubbed his upper arms nervously.

"What was Jesus' message again?" he asked.

"For God so loved the world that he gave his only begotten son, that whoever believes in him should not perish, but have everlasting life."

Nidal dropped his eyes. Compassion for the poor man grew in my heart. At first, I was angry with him, but God showed me something I didn't expect.

In smugness, I'd considered myself better than Muslims because of Jesus. How wicked my thoughts. Witnessing Nidal's struggle to understand love and forgiveness, something unknown to him, was heart-wrenching.

Nidal took a deep breath. "I almost hate to ask you this question because—well, I don't want to disrespect you."

Daniel drew closer. "Nidal, you've been given a gift. We've both been given a gift."

"What's that?" Nidal asked.

"We've witnessed the giving of the Comforter, as recorded in the book of Acts. I don't think you could say anything to diminish that."

"If I may be so bold to ask…"

Daniel waved his hand. "Ask."

"Many Imams say the Bible is corrupt because there are many translations, but you can believe the Quran because it's written only in the original Arabic."

"The Bible is made up of many books," Daniel said. "The translation of the Tanakh and New Testament into different languages allows people to read God's Word in their own language. The Bible gives many warnings concerning Scripture.

"In the Book of Revelation, the disciple John wrote, 'If anyone adds to these things, God will add to him the plagues that are written in this book.' Moses wrote the same thing in the Torah. 'You shall not add to the word which I command you, nor take from it, that you may keep the commandments of the Lord.' Two centuries later, Solomon wrote in the Psalms, 'Every word of God is pure. Do not add to his words, lest he rebukes you, and you be found a liar.'

"The books of the Bible were written by many people with great care. Doesn't the Quran attest to the authenticity of the Scriptures that existed even before Muhammad wrote the Quran?"

"Yes," Nidal said, "in Quran 5:43."

"I can give you the Bible in your own language, and you can read it for yourself and understand. There are no contradictions. The greatest story ever told covers the pages of the Bible—God's plan of salvation found in Jesus Christ. In the Tanakh, it is revealed through hundreds of prophecies. Many were fulfilled at the first coming of Yeshua."

Nidal leaned toward Daniel. "That seems fair enough. May I ask one last question? How do you know Jesus rose from the dead? I mean, if he didn't rise from the dead, then there is no Christianity."

"That's true," Daniel said. "However, there is plenty of evidence that he did. Yeshua appeared to Peter and the women three days after his crucifixion. He preached to hundreds of eyewitnesses on the shores of the Sea of Galilee a couple of weeks later. During the past forty days, he's spent time eating and drinking with his disciples before returning to Heaven. That's many eyewitnesses. It's not like only one person saw him after his death.

"All the Gospels were written within the first seventy-five years of the life of Jesus. What was written could be verified by those who heard him preach."

Daniel waved his hand at the multitude. "You witnessed God's spirit come upon the disciples. Jesus longs to know you, Nidal. He wants to have a relationship with you."

Nidal was quiet, taking in Daniel's words.

"You know, Nidal, if you follow Islamic tradition since I've shared Jesus with you, as a Muslim, you should kill me, even though I saved your life. Do you want to kill me?"

"Of course not. That would be wrong."

Daniel edged closer. "That tells me Jesus has already touched your heart. He is speaking to you even now. He is showing you hope, forgiveness, and love. He is putting that longing in your heart."

"You knew who I was when you rescued me, didn't you?"

Daniel nodded.

"You must have known at some point I was involved in your father's kidnapping, and still, you saved my life."

"I forgave you because God forgave me."

Nidal stood and offered his hand. "I need time to think. I must go."

Daniel clasped Nidal's hand. "If you don't remember anything else, remember Jesus loves you."

Nidal bowed slightly. "And you, ma'am, peace on you." His voice cracked, and he wiped his eyes. Then he took off, hurrying through the crowd, and we lost sight of him.

"Are you just going to let him go?" I asked.

Daniel placed his hand on mine. "He has a lot to think about."

We sat for a while in silence.

At last Daniel stood. "We need to go back and check on my mother."

I wrapped my arm around him. "Remember what Jesus said about your father. You need to trust him. Our hope in Jesus never disappoints."

"Yes," Daniel said. "I must wait on God and not force his hand. I keep insisting on things happening the way I want them to."

I laid my head on his shoulder. As we walked, Daniel pulled out the necklace his mother gave him. "I need to return this to the owner."

"Who is that?"

"My great-grandmother."

"Where is she?"

A faraway look entered Daniel's eyes. "She's on a train to Auschwitz."

CHAPTER 30

AS QUICKLY AS Daniel said "train," I heard chugging and a whistle blow. The power of suggestion was so strong that goosebumps covered my arms. "What did you say?"

"She's on a train to Auschwitz."

The haunting sound of the Temple shofar couldn't eclipse the train's arrival as it blew across space and time, but I didn't see a train—in the first century. All I saw was the afternoon sun bearing down on weary people. Many stood in line to be baptized as musty donkeys pressed in around us.

Daniel took me by the arm and led me away from the Temple Mount. I followed him through the city gates, past the cemetery, and along a dusty trail that led to the Mount of Olives. The road split, and we took the one to the garden. The ascent wasn't steep, but it was enough to make me winded. Within a short time, we reached a secluded area in the garden.

Daniel stopped to rest on a large boulder. I sat beside him as he held up the necklace. "This belongs to my great-grandmother."

"She was wearing it in that photograph beside your mother's bed, wasn't she?"

"You saw it?" Daniel asked.

"When you picked up the picture frame and examined it. I couldn't imagine its significance."

Daniel ran his finger along the edges of the Star of David.

I admired the necklace over Daniel's shoulder. "How did your mother get it in the first century?"

Daniel stood, reaching for my hand. "Follow me."

"Where are you taking me now?"

"Where the soldiers bound Jesus and took him away."

"Why?"

"I want to tell you a few things before we go back to the apartment."

We continued along the edge of the Garden of Gethsemane overlooking Jerusalem. Beyond the city walls, the desolate Judean wilderness revealed waves of mountains in an ocean desert.

After a few minutes, Daniel pointed. "There the angel ministered to Jesus and strengthened him before the Temple soldiers arrived and carted him off to Caiaphas."

I imagined what that night must have been like. "You saw it happen, didn't you?"

Daniel nodded. "Mark was with me. Then some guards discovered us. Mark escaped, although he left behind his clothes."

"I remember that story in the Gospel."

Reminiscing, Daniel swiped his hair from his forehead. "I thought we would suffer the same fate as Yeshua."

"How did you escape?"

"It wasn't my time."

Neither of us said anything for a minute, and then I broke the silence. "You don't want to go to Auschwitz, do you?"

Daniel didn't hear my question. "I think we're being watched."

I froze, and my heart beat wildly. I wanted to run away, but I couldn't move. "Who is watching us?"

"Whoever it is, he's behind that clump of olive trees."

I didn't see anybody.

"See the movement in the branches?" Daniel whispered. "It's as if it has invisible legs."

I searched hard as fear gripped my heart. There was no wind, nothing to make the trees sway so violently. "I don't see anything."

"Whoever it is, I can't read his mind, and I can read the mind of any human."

My eyes dropped to the ground, and I saw a snake wrapping its body around Daniel's ankle. I screamed.

Daniel grabbed the reptile and flung it toward the trees. The snake slammed into one of the trunks and then disappeared inside the bole. I blinked. Did I really see what I thought I saw?

Seconds later, the tree turned into a reptilian creature. It had a humanoid body, but its freakish appearance reminded me of the Shambhala demons. As it emerged from its shadowy cover, I trembled. I'd never seen a reptilian human. The evil eye on its forehead stared at me as it started to approach.

"Fallen angel," Daniel whispered.

Suddenly, a white dove swooped down and flew toward the demon. Immediately, the fallen angel disappeared, as if it were swallowed up in another dimension.

I gasped. I recognized the bird.

The magnificent creature grew in size as it flapped its wings and circled overhead. Soon it morphed into an eagle and disappeared into the heavens. I'd hoped it would speak, but it didn't. Within seconds, it was out of sight. Neither of us moved. Several seconds passed as we waited for something to happen—for the bird to return or to see if the underling reappeared, but all we heard were a few songbirds chirping.

Daniel drew in a long breath, and I realized I hadn't breathed either. His eyes met mine. "Did you ask me something?"

I shook my head, "I don't remember asking you anything."

"I could have sworn you asked me something."

I followed his gaze and noticed the branches weren't swaying anymore. Everything looked normal, but I knew we had witnessed a fallen angel.

"This must be the evilest place on the planet, where Judas betrayed Yeshua!" Daniel exclaimed.

I wrapped my arms around myself, still feeling fearful. "If we could see the whole spiritual world and not just an opening, I bet the devil's minions are everywhere."

Daniel rubbed his forehead. "I'm glad we can't see more. That was enough."

I touched his arm. "Doctor Luke gave Shira a wooden dove as a gift. The doctor said Jesus made it when he was a carpenter. The bird came to life and brought us here from Dothan. Along the way, the dove fed the lepers and kept away the vultures. Once we arrived at your mother's house, he flew away. That's the same bird."

"That's amazing." Daniel tugged at his toga as his eyes scanned the horizon. "God must be looking out for us. Even here." He took me by the hand, and I followed him back to the garden entrance. "By the way, I remember your question."

"What was it?"

"You asked me if I wanted to go to Auschwitz."

"Oh, yeah." I inched forward. "It's strange that we both forgot—as if the fallen angel could steal our thoughts."

"I know," Daniel said, "but to answer your question, no, I don't want to go to Auschwitz, but I need to tell you what happened."

"I'm listening."

Daniel helped me down a more difficult incline. "When I left Caesarea for Passover, I didn't have enough time to make it to Jerusalem before Shabbat. God sent a train to take me to Jerusalem, but it wasn't an ordinary train. Jewish families were crammed in like sardines. I couldn't move, and the odor was nauseating. When I couldn't take it anymore, a woman cried, 'Fire.' I think she saw the flames of Auschwitz, even though there were no flames visible from the train."

"She saw the future," I suggested.

Daniel wiped his nose with the back of his hand as if he could smell burning flesh. "But it was the children on the train that bothered me. Most of them had kittens in their laps. Later, I saw the same children in the garden holding the kittens."

"Did you ever find out their meaning?"

Daniel placed his hand on his chin. "Animals bring comfort to young children. Perhaps the kittens symbolized the Holy Spirit, but I don't know for sure. There was an older girl on the train sitting near me, perhaps twelve or thirteen. She didn't have a kitten." Daniel held up the necklace. "She was holding this in her hand."

"Did she give it to you?"

Daniel shook his head. "At that moment, a large man with a menacing dog opened the boxcar. As he was about to enter our cabin, the train disappeared, and I was on a hill overlooking the Temple. When I looked down, I saw the necklace lying in the road as the Star of David glistened in the sun. The young girl must have dropped it when she got off the train."

I stopped Daniel. "You want to return the necklace to the girl who you think is your great-grandmother?"

"Yes," Daniel replied.

"What difference does it make now? That happened almost eighty years ago. God must have allowed it to fall out of the train."

Daniel furrowed his brow. "Her parents died in the gas chamber. Perhaps she didn't leave the train. How else did she live through the holocaust?"

"You mean the Nazis didn't see her on the train?"

Daniel crossed his arms. "The photo was taken after World War II, and she was wearing the necklace. If she lost it getting off the train, then how could she have worn it when the picture was taken?"

I threw up my hands. "Daniel, this whole idea seems implausible. How could you find this train? Or find her?"

Daniel ignored my questions. "I need to find the place where the train stopped. If we can find the lion, I'll know I'm in the right place."

"Lion?"

"Yes, a lion."

"What about Shira? We can't leave her here if we go on this train. Should we bring her along?" I let go of Daniel's hand and walked a few feet in front of him, torn between my longing to be by Daniel's side and worry about Shira. "It's one thing to put our lives in danger, but quite another to put an innocent child in harm's way."

Daniel came up from behind and wrapped his hands around my waist. "You can stay here if you prefer."

I turned and faced him. "No, Daniel." Tears came to my eyes. "I don't want to stay here. I want to be with you. I want to marry you, but what about Shira? You know what you must do, but what does God want me to do?"

Daniel lifted his hand toward the heavens. "God is on our side."

I glanced up, pleading my case. "I don't want to go to Auschwitz, anywhere but a concentration camp. Suppose we end up there —permanently?"

"The train should take us to Caesarea."

"Should?" I rubbed my teary eyes. "How can you be sure?" I backed away. Heavy indigestion made me feel like I was on the verge of throwing up, and panic filled every fiber of my being. "You're talking about Auschwitz, Daniel. It doesn't get any worse than Auschwitz."

Daniel persisted. "I need to give the necklace to my great-grand-mother, and I don't know of any other way to make that happen."

"We're really not back in time, Daniel, as I said to Nidal. We're in the seventh dimension, a spiritual reality. I don't think you literally need to give it back to her."

Daniel began pacing back and forth, something I'd seen him do only a couple of times. "That photograph meant more to my mother than anything else, probably more than us."

I prayed under my breath. "Jesus, please show me what to do."

Daniel came alongside me, gently touching my arm. "We don't have to figure this out now. Let's leave it with God. We should return so I can check on my mother."

Patience in solving what seemed unsolvable was not my strength. I was glad Daniel put this off for another day.

Daniel kissed me lightly on the forehead.

"I'm glad you found out about your father," I said, focusing on God's answered prayer.

"Yes. Let's keep praying God is with my father, wherever he might be."

CHAPTER 31

AS WE ENTERED through the city gates, the Temple environs appeared less crowded. The Roman guards were more visible with the multitudes leaving, and the baptismal lines at the mikvehs were short. Even the grain offering stations inside the Temple were closed. An exquisite aroma filled the streets. "What is that smell?"

"Frankincense," Daniel replied. "The priests add it to the grain."

I'd never smelled it before and found it uplifting. Signs displayed at nearby inns read "no vacancy." Even with the grain shared at the Temple and the fruit brought into the city, beggars still begged. I wished we could linger, but Daniel seemed hurried to check on his mother.

We passed through the wealthy Upper City, and as we neared the apartment, I noticed many people gathered outside. Bouquets of black flowers were displayed prominently on the porch.

I saw her and shook Daniel's arm. "Look!"

Daniel started running, and I followed on his heels. As we approached the house, the demon started toward us. What few whiffs of white hair there were on her head blew wildly in the breeze. She smiled and extended her hand, offering us black flowers. Daniel pushed her arm out of his way. The flowers fell on the ground and wilted.

"She's mine," the ventriloquist announced.

"Shira!" I cried.

We raced up the porch steps, sidestepping mourners dressed in black. Daniel pushed the door open. Inside was dark, and it took a moment for my eyes to adjust. A multitude of people filled the small room.

"She died," I heard someone say. "She's gone."

Who died? Who...surely they didn't mean...my God! I searched frantically for someone I recognized amongst all the strangers. When I saw Daniel's sister, I rushed to her. "Where's Shira?"

Martha pointed. "She's playing over there."

I ran over and scooped her up in my arms.

"Auntie," she said excitedly. "Look what I made."

I saw a white rock in her hand but could make out the faint impression of a bird. It was a poor imitation, but I praised her. "It's beautiful."

"Do you think it will come alive?" she asked.

I chuckled. "Probably not, but you can always pretend."

As I held her, in an instant, I realized how much I loved her. She was mine—or rather, God's. But never would she belong to the ventriloquist. Never!

I realized then that Daniel's mother was gone. I mistakenly thought it was Shira. My eyes met Daniel's. "I'm sorry," I mouthed.

Daniel sat in a chair overwhelmed with emotion.

The rest of the late afternoon and evening was a blur of activity. Kitty's body was taken to its resting place. Burial couldn't happen during the festival. I threw out the black flowers.

"You don't bring flowers to a Jewish funeral," Daniel said.

Friends and mourners dropped off food late into the night. A few hymns were sung, and I tried to comfort Martha and Daniel, but words fell short. How much did this dimension impact the world we left behind? Was there still time to change the future?

Based on Daniel's insights, I doubted his mother was in the presence of the King. I didn't want to dwell on it.

Late that night, when the visitors and mourners were gone, and Martha was asleep, Daniel and I sat outside on the porch steps. The stars shone brightly in the clear sky, and torches along the street lit up the area around the Temple. Neither of us said much. I laid my head on his shoulder.

"I talked to the rabbi," Daniel said. "The funeral is tomorrow morning, but you don't have to come."

I nodded. "I should spend time with Shira. I think she missed me today."

My betrothed pressed my hand. "Shira loves you. You're her mother now."

I started to resist. "I can't—"

"That's not your choice. God chose you."

I bit my lip, feeling overwhelmed by the thought.

Daniel put his arm around me and wistfully said, "If only…"

"If only what?" I asked.

Daniel shook his head. "Nothing."

After a few minutes, Daniel stood. "We need to get some sleep."

I nodded.

Daniel embraced me but didn't kiss me. "I want to watch you until you close and lock the door."

I glanced around, half expecting something to pop out from behind a tree.

"Good night, Daniel."

Upon reaching the top of the steps, I turned once more and repeated myself. "Good night."

"Good night," he echoed back. True to his word, he stood and waited as I closed the door.

Once inside, I leaned my back against the doorframe and finished his sentence. "If only we were married."

CHAPTER 32

THE NEXT MORNING, I rolled over on my stomach, pulled the pillow over my head, and groaned. Of course, I couldn't sleep off my depression. I needed to take care of Shira.

More visitors arrived from faraway villages to drop off food and offer condolences. Sadness that Daniel's mother didn't know Yeshua added to my gloominess.

Shira bounced on the bed. "Wake up, Auntie. I want to go play."

She jumped out of bed and ran to the door, waiting for me to open it.

"First, let me get dressed."

I was glad to take Shira outside. Many had already left for the funeral. Rain dripped from clouds that meandered across a partially blue sky. An unexpected rainbow popped out and arched through the heavens. How long had it been since I'd seen an unbroken one?

Longing pricked my heart. I missed my mother. Thinking about the train ride to Auschwitz sapped my strength. How could Daniel be sure we would return?

Could I claim the rainbow as a promise from God he would bring us back?

I pointed up at the sky. "Look, Shira, a rainbow."

She stopped to look up. "Can we walk on it?"

I chuckled. "No."

If only life was so simple as to walk on rainbows, but my mind was stuck in quicksand. If Daniel's mother rejected the truth here, was that the real condition of her heart in our time? If Kitty didn't believe Jesus died for her sins, she would pay the penalty for her own sins—through eternal death.

Most of the spectators were gone, probably headed home to outlying communities and towns. The city seemed deserted compared to when we first arrived.

Soon we approached a young girl playing along the roadside. Shira struck up a conversation, and I sat on a nearby bench. I pulled out my diary from the bag and began to write.

"Dear God, I pray we can visit Lowly and Baruch before returning home. I promised the pig I would return, and the donkey would be so happy to see me."

I reflected on the last few weeks. Thank goodness Scylla was gone, according to Daniel. My father's fourth wife was cruel, ridiculing me and locking me up for days at a time. I sighed. If it weren't for the farm animals and my half-brother, Nathan, I never would have survived.

I set down my pen. Despite my attempt to think only positive thoughts, my depression wouldn't lift. I wanted Jesus to return. I was tired of dealing with thorns and thistles. As I wallowed in self-pity, I saw someone approaching. When she was close enough, I recognized her.

Lilly came over and sat beside me on the bench. She remained quiet for a moment, perhaps not sure what to say. At last, she offered, "I'm sorry about Daniel's mother. I came to bring some bread."

I forced a smile. "Thanks for the food. Martha will be glad not to cook today."

Lilly rocked her feet back and forth. "How is Shira doing?"

"Oh, she's fine."

More silence followed. I wasn't in the mood for small talk. I sensed Lilly wanted to encourage me. "God is going to use Daniel in a mighty way," she said.

Was she a prophetess? "Thank you for your kind thoughts."

After another long pause, she stood. "Come by and visit me anytime. I'm here for you if you need me."

I furrowed my brow. "You know, the funeral has already started, but you can still make it."

Lilly smoothed her long dark hair with her hand. "I just came from the funeral."

"Really?" I didn't know it was over.

"Yes. Some have lingered, but I wanted to drop off this bread."

I searched for the right words. "That's thoughtful of you."

Lilly hesitated. "You know, I don't think Martha is far from the kingdom of heaven."

"I appreciate your prayers."

More silence followed. Lilly's eyes focused on the street toward Kitty's apartment. Her feet started moving in that direction. "Come by and visit," she said over her shoulder.

"Thanks, I appreciate it."

Later that evening, when everyone had left to go to their own homes, and Shira and Martha were resting, doubt crept into my mind. "Do you think we did the right thing coming here?"

Daniel took my hands in his and whispered. "I know God is with us. We're in a tough place right now."

I nodded. "I miss my mother."

Daniel wrapped his arms around me. "Losing my mother has reminded you of yours. We'll leave in the morning. I told Martha we're going to Caesarea. Before going to bed, she packed up some food for our trip."

"By way of Auschwitz," I added. I stared at the floor. "I'd like one more chance to witness to my mother. Death is so final, you know."

Daniel's eyes bore into mine. "God gives us the desires of our heart."

I didn't know how to respond. I followed Daniel as he walked to the door, again wishing we were married. When would that happen? Maybe in Caesarea, I would bring it up once more.

CHAPTER 33

WHEN DANIEL ARRIVED the next morning, Shira and I were waiting on the front steps. We said our goodbyes to Martha, tearfully hugging and promising we'd be back after our trip.

Daniel kissed me on the lips for the first time in a while, and then lifted Shira in his arms. "How is my princess today?"

"When do we get on the train?" she asked.

Daniel glanced at me.

"Kids love train rides." The issue was settled. We would trust God for her safety.

"Let me say goodbye to Martha," Daniel said.

He disappeared inside the house and returned a couple of minutes later.

"You have our snacks?" he asked.

I held up the bag.

"Good." As we started down the road, Daniel said, almost as an afterthought. "I want to stop by the Temple."

I was anxious to accomplish our immediate purpose without delay. That seemed like a waste of time. "Why?"

"The disciples and followers are praying and breaking bread together."

"Oh, all right," I muttered. That shouldn't take too long.

We entered through the Beautiful Gate and found a couple of dozen or more followers and disciples gathered at Solomon's Porch. I noted Peter, whom I recognized. The others I wasn't sure about. Then I saw Lilly. I walked over to greet her. "Thank you for your kindness yesterday."

Lilly gave me a quick hug and returned to setting out the food. "You seemed depressed. After dropping off the bread, I went home and prayed for you."

I watched her in amazement. Could I ever be that caring? "Thank you," I said again.

Everyone brought plenty to share, and we added ours that Martha packed for the trip. There was more food than everybody could eat, so when we finished, several of the women gave the leftovers to the beggars by the Beautiful Gate.

For the first time, a sense of awe struck me. The power and strength of the early believers was a force with which no one could reckon. Not Rome, not the Sanhedrin, not the unbelievers, not the dark powers of the netherworld that would wreak havoc with every generation to follow.

The early Christians would turn the world upside down one martyr at a time. Did I have that much faith? My uncertainty compelled me to try harder to be like Jesus, remembering faith without works is dead. As the prayers and praise of the new believers rose into the heavens, gladness filled me with thanksgiving. When the crowd began to disperse, I was sad to leave.

As we exited the Temple, I confided to Daniel. "You know, I didn't want to stop here, but I'm glad you insisted. I needed that."

Daniel squeezed my hand. "Me, too. Prayer changes things—especially perspective."

He turned to Shira. "Have you ever met a lion?"

Shira's eyes grew big. "No."

"Would you like to meet one?"

"Is he a nice lion?" Shira asked.

"Yes, he's a good lion," Daniel replied.

Shira tugged on Daniel's hand. "Is he Aslan?"

Daniel and I exchanged glances. How did she know who Aslan was? She must have seen the movie, or perhaps her mother or someone read the *Narnia Series* to her.

Daniel smiled. "If you want him to be."

"Where is he?" Shira asked excitedly.

Daniel pointed to the heavens. "He's on his throne."

We crossed the Kidron Valley and continued along the well-worn path to the Mount of Olives. Once we reached the top, Daniel stopped to rest.

The Temple stood tall and majestic surrounded by the walls of the city. Its golden hues glistened in the morning sun as the Judean wilderness and mountains framed it as a center masterpiece. I couldn't think of anything that compared to its beauty. I forced myself to return my focus to Daniel and Shira.

"I think we're pretty close," Daniel said. "Perhaps we should hold hands and pray."

Before we could, Shira let go of my hand and pointed. "Look, Aslan."

Several yards away, a magnificent lion appeared. A strong wind rippled through his brown and golden mane, and his amber-colored eyes pierced my heart with supernatural intelligence.

My lack of faith convicted me. The animal roared. Trembling, I covered my ears and dropped to the ground. Shira forced her body into my lap, and I wrapped my arms around her. Seconds later, I felt the chugging motion of a moving train.

I expected to be sitting in an overcrowded, dirty boxcar with Jews headed to Auschwitz, but when I was brave enough to open my eyes, I saw an old freight car with green walls and faded green seats. While old, it wasn't anything like the Nazi Holocaust trains.

A young girl sat across the aisle from us who couldn't have been more than thirteen. She wore a plain white dress, brown loafers, and white socks. Her dark brown hair fell loosely over her shoulders.

I nudged Daniel. "Is that her?"

"I think so, but this isn't the way it was before. The last time the car was filled with too many passengers, and there was no place to sit except on the floor. Most of the men stood, holding onto a steel bar to keep from falling."

I whispered, "Why don't you ask her if the necklace is hers?"

The girl turned. Her questioning eyes revealed surprise that we were on the train. She smiled faintly but didn't say anything.

Daniel held up the necklace. "Did you drop this?"

Her eyes went from surprise to recognition. "Yes, somehow I lost it."

Daniel handed it to her.

"Thank you," she replied.

I asked the young girl, "Would you like for me to help you put it on?"

She nodded. "Yes, please."

Shira and I exchanged seats, and I latched it around her neck. The Star of David shone brightly against her olive skin. "You look beautiful."

The young girl returned my smile. "The angel told me to stay on the train until I found my necklace. I looked and looked, but I couldn't find it. For some reason, the guards didn't see me."

Her eyes twitched with sadness. "They took the others, even my parents, but for some reason, they didn't see me."

"Is the angel on the train?" Daniel asked.

The young girl nodded. "I think he's in another compartment."

My attention was drawn to the passing scenery outside the window. The train was moving so fast, everything was a blur. After what seemed like a short time, although I couldn't be sure, the train came to an abrupt stop. The view through the window stunned me. I whispered to Daniel, "I think we're in the garden, in the garden of the King."

CHAPTER 34

I LEANED OVER, straining to see out the window. The old boxcar from World War II came to rest in a lush green meadow. The door to the almost hundred-year-old train scraped open grudgingly, and an angel of immense stature appeared in the opening. I knew he was an angel because he was dressed in pure white linen that dazzled in the sunlight through the rustic doorway. The angel's shimmering robe and striking features sent chills down my spine. His soft eyes, however, captured my heart, and my panic evaporated.

God's messenger gestured with his hand at the breathtaking world that beckoned us. "Welcome to the garden."

We rose from our seats and disembarked. The young girl exited first, followed by Shira, myself, and Daniel. Awe filled my heart as the strength to speak left me momentarily. As we stepped down the stairs, my significance and insignificance convicted me. Why did the King bring us here?

Our guide proclaimed, "The kingdom of heaven is like a grain of mustard seed. Though smaller than other seeds, when sown in love, it multiplies, filling the entire universe." His hand swept through the air. "Nothing can stop the expansion of God's kingdom."

The rolling hills and gentle valleys stretched far into the distance.

Trellises of green, yellow, blue, purple, pink, and white flowers filled the meadow. Fruit trees laden with heavenly fruits of love, joy, peace, patience, kindness, goodness, faithfulness, and gentleness basked in the sunlight. Limbs amassed with healing leaves fluttered in the gentle breeze.

Herbs, sanctified with a heavenly fragrance, quickened my anxious spirit. The sweet aroma of God's holiness filled every corner of the garden.

For a fleeting second, I felt the presence of the King. My anticipation soared. I knew the King was with us. The brevity of time, however, seemed like a sweet piece of chocolate. I imagined a large box of gift-wrapped heavenly chocolate awaiting my imminent arrival.

Another angel appeared and took the hand of Daniel's great-grandmother. I knew the young girl's life was spared. She turned toward us, mouthing the words "thank you" to Daniel. Hand in hand, she accompanied the angel down a path that faded from our view. A momentary silence followed as we tried to catch one last glimpse.

Shira's voice interrupted my musings. "Look, Auntie, there is my bird."

I glanced up and saw the familiar dove flying overhead. "It is your bird!" I exclaimed. We watched as the bird circled overhead, once again appearing to morph into an eagle.

"Are you an angel?" Shira asked our guide.

The garden messenger nodded. "Follow me."

I took Shira's hand and clasped Daniel's upper arm. We followed the angel deeper into the magical land. He took us to the top of a mountain, and my eyes feasted on the breathtaking view. Little by little, more of the garden's treasures became visible.

He lifted his right hand. "Explore the secrets of God's kingdom. Seize the moment, remembering the present will pass quickly. It may seem short, but it will be longer than you think."

Then the angel was gone.

I started to say something to Daniel, but before I could, Shira took off. "Look, a rabbit."

I caught a glimpse of something white zigzagging down the knoll.

"Cherios!" I started to run after the rabbit, but when I realized Daniel wasn't following us, I stopped. "You're coming, aren't you?"

Daniel shook his head. "I want to explore the castle."

"What castle?" My eyes followed his gaze. A magnificent fortress floated above the horizon. A round sphere in front of the citadel illuminated the structure in white luminosity.

For an instant, emotions overwhelmed me, so much so that I couldn't speak. When my voice returned, I exclaimed. "Wow! You've talked about the castle, and now I get to see it. It is beautiful."

I turned my attention to Shira who was still trying to catch the rabbit. I hesitated. I hated for us to separate, but I wanted to be reunited with Cherios. Four years had passed in the twenty-first century since we parted ways.

I smiled. "Don't stay gone too long."

Daniel's eyes twinkled. "Remember, time is an illusion."

I nodded. "Yes, until God's appointed time."

Daniel kissed me on the cheek and took off.

"Godspeed," I uttered under my breath as I watched him disappear.

My focus returned to the rabbit. "Cherios, is that really you?"

The bunny hopped toward me with an exhausted Shira close behind. She twitched her nose as she spoke, bringing back sweet memories. "Shale, you returned. My goodness, you've grown tall."

"Have I? Well, I am four years older."

The rabbit's voice quivered. "Oh, me, oh my! It's been that long?"

I nodded, finding it hard to believe myself.

Cherios lifted her head catching a sweet aroma that drifted by. "Time is too deep for me. In the garden, there is no time—only endless eternity."

I tried to imagine that.

The furry animal bowed. "Shale, my dear friend, who I knew before the King journeyed to earth and fought the great battle. I want to give you something."

"What's that?"

"I'll be right back."

Cherios took off on one of the many garden trails and disappeared from view.

I sat on the grass to wait. Shira plopped down beside me and rested her head in my lap. "Auntie, this is the most wonderful place. Can we stay forever?"

I inhaled deeply, tasting the heavenly air. "If God wills it," I replied.

Soon my old friend returned with something in her mouth.

When she was close enough, I saw she held two fluffy white flowers.

"One for each of you." She dotingly set the flowers on the ground.

My heart leaped. Cherios gave me the same white flower when we met the first time. She and Baruch were enjoying a picnic under the apple tree when a gryphon sky-bombed me. "Oh, Cherios, thank you." I picked them up and handed one to Shira.

She twirled the blossom in her hand. "Do you hear it?"

I shook my head. "Hear what?"

"The singing," she replied.

I shut my eyes, but I couldn't hear anything.

"The flower is singing."

I tried again, but I still couldn't hear anything.

Shira stood and danced in a circle, lifting her hands over her head. I smiled as my thoughts returned to Daniel and the castle. I glanced back, but it was no longer visible on the horizon. I missed him already.

When Shira tired of dancing, she reached over and grabbed my hand. "Can we go for a walk?"

I stood. "Sure."

Cherios was so busy sniffing the air that I didn't think she heard Shira's question.

"Can you show us around the garden, Cherios?"

She stopped long enough to sneeze. "Oh, dear, excuse me for my poor manners." She quickly wiped her face and brushed down her beautiful white coat. I remembered how she always kept herself fastidiously clean.

"The garden has been busy with much activity now that the underlings are gone and the King has returned. I have much to show you," Cherios said.

I found it reassuring we no longer needed to worry about demonic creatures. I took Shira's hand in mine. "We'll follow you if you lead the way."

CHAPTER 35

WE FOLLOWED CHERIOS past crystal clear streams, spectacular waterfalls, and fascinating heavenly creatures. If God filled the earth with his glory, how much more would he fill his heavenly kingdom with love? In my heart, like Shira, I didn't want to go back, but embracing God's will meant blessed surrender.

Soon we came upon a trail I remembered from before. Only this time it was different. No longer did I see fearful things—flowers that moved like snakes, gryphons that sky-bombed seekers of truth, evil crows that gathered on the wings of dead trees, and black clouds that chased away the breath of life.

The trail opened to a secret place in the garden. Straight ahead stood the apple tree where I spied on Baruch and Cherios. Plump red apples weighed down the branches. I longed to pick a few and put them in my bag. "The tree has grown since I was here."

The rabbit twitched her nose. "Everything here grows fast." She snatched a brown blanket from a hidden spot nearby, laid it on the grass, and plopped down. Shira and I snuggled up beside her.

A small tear fell from Cherios's eye. "I miss Baruch, my favorite donkey, and our picnics."

I reached over and wiped her tear. "Baruch misses you, too. I'm sure you'll see each other again."

Cherios nodded. "At the end of days." She composed herself and raised her front paws. "Long live our Lord and King." Overcome with emotion, she cleared her throat. "I almost forgot. I want to show you something else."

Cherios hopped off the blanket and darted past a clump of trees. Shira and I followed her to a wood and stone building under construction. Exquisite, colorful stones decorated the foundation of the house. I couldn't take my eyes off the structure that basked in radiant beauty.

"Do you want to go inside?" the rabbit asked.

I hesitated. "Do you think it's okay?"

"I think so," Cherios said.

I pushed opened the door. Bright light flooded the room penetrating the walls and roof. I ran my hand along the wooden doorframe as I admired the intricate woodwork. The attention given to the minutest detail spoke of a masterful builder. "This looks like someone's future home."

Cherios hopped around the room, and Shira let go of my hand to explore.

"Whose house is this?" I asked.

The rabbit cocked her head. "I don't know. The King has been building houses ever since he returned. Thousands and thousands of houses are under construction. I think he's preparing a home for everyone."

As I thought about what Cherios said, Shira returned from an adjoining room holding something in her hand. She handed it to me without saying anything and went about exploring.

When I examined what she gave me, I almost fainted. Inside the magnificently carved picture frame was a familiar photo. I held it closer not believing what I saw.

The photograph was of Daniel's great-grandmother wearing the Star of David—the young girl we met on the train. How could I be seeing this photograph? Was God validating that we'd restored history to its proper order?

I called to Shira. "Where did you find this?"

She came to the doorway and pointed. "On the table—over there."

I rushed into the room with Cherios. A pristinely-cut table surrounded by unfinished chairs decorated the center of the room. I studied the picture again with my hand visibly shaking.

I turned to Cherios. "You say there are many houses under construction?"

Cherios twitched her nose. "Yes. Would you like to see?"

"Yes, please."

We followed Cherios outside, and she took us along a scenic path of extraordinary beauty. Colorful birds greeted us, and exotic butterflies swooped along beside us. Soon we came to many houses under construction.

Some were more ornate than others, but they were all charming and delightful. Shira tried to count how many she saw, but couldn't get past nine. I helped her for a while, but when we reached ninety-nine, I stopped. "Cherios, you're right, there are more than we can count."

After a long walk, nearing exhaustion, I stopped to rest on a bench. One thing puzzled me. "Cherios, where are the people?"

The rabbit cocked her head. "Why, I don't know. I never thought about that. I mean, they're here, I smell them, but I don't see them. More humans are coming soon—very soon, like you. Only people live in houses. Bunnies don't need houses."

I laughed. That was true. I took a deep breath as I studied the photograph once more. God put this photo in the house but why? Was this our future home?

Now I was anxious to find out what Daniel had discovered. "Maybe we should head back to the entrance."

Cherios hopped a few feet in front of us. "Follow me, so you don't get lost."

Shira took my hand and whispered. "Auntie, I think Cherios understands everything you say. She is a very smart bunny."

I squeezed her hand. "I think you're right."

When we arrived at the garden entrance, I didn't see Daniel. I sat on the grass to await his return. Overcome with fatigue, I laid back, staring into the heavens. Within seconds, the sky rolled back.

Shira pointed. "Look."

I pulled myself up and held Shira in my lap. I wanted to cover her eyes, but she pushed my hand away.

The heavens burst forth and revealed the earth hanging precariously in space.

The rabbit jumped up and down. "The prescience!"

"The what?" I asked.

Cherios added, "I needed to practice saying that word a long time. That's a very big word."

Lightning flashed in a display of immense power and blinded me temporarily.

Shira turned her head and clutched me. I covered her eyes.

"Tell me when I can look."

I patted her on the back.

The earth rocked back and forth like a grandfather clock that could no longer tell time. Its distorted surface writhed in pain. I wanted to hide my own eyes, but part of me was too afraid I'd miss something God wanted me to see.

Four mighty angels appeared at the four corners of the earth. Another angel ascended from the East bearing a seal on his forehead. He shouted to the four angels, "Do not harm the earth, the sea, or the trees till we have sealed the servants of our God on their foreheads." I heard another voice say that the number to be sealed were one hundred and forty-four thousand.

I sensed time passing when a heavenly magnifying glass focused on Israel, zooming in on Mount Zion. A vast multitude of men stood before the King. To my surprise, I saw Daniel. He told me he was one of the chosen, and I saw the unusual mark on his forehead, but to be shown this vision of him left me speechless.

Cherios bounced up and down. "The King is coming." She bowed her head. "My heart goes pitter-patter when I see my risen King."

Then I heard a voice. "These are God's servants, commissioned by the High King to bring into his kingdom every soul possible before it is too late."

Harpists played in the throne room, and the voices of God's servants filled the heavenly chambers. I tried to sing along, but I couldn't. No matter how hard I tried, I couldn't follow the tune or the words.

When the saints finished singing, hundreds of stars fell from the heavens upon the earth, scorching the surface of the planet. Large portions of the land erupted in sheets of fire. A deep gash tore open the earth's crust as lava spewed forth. I heard the earth mourn as the judgments of God fell on a world that was not worthy of his glory. Scarred, plundered, and emptied—the curse devoured the earth.

Then, as unexpectedly as the vision began, the heavens closed.

CHAPTER 36

I REACHED INTO my bag and pulled out my Bible. I found Revelation 7 where John wrote about the one hundred forty-four thousand and the multitudes that stood before the throne. "They cried out with a loud voice, 'Salvation belongs to our God who sits on the throne, and to the lamb!'"

I looked for Rachel among the martyrs. Why didn't I witness to my mother until she believed? Now it was too late. Did Much-Afraid escape God's wrath? How many people died?

I flipped through the pages of the book of Revelation and read Revelation 16:20-21: "Then every island fled away, and the mountains were not found. And great hail from heaven fell upon men, each hailstone about the weight of a talent. Men blasphemed God because of the plague of the hail since that plague was exceedingly great."

Stunned, I closed my Bible. How many times did I read those words without understanding the depth of their meaning? How could anyone blaspheme God? Even now, if the earth-dwellers would turn to God, they could still be saved.

Shira reached up and touched my face. "I saw Daniel singing." She clapped her hands. She couldn't sing the song, but she tried to imitate the beat.

I smiled. "It's the most beautiful song I've ever heard."

Cherios hopped over and placed her head on my lap. "While you wait for Daniel, can Shira play with me?"

I repeated to Shira what Cherios asked. Shira's eyes grew big as anticipation crossed her face. She patted Cherios on the head. "Let's play." They floated across the heavenly carpet as they ran to the bottom of the hill. Uncontrollable tears welled up. How could I cry now?

I forced myself to pray. "Dear God, what happens on earth is your perfect will. Please help me to trust you."

When I opened my eyes, I still didn't see the castle or Daniel. Perhaps I should follow Cherios and Shira. They were probably going to the apple tree. How many apples could I squeeze into my bag? Maybe a dozen, though my bag would be quite heavy.

I jogged down the knoll and caught up with them. As I started picking apples, I heard my name echo across the garden. "Shale."

My heart leaped. "Daniel."

I dropped my bag and rushed back up the hill. When Daniel saw me, he waved. Within seconds, he swept me up in his arms. "You won't believe where I've been," Daniel said. "I was gone so long I was afraid you wouldn't be here when I returned."

I looked up into the heavens at the position of the sun. "You were only gone a few hours."

Daniel shook his head. "No, it's been many, many days."

Then I remembered what the angel said—that our time here may seem short, but it would be longer than we thought.

"I saw you on the Mount of Olives." I lifted his hair off his fore-head. "You have the seal—the mark of the one hundred forty-four thousand."

Daniel's face turned serious. "I had a scar there before, but now that the time has come, it's a seal."

I buried my head in his chest, listening to his heartbeat. "I love you."

Daniel stroked me on the back. "I love you, too."

I stepped back and admired him. "God truly has chosen you. I'm humbled to play a small part in what he's doing."

Lifting his eyes, he smiled. "I see Shira and Cherios have become friends."

I bit my lip. Should I show Daniel the photograph I found?

Before I could decide, Daniel placed his hand on my shoulder. "I want to tell you some things."

My thoughts turned to Daniel's adventure. "Tell me everything, starting from the beginning."

Daniel pointed. "Let's sit over there."

I followed him to a spot where we could keep an eye on Shira and Cherios. I made myself comfortable beside him on the silky grass, leaning my head on his shoulder.

Daniel took my hand in his and began. "I took the same trail as before, passing cascading waterfalls and water gardens. I didn't see any children this time, but at the end of the trail, it opened up to a white sandy beach that bordered a crystal clear river. This time a small boat was on the shore. A guide sat in the back of the boat holding an oar."

Daniel peered intensely into my eyes. "Last time, you met me on the other side with dry clothes because I swam across."

"I did? How could I have done that when I've never been to the castle, and I have no memory of giving you clothes?"

Daniel shook his head. "I don't know, but I think we have many futures, and God allows us to choose."

"What does that mean?"

Daniel smiled. "Remember, when you asked Yeshua if you could marry me? I think you changed your future."

"How?"

Daniel hesitated before replying. "You missed the rapture."

"Oh." Could that be true? "And Shira, too?"

Daniel inched closer. "There are no children on the earth now."

My mind struggled to embrace Daniel's revelation. "Did you learn anything else about me?"

"First let me finish this part of the story."

I glanced up at the sky, hoping to catch another vision, but the heavens were blue. I noticed Shira and Cherios resting. Shira would sleep well tonight.

Daniel continued. "I walked up to the boat, and the man in the boat called out to me. 'Get in the boat, and I'll give you a ride.' I jumped in, and he took me across the river. I wanted to ask him who he was, but I knew, even though he didn't tell me."

"Who was it?"

"I knew it was the Lord."

"Wow!" I exclaimed. "You saw Jesus."

"When I reached the other side, he told me to make sure I visited the library. I knew then it was the Lord. He met me in the library when I came to the castle the first time."

Daniel inclined into me. "When I went inside the castle, the first thing I did was run up the stairs. When I reached the top, I opened the door..."

CHAPTER 37

"**A**N IMMENSE LIBRARY filled the room, just as before. This time, however, Yeshua was not waiting for me. Neither was there a burning fire or prepared food. Still, books lined the walls as far as I could see."

Daniel reflected. "I didn't expect to see my father, but part of me hoped I might."

I assured him. "I'm sure he's no longer in the castle."

Daniel shrugged. "Probably not, but in the garden, anything is possible."

"What happened next?"

Daniel stretched his legs and leaned back, propping himself up with his arms. "I wasn't sure what to do. Then I remembered your diary. Why not put it on one of the shelves?"

The thought of my diary being in God's library thrilled me.

"Did I ever tell you I found a scroll at the Temple with my name on it?" Daniel asked.

I shook my head, surprised.

"Well, the strange thing was, I was unable to open it, but Yeshua unsealed it for me before placing it on a shelf. He said it was my life from beginning to end. I tried to remember where he put it because I wanted to see if it was still there, but the library was so vast, I couldn't remember."

"Did you put my diary on a shelf?"

Daniel seemed reluctant to continue. Finally, he said, "When I tried to place your scroll on the shelf, it fell on the floor."

I placed my hand over my heart. "What do you mean?"

Daniel pulled my scroll out of his bag. "I tried several times, up high, down low, in several places, but as I said, the scroll fell onto the floor."

Did God not like my diary? Panic filled me. "What's wrong with my scroll that God would reject it?"

Daniel ran his fingers through his hair. "About that time, an angel entered the room. I knew he was an angel because he was tall, ten feet or more, and similar in appearance to the one that greeted us when we arrived."

I would have been excited to hear about Daniel's encounter with an angel if I wasn't so upset that God rejected my scroll.

Daniel sat forward, clasping his knees. "I told the angel I was trying to put your scroll on the bookshelf. The angel walked over and opened it."

My heart lodged in my throat. "And—"

"The angel pointed to the first entry. "The diary is addressed 'Dear Dog,' not 'Dear God.'"

My heart sank. "No." I covered my eyes, dismayed at how Daniel's words sounded. "I didn't mean it like that. I didn't want Scylla to know who I was writing to because I was afraid. Plus, I was imitating Anne Frank. She addressed her diary, 'Dear Kitty.'"

Daniel squared his shoulders. "I know, you told me that, and that's what I told the angel."

Tears flowed. "What did the angel say when you told him that?"

The angel replied, "Jesus said, 'Whoever acknowledges me before men, I will acknowledge him before my father in heaven.'"

I dropped my head. "Oh, Daniel, I've made a terrible mistake. Do you think God will forgive me?"

Daniel lifted my face to his. "You know God will forgive you."

I sat frozen, overwhelmed, thinking about my mistake. "Dear Jesus, please forgive me for my pride. How many things like this have I done? Please forgive me."

We both remained quiet for a moment until I softly touched Daniel's hand. "You know, everyone has wanted my scrolls—my father, the Illuminati, the scientists, Nidal, even the media if they could get their hands on them. What everyone values here means nothing to Jesus. How foolish of me, trying to avoid Scylla's scorn, pretending to be another Anne Frank—what horrible stinking pride. How wrong I've been. I didn't even know my own sinful heart."

Daniel put his arm around me. "You have confessed your sin, Shale. That's all God requires. He's already paid the price on the cross."

I knew that, but guilt shot through me. Why did I not see my own sin? I looked up at Daniel. "Do you have a pen? I want to change those entries."

Daniel opened his bag to look for one.

Then I remembered I had a pen, but I left my bag by the apple tree. "I have a pen in my bag. I started a new diary in Dothan. This one is written to God."

Daniel smiled. "See, you've grown in your faith, probably more than you realize."

I stood. "Can you come with me to get it?"

Daniel followed me down the knoll to the secluded part of the garden. We passed Shira and Cherios that were still sleeping. I was glad Shira was taking a nap.

After opening my bag and finding my pen underneath several apples, I changed the pages where I wrote "God" backward as "dog."

Daniel opened his Bible. "The angel also told me to read Isaiah 5:20."

"Do you know what it says?"

Daniel shook his head. "I'll look it up."

I waited as Daniel turned to the passage and read it out loud. "Woe to those who call evil good, and good evil; who put darkness for light, and light for darkness; who put bitter for sweet, and sweet for bitter!"

My hands trembled. "God doesn't like for things to be reversed."

"It's a form of divination," Daniel said.

I cried again, bowing my head once more. "Dear heavenly Father, please forgive me."

After several minutes, I felt God's forgiveness. I was also thankful that Shira slept through my pain.

Daniel placed his hand on mine. "I hear the train coming."

I perked up through my tears. "I do, too."

I stood and called to Shira. "Wake up. The train is coming. We need to go."

Cherios awoke immediately, and Shira stood, still half-asleep. She rubbed her eyes as she ran to me. "I'm so glad I got to play with Cherios. Can we come back to the garden?"

I smiled. "I hope so." I wanted to see if God would accept my diary.

Daniel carried my bag laden with apples up the hill as I helped Shira to the top. In the distance, an immense angel waited beside the train. Cherios hopped beside us, and I stopped to pat her on the head. "We'll come back soon."

Cherios twitched her nose. "There is no place like home."

I peered out over the garden where one house was under construction and remembered the photograph. "Yes, there is no place like home."

CHAPTER 38

ONCE WE REACHED the top of the plateau and approached the train platform, I didn't see the angel. I saw other things —things I didn't notice before. Perhaps this was a different train. Or maybe my eyes were playing tricks on me. I noticed a swastika on the side of the boxcar. I remembered what Daniel shared, how Satan perverted things, reversed words, printed backwards, or displayed objects upside down. In the swastika, I saw a hideous cross.

I picked up Shira and called out to Daniel who was a few steps in front of me. "Daniel, that's not the same train we rode. And where's the angel? Maybe that wasn't an angel we saw."

Daniel studied the train. "It's definitely not the same one, but that doesn't mean anything. Let's wait for the angel."

We waited a few minutes. By this time Cherios had arrived and hippity-hopped in front of us to get Shira's attention. Shira squirmed. I set her down, staring at the train and then at Daniel. Steam poured out the top of the engine.

Soon a man stepped out of one of the old freight cars and waved. He didn't look like a Nazi, but he wasn't the angel we'd seen from the bottom of the hill.

"Welcome aboard," the man shouted.

Daniel and I exchanged glances. I studied the middle-aged man with a receding hairline. He was a little too thick around the middle and wore baggy pants and a stained, long-sleeve shirt.

Daniel hesitated. "I'd rather see the angel and make sure we're boarding the right train."

I called out Cherios to come closer. She hopped up to me, wiggling her nose. Shira was beside her.

I squatted and whispered in her ear. "Cherios, have you ever seen that man before?"

Cherios stood on her hind legs to get a better view. Then she made a shrill squeaking sound, jumping up and down. "Why, that's Mr. Clover. Best angel friend animal kind could have."

I laughed lightly, partly from relief, partly from the embarrassment that I so quickly doubted God. Why would he send a bad man to rescue us from his garden? Still, I'd felt better if the train didn't have the Nazi symbol on it.

I relayed to Daniel what Cherios told me. "She said that's Mr. Clover, the best angel friend anyone could have."

Daniel smiled. "Then I guess we better get moving."

We climbed the platform, and Mr. Clover shook our hands. "We'll be off in no time." He beamed. "However, we'll have to wait a few minutes for some other passengers to arrive."

I glanced back at the garden. I hadn't seen any other people. "So who is coming?" I asked, making conversation.

Mr. Clover wiped his hands on a handkerchief he pulled out of his pocket. "We have to wait for the sheep and the goats."

"Oh." Would we have to share our cabin with a bunch of animals?

Mr. Clover went back into the engine room. Shira, Daniel, and I found our seats and waited for the arrival of the passengers. Several minutes later, a long line of sheep and goats appeared. There weren't just a few. There were dozens. Were all these animals coming with us to Caesarea?

Daniel reached over and patted me on the arm. "It looks like we're going to have lots of company on our trip."

I leaned my head on his shoulder. "Yeah."

Soon the animals started entering our rail car. They were dirty and smelled. I held my nose. How long would we have to share our cabin with these odorous creatures? Still, I tried to be patient despite my impatience. I held Shira in my lap so she wouldn't get soiled.

Once our compartment was full, I expected the door to shut, and we'd be on our way. However, nothing happened. Where was our conductor?

I stared impatiently at Daniel. "How long are we going to be stuck here?"

Daniel's eyes got wide. "I don't know."

We waited, and we waited some more. Where was God, or the angel? Why did he abandon us on this Nazi train with smelly sheep and goats and a conductor who forgot about us?

Daniel stood. "Maybe there is a problem of some sort. Let me go see if I can find the conductor and offer him some help."

I laughed. "Yeah, like you know anything about Nazi trains."

Daniel's eyes grew stern. "Shale, be patient. I'm sure there is an explanation for the delay."

I puckered my lower lip. "I am being patient."

Daniel disappeared when he entered the compartment in front of us. I focused on Shira.

However, the bleating and baaing and bodily fluids making an appearance on the floor irritated me even more. The train wasn't sanitary now, and Daniel was taking far too long talking to Mr. Clover. Why didn't he come back and tell me what was going on?

After several minutes, Daniel reappeared in the doorway with Mr. Clover trailing him. While Daniel approached me, I noticed the conductor walking around talking to the animals. Mr. Clover's lack of desire to get the train going and being more worried about farm animals was so distracting I had a hard time focusing on Daniel.

Daniel sat beside me. I was glad he avoided the urine that was edging closer to us.

I glared at him. "What in the world is going on?"

Daniel squinted. "Why are you so upset? Calm down. It's not the end of the world."

"Okay. Tell me, what's going on?"

"The train coupler is broken, and Mr. Clover is waiting on some-body to deliver the part so he can fix it. It's a minor delay, maybe an hour."

I felt my face getting hot. "An hour? Well, can we get off the train and wait outside instead of being stuck inside with these stinky animals?"

Daniel did a double take. "Animals? I don't see any animals."

My voice went up several notches. I pointed. "Are you blind—those sheep and goats."

Daniel shook his head. "Those aren't animals, those are people."

"What?" Slowly, as I allowed my emotions to calm down and my eyes to focus, the animals become more apparent to me. In fact, they weren't animals. They were people.

I started to explain. "Daniel, I know I saw farm animals getting on the train."

Daniel rubbed his chin. "It was a test."

I felt my face growing hot. "What?"

Daniel scooted closer, patting Shira reassuringly on the back. "When you are selfish, only thinking about yourself, people become like animals, nuisances. People are—well, like sheep and goats. You should have listened, and you wouldn't have heard bleats and baas. You would have heard their stories, their hearts, and their journeys. Every person has value, but when you live in a selfish world, no one has value. Not even yourself."

Before I could respond, Mr. Clover approached, taking away any opportunity to wallow in self-pity. I glanced at the floor wondering if there was manure or urine on his shoes, and then remembered. It was an illusion. He held out his hand. "Shale, I'm glad to meet you."

I shook it and smiled meekly, ashamed of my selfish attitude. "I'm glad to meet you, too."

He handed me a pencil and a piece of paper. "Would you mind going around and finding out what our guests would like to eat? We'll celebrate with a big meal. That way, when we get the coupler fixed, everyone will be full and lacking in nothing."

I stood, my heart fluttering. Even after all my disasters in one day, I still could make up for it. "I'd be glad to. Shira can help me."

After a couple minutes of private conversation, Daniel and Mr. Clover returned to the engine car to wait for the new coupler. Shira and I went through the various rail cars taking orders of food. To my surprise, every person did have a story.

What did I miss in my journey through life because I was in too big a hurry, too impatient, or too selfish to care about others? It wasn't that I didn't love Jesus. I just didn't know how to love his sheep and goats.

CHAPTER 39

THE HEAVENLY BANQUET featured some of the most exquisite cuisines I'd ever eaten. Flavored with love, joy, peace, patience, kindness, goodness, faithfulness, and self-control, I leaned back and closed my eyes. I couldn't imagine life ever being hard again.

In the garden, no thorns or thistles compromised God's love. No disease could kill the body. No temptation would torture the soul. Suffering was held at bay as we were allowed to taste the goodness of the Lord if only briefly, making the longing for our permanent home even sweeter.

Miss Jeanne, a retired teacher from Alaska, told me she was on her way to Seattle to attend a conference. Another woman was on her way to Hauppauge, New York, for a house sale. Everyone had a story—from all over the world. Along the way, each soul met the King.

While the boxcar was quite old, instead of perceiving it as ugly and offensive, now I saw it as an antique made more elegant with age. How many millions of wandering travelers took this train, looking for the narrow road leading to the heavenly gate? Even the swastika on the engine was transformed into a beautiful cross.

Gold trim embossed the immaculately inlaid wooden ceiling. The stainless steel siding shone with such luminosity I could see my reflection, and the windows were so transparent I couldn't see the glass.

I cuddled up to Daniel when he returned from helping Mr. Clover fix the broken coupler. I lifted my eyes. "Daniel, why didn't we see these people in the garden?"

Daniel gazed around the rail car. Every seat was filled.

"It's a spiritual journey, Shale. Every day, millions of people travel somewhere. Some come to the garden. Too many visit other places, not good places, drawn by their human hearts.

"When you pray, millions of people around the world are also praying. You don't see them, but they are in God's presence with you."

I tried to understand. "So there were people in the garden with us, and I couldn't see them because they were on their own spiritual journey that didn't intersect with mine?"

Daniel nodded. "That's a good way to look at it."

"How do you know this stuff and I don't?"

Daniel's eyes twinkled. "Because you didn't ask God."

I lifted my head off his shoulder. "I asked Cherios where the workers were."

Daniel smiled, peeling away strands of hair from my face. "The reason we need the body of Christ and the different parts is because no one is righteous enough to see everything. We see through a glass darkly, but someday, we'll see Yeshua in his glory. Eternity awaits."

Shira reached over and placed her hand on Daniel's knee. "Papa, can I sit in your lap?"

Daniel and I exchanged glances. He smiled. "Sure, Princess, come here."

Shira climbed into his lap, and I leaned over and saw Cherios perched on her hindquarters looking into our window. She caught Shira's attention.

"Why can't we take Cherios with us?" she asked.

I waved at the bunny as I thought about Shira's question. "She wouldn't want to come, honey. Why would she want to go back to thorns and thistles when she already lives in the King's garden?"

Shira poked out her lower lip. "I already miss her."

I stroked Shira's arm. "I know, but she'll be here when we return."

I nudged up closer as we waited for the train to start. "Daniel, you didn't tell me what else happened. I saw you on earth singing with the one hundred forty-four thousand."

Daniel raised his eyebrow. "That's how I know I was gone more than a couple of hours."

"Tell me more."

"When I was in the library after the angel left, I put your scroll back in my bag and started to go, but a particular book caught my attention. It had a curious title.

"What was that?"

"The Prescience."

"That's sort of an unusual word," and then I remembered Cherios used that word in the garden.

"When I opened it," Daniel said, "I was taken someplace else. I'm not sure if I was in my body or out of my body, but I know I was in the spirit. I was with thousands of men in the throne room of God."

I noticed Daniel's excitement mounting.

"Yeshua was opening the fifth seal. I distinctly remember it was the fifth. I felt like events were happening on earth that defied description."

He paused as singing filled the compartment. We joined in and added our voices to the others.

"Amazing Grace, how sweet the sound,
    That saved a wretch like me.
    I once was lost but now am found,
    Was blind but now I see."

We sang all the verses and tears came to my eyes. If only this moment could last forever. Of course, we would have all eternity to praise our King.

When the singing ended, I stroked Daniel's arm. "What happened after that?"

"Ah. My spiritual eyes were opened, and I saw under the altar the souls of thousands who had been slain. They cried out, filling the halls of heaven with such sadness and heartache, I was overwhelmed with grief. The martyrs were given white robes."

Tears came to my eyes.

"I heard a voice answer," Daniel said. "'Wait a little bit longer, for many more of your fellow servants must be killed first, as you were.'"

I laid my head on Daniel's shoulder. "Sometimes I think if we were aware of all the pain and suffering in the world, it would kill us. We simply couldn't handle it, but in heaven, nothing is hidden. God sees all, feels all, and endures all. Only pure goodness could endure that kind of pain."

Daniel's eyes teared. "God is just. In the end, he will make everything perfect, and that gives me hope."

Unexpectedly, the train jerked forward.

Shira asked, "Are we leaving now?"

We waited, but nothing happened. I noticed other seventh dimension travelers peering around the cabin and looking out the window.

I reassured Shira. "It might be a couple more minutes."

Daniel continued. "The sixth seal was opened, and an earthquake struck the earth. The sun turned as black as sackcloth, and the moon turned to the color of blood. Stars fell from heaven, as a fig tree flings down her figs when she is shaken by the wind.

"Heaven departed like a scroll, and every mountain and island moved out of their assigned places. The earth-dwellers—the kings, the rich, the poor, the mighty, and the common—hid wherever they could find a place, even in the rocks of the mountains. The people cried out to the stones and the rocks. 'Fall on us, and hide us from the face of him who sits on the throne, and from the wrath of the Lamb.'"

Daniel's eyes watered. "I knew at that instant, the great tribulation was already at hand."

Chills swept through my body. "Daniel, the end is so scary no one in my school would read the book of Revelation. When Shira and I were in the garden, I saw Earth rocking back and forth. The planet didn't know which direction was north and which was south."

Daniel reached into his bag, pulled out his Bible, and handed it to me. "Read Daniel 2:21."

I flipped to the book and verse and read out loud. "'He changes the times and the seasons; he removes kings and raises up kings; he gives wisdom to the wise and knowledge to those who have understanding.'"

I closed the Bible. "Doesn't it seem strange the changing times and seasons would be mentioned in the same sentence as removing kings and setting up kings?"

Daniel peered deeply into my eyes. "If the earth is teeter-tottering, imagine what is happening to the earth-dwellers? Seas are being emptied, and mountains are being brought low. Chaos would be the order of the day, and no king stays in power when the world is coming apart. Of course, this is God's judgment on an unrepentant generation. Only the wise will understand."

The steam engine came to life, and the train, while not yet moving, was alive. We'd be taking off soon. I glanced out the window and waved one last time at Cherios. She was hopping up and down.

"Cherios is funny," Shira said. "Look."

I watched her, amused, waving at her through the window. I couldn't wait to come back.

"After that," Daniel said, "four angels went down to earth and stood at the four corners. God told them to hold back the four winds. Fire poured down upon us like at the Temple on Pentecost. I felt the hand of God sealing his name on my forehead.

"A voice said, 'You are the first fruits of Shavuot'—just like we witnessed with Nidal on earth. The festival is repeated in heaven before Yeshua's return."

I briefly thought about Nidal. Where was he now? "Jesus must have wanted us to return to the first century for many reasons."

Daniel nodded. "I don't think Christians appreciate how important God's festivals are. That's when everything happens. I never understood that before."

"What happened after that?"

"A voice said, 'The one hundred forty-four thousand are sealed,' and the throne room erupted in worship.

"Instantly, we stood on the Mount of Olives. A voice told the harpists to play, and we began to sing. I knew the song, although I don't know how. Yeshua said no one could learn the song except us. And then, as quickly as it happened, I was back in the library."

"Do you think we should go back to the twenty-first century?"

Daniel frowned. "No. I think we're where God wants us. He'll call us back when the time is right. Yeshua told me it wasn't my time yet."

I nodded and closed my eyes, suddenly realizing how tired I was. Soon I felt the train chugging along at a good clip.

"Auntie, we're moving," Shira said excitedly.

"Yes, we are. Hang tight."

I opened my eyes. "I assume we're going to Caesarea, right?"

Daniel sighed. "I think so. Maybe we should have asked."

I glanced around the cabin, but the angel was nowhere.

CHAPTER 40

I FELT A thump and a whoosh as we ascended into the heavens. "Whoa!"

Applause erupted in the cabin. Shira climbed back into my lap as contagious excitement spread. I tried to imagine what a flying train would look like if I were on the outside looking in.

A man's voice a few rows behind us exclaimed. "Look down."

Clouds and bright glare from the sun made it impossible for me to see. Then everything turned pitch black. Were we in a tunnel? Flickering stars appeared across the heavens, and celestial music filled the cabin. I turned to Daniel. "Where are we?"

"We're crossing dimensions."

Oohs and aahs came from several travelers.

Shira tapped me. "Do you hear music, Auntie?"

I touched her hand and smiled. "Yes, this time, I hear it."

As quickly as the angels of the night sky appeared, they disappeared and the music faded. I couldn't tell if we were moving, but a light breeze caressed my face, and soon a sweet aroma filled my nostrils. I recognized the scent, but did Daniel? I cuddled close to him. "Do you smell it?"

He whispered back. "The Opobalsamum perfume."

"Did you open the bottle?"

"No, it's underneath our seats in the bag."

I checked to make sure Shira hadn't opened the bag and gotten into the perfume, but her hands were empty.

Was that not like God, to throw in a surprise when least expected? He delighted in creating special moments that would remain with us.

Daniel whispered, "I can't wait until you wear the perfume on our wedding day."

I smiled. Then Shira repositioned herself, and I felt her sandal digging into my stomach. "Ugh," I muttered.

Seconds later the sun shone through the windows, and we arrived. When I surveyed the cabin, I discovered we were the only passengers on board. I imagined the train stopping in multiple locations at once —Seattle, Hauppauge, Rome, Kenya—who else did I meet on the trip?

My ponderings were interrupted by blinding light when the cabin door opened. Mr. Clover wasn't here this time to help us.

Daniel stood. I set Shira down in the aisle and grabbed her hand. We stepped back to let Daniel out as steam from the train expired, and warm air poured in through the doorway. I assumed we were in Caesarea, although I didn't know what Caesarea looked like.

We disembarked by way of the outside platform as brightness engulfed us. I paused to allow my eyes to adjust. Before I said anything, Daniel mumbled under his breath, "We aren't in Caesarea. We're in Galilee."

His comment jarred me. "Really?" I studied the road in front of us. "How do you know?"

"I recognize this as the road to your father's estate."

I reached down to hold Shira's hand, but she had taken her stone dove out of her bag and dropped it. "Honey, you might want to put that back. We have much to see."

She brushed the dirt off and tucked it in her bag. "Can we get something to eat?"

I did a double take. We'd just eaten. How could Shira be hungry? I dug into my bag and handed her an apple.

That satisfied her, and I focused on the road. Daniel was right. This was the same road Baruch and I traveled when I came the first time.

My anticipation at seeing the donkey and the pig soared. As we walked, though, Daniel grumbled. "I don't know why we came to Galilee. We should have gone to Caesarea."

I shrugged. "It's a beautiful day without a cloud in the sky. God is in control. He must have brought us here for a reason."

Daniel smiled. "I suppose you're right."

We approached the dirt road leading to my father's estate, and I noticed a "for sale" sign with the word "sold" etched across it. I clasped Daniel's arm. "Did my father sell his property?"

"I guess so," Daniel said. "We'll find out more from Judd—if he's here."

My heart pitter-pattered. What about Baruch and Lowly? My voice trembled. "Suppose we're too late? Suppose some Gentile ate my favorite pig?"

Daniel squinted. "Are you having a panic attack? I'm sure that's not the case."

I started to enter the gate that led to the cave where the animals slept at night. I wanted to find Baruch and Lowly as I didn't see them in the pasture, but Daniel encouraged me to go with him to the front door. "We don't know if the new owners have already moved in."

I reluctantly followed him. Daniel knocked and within seconds, we were ushered into the familiar dwelling. "What a delight!" the woman exclaimed. "Come in, please, come in."

CHAPTER 41

WE ENTERED THE home of my father—a wealthy diplomat of the Roman government. I hoped he wasn't here, but then, he never was.

I remembered the layout of the house to the tiniest detail. Off the main room, three small adjoining rooms abutted. Expensive rugs from Egypt covered the wooden floors, and the cold stone-hewn walls would have looked less severe if fireplaces were built in homes in the first century.

I glanced through a side door and saw the stairs that led to the second floor. For a time, my stepmother, Scylla, imprisoned me up there.

The young woman who opened the door, Mari, motioned for us to sit on the sofa. She sat on a chair. Her curious eyes studied me, but her warmth filled the room. I imagined what she was thinking. How could I look so much older after only a couple of months? Well, everyone knew kids could grow an inch in a week. Or maybe she never expected me to return. I left in such an unfortunate way. I never even said goodbye.

Mari was the one who cared for me when I was sick, who helped Daniel and me to sneak Nathan, my half-brother, out of the house when we took him to be healed by Jesus. She cooked all the meals. Most of all, she loved me like a sister.

I broke the momentary silence. "Mari, I'm sorry I left so suddenly. I never meant for things to turn out that way."

Mari burst into a big smile. "Oh, my goodness, Shale. I'm glad you left." Her smile faltered. "The Romans came. You wouldn't have wanted to be here. They did terrible, unspeakable things."

She stopped herself from elaborating after glancing at Shira. Conversation in front of our princess would need to remain suitable for young ears. Mari's eyes stayed focused on Shira as if trying to figure out what our relationship was.

"Did they hurt you?" I asked.

Mari shook her head. "Judd saw them coming, so we had time to get Baruch and Lowly into the cave. I hid in there with the animals until they left."

"Thank goodness God protected you," I exclaimed.

Daniel made the introductions. "Sis, this is Shira through whom God has blessed us. And Shira"—Daniel pointed to his sister—"this is Aunt Mari."

Mari interrupted. "Did you, you know…?"

I covered my mouth, giggling.

Daniel laughed. "No, we aren't married—yet. However, we are given to each other, and God has given us Shira for a time."

Mari's eyes beamed. "I'm so excited for you." She clasped her hands, obviously not sure how the pieces fit together, but glad somehow they did.

I glanced at Daniel. "Sis? Is Mari your sister?"

Daniel replied, "Yes!"

"She is?" How could I be the last to know?" I thought for a minute and put it together. She was his half-sister who was adopted by Theophilus.

Mari stood. "Please wait here, and I'll make us tea."

As she hurried off to the kitchen, I edged closer to my betrothed. I needed a reassuring hug. I didn't expect this many buried memories to be stirred by coming here. Until I walked into the house, my thoughts were focused on Baruch and Lowly.

Shira wanted to sit in my lap, perhaps also feeling insecure, but I knew she would quickly warm up to Mari once she got to know her.

I clarified. "Mari is your half-sister?"

Daniel nodded.

I would have to ask Daniel more about it later. He couldn't have known that when he was Nathan's teacher—or did he?

Mari returned with a brew of tea and herbs, rattling the hot teacups as she set them down. Also on the serving plate were bread, figs, and dates. Shira wasted no time reaching for the fruit.

I spoke to Shira. "I think Aunt Mari made you a very special tea, but let's let it cool."

She nodded.

Daniel spoke first. "We saw the sold sign out front. Has somebody bought the farm?"

Mari nodded. "Yes. We have to have everything out of the house in the next few days."

"That soon?" I asked.

"It's what Mr. Snyder ordered. After the Romans came, everything changed."

"What are you going to do?" Daniel asked.

Mari's eyes danced. "First, I have some news to share with you."

"What's that?" I asked.

"Judd and I are betrothed."

"Congratulations!" I exclaimed. That meant the prenuptial contract was void. I would never have to marry Judd, and I was free to marry Daniel. That must have been why God brought us to Galilee. I tried to imagine Judd and Mari getting married. Judd wasn't nearly good enough for her.

Mari laughed. "Yes, it came on rather suddenly. We realized we were in love with each other."

"When is the wedding?" Daniel asked.

Mari's eyes glowed as she rattled on about their wedding plans.

The Opobalsamum perfume lingered in my mind. Was I jealous

that she was getting married and I wasn't? I said a silent prayer for God to help me to be happy for Mari's good fortune. As she discussed their immediate plans, I tried to share her excitement.

"We're going to get married and live in Caesarea." Mari glanced in my direction. "Your father said we could keep anything we wanted. The rest he would give to the poor. He just asked us to bring his scrolls to him in Caesarea."

Daniel looked disappointed. "Why does he want the scrolls? I never saw him read them."

Mari smiled. "I think he wanted to, but he never found the time."

I admired Mari. She always thought the best of people, even when they didn't deserve it. Sadly, though, Daniel had said he'd love to keep a couple of them. Apparently, that wouldn't happen now.

I was almost too afraid to ask, but I couldn't wait any longer. "Are Lowly and Baruch still here?"

Mari laughed. "Of course. As I said, we hid them in the cave when the Romans came. And my father has agreed to take them as well as the horses. The rest of the animals Mr. Snyder said he'd give to the needy."

I was relieved. "I can't wait to see Baruch and Lowly again,"

"They will be excited to see you and meet Shira."

I took a sip of tea reflecting on the drama that lay in Mari's future.

"Is Much-Afraid with you?" Daniel's half-sister asked. "I thought she went with you when you went back home."

I smiled. "Oh, Much-Afraid is fine. She stayed with my mother this time."

Shira was getting antsy sitting through the small talk. I took another sip. "Can I take Shira out back to see Lowly and Baruch?"

Mara stood. "Sure. They should be in the pasture since it's a sunny day. Judd is cleaning up the cave before we move."

We followed Mari around to the back portico.

"Does Scylla still live here?" Daniel asked, following us.

I'd conveniently forgotten about her.

"She moved out a couple of weeks ago. I heard she went back to practicing her old profession."

"What's that?" I asked.

"She was a fortuneteller. She found a place to live," Mari added.

I wanted to say something unsavory, but God spoke to me so sternly, I stopped. After my mistake with the scrolls and the sheep and the goats, I knew I needed to deal with my hard heart.

I scanned the pasture. The tall green grass glistened in the bright sunlight. To my delight, I saw Baruch and Lowly. I took Shira by the hand. "Come with me. I want to introduce you to some old friends."

CHAPTER 42

THE SWEET-SMELLING flowers that covered the patio area brought back memories—and nostalgia. I never dreamed I'd be back—but now redemption seemed so near, I could taste it.

I remembered Scylla confronting Daniel and me over my ill behavior—which wasn't true. I remembered how upset Scylla was when we snuck my half-brother, Nathan, out of the house so Jesus could heal him, and I remembered when Daniel left without saying goodbye. How deeply I was hurt. Now that was all in the past.

"This way, Shira." We hurried through the gate that opened to the pasture. I noticed a grating sound as it swished back and forth. The Romans must have damaged it. My emotions tugged at my heart as we trekked through the knee-high grass.

"Heehaw!" Baruch brayed. "Miss Shale, is that you?"

"Yes, Baruch. It's me."

The donkey's ears quivered at the sound of my voice. "You came back."

I picked Shira up in my arms as the gray donkey bolted toward us. Seconds later, Baruch greeted us with happy donkey sounds, and I was sure I saw a large teardrop out of the corner of his eye. I ran my hand along his back and patted him on the head. Shira imitated me, making me smile. "I'm so glad to see you, Baruch."

"And you, too, Miss Shale, although you seem to have grown."

I laughed. "Maybe a little. I want you to meet Shira."

She reached out her hand and touched his ear. "Is this Baruch?"

I smiled. "Yes."

"He came back home?"

"Yes, he returned from the garden to be with his old friends."

After a moment of delightful affection, Shira pointed across the meadow. "Is that Lowly?"

"Yes."

It took a little longer for Lowly to ramble over as he'd put on a few extra pounds. I covered my mouth with my hand, delighted to see my favorite pig again. I flung my arms wide. "Lowly, I'm so happy to see you."

"And you, too, Sh-shale. You kept your promise."

I winked. If only I could keep all of my promises to everyone. "Let's go sit under my old tree."

We edged over to the grassy knoll that I considered my very own, at least for a little longer. We plopped down in the spot where I used to pray. It hardly seemed like a minute had passed since we were together, reminding me of the illusion of time.

Baruch looked like a little old man with hair on his nose and big ears. He started the conversation. "Things haven't been the same since you left."

"I'm sorry, Baruch. I needed to leave in a hurry and didn't get to say goodbye."

Tears puddled on the dirt under the donkey's face. I rubbed his head. "I'm glad I could visit, even if it's only for a short time."

"You aren't staying?" Lowly asked.

I shook my head. "Neither are you. The farm has been sold."

Surprised eyes reflected back at me. Baruch dropped his head. "No one can talk to us except you, Miss Shale. People think we're stupid animals. We aren't dumb, you know. We just can't make people understand us."

For a moment, a lump of sorrow got stuck in my throat. I wanted to cheer up my friends. "This should make you happy."

"Wha-what's that?" Lowly asked.

"Theophilus wants you and Baruch to live at his farm. That's Mari's adoptive father. You'll have a kind owner and all the oats you want. Isn't that wonderful?"

"That's more than wonderful," Baruch piped up. "I was afraid. I knew some mischief was in the air, but I didn't know how to find out what."

We sat on the grass and talked for a long while. Shira picked flowers and put them in a small vase she found by the fence. Baruch and Lowly shared about the Romans coming and ransacking the farm, how Scylla left and didn't return, which that part they were quite happy about. And, as they said about five times, they thought something was up because important people visited the farm.

"Do you know who bought the farm?" Baruch asked.

"No, I don't." I glanced around. "It's kind of sad because it's such a beautiful place."

I lifted up my hair to cool off my neck. It felt like summer had arrived early. A butterfly checked out Shira's vase of flowers and then moved on.

"I hope you haven't wandered into the wilderness again," I chided Baruch.

"No, since I know there aren't any apples down there."

"Oh, I almost forgot." I opened my bag. "Look what I brought you." I showed him a red apple.

"You've been to the garden?" Baruch asked.

"Yes. We even saw Cherios."

"Oh," Baruch cried.

I reached over and patted his head. "You'll always be my favorite donkey."

"And you, my favorite human, Miss Shale."

Shira whispered in my ear. "I wish I could talk to the animals like you can."

"Talk to them in a sweet, tender voice," I encouraged her. "Animals know what you are saying. They feel your compassion through your gentle words, and they want to be loved and accepted just like people."

"Can I give Lowly an apple, too?"

"Sure."

I handed one to Shira, and she put it in Lowly's mouth. He took the apple like a gentleman and wagged his curlicue tail. Of course, Lowly never forgot his manners in matters of extreme importance.

"Thank you, Shira, you—you are a kind young lady to give me such a big red apple."

I told Shira what Lowly said, and a big grin crossed her face.

After a while, I saw Daniel approaching. He motioned for me to come over to the fence.

"Let's go see what Daniel wants." I stood and reassured Baruch and Lowly. "We aren't leaving yet."

Baruch heehawed. "Tell Daniel we said hello, Miss Shale."

"I will," I promised.

As I approached, Daniel smiled. "Reunions with old friends are always sweet."

I laughed. My betrothed was reading my mind.

Daniel's eyes twinkled. "Mari fixed us dinner. Come and eat."

"I didn't realize I was hungry."

Daniel touched me on the shoulder. "Are you all right eating with Judd?"

I cleared my throat. "I'm fine."

CHAPTER 43

F RESH POMEGRANATES, FIGS, dates, olives, and bread filled the serving dishes.

"May I say the blessing?" Judd asked.

It would take me a while to get used to the new Judd. The one I knew from my last visit here was a jerk. Of course, I did see him sharing bread at the feeding of the five thousand. But this was all new to me—a redeemed Judd who wasn't a pervert.

Daniel bowed his head. "Please."

The words flowed smoothly from Judd's lips. "Dear Jesus, thank you for bringing our friends safely back to us. Thank you for this food, and thank you for the blessings you give us each day. Help us to place our burdens on you, and give us hearts to reach others for your king- dom. In Jesus' name. Amen."

I nodded. "Amen."

After a bit of small talk, Daniel told me what he and Judd discussed in the cave. "Judd is planning to take the donkey and the pig to Caesarea. Shira can ride on Baruch with you. I'll take one of the horses."

I was already worried. "That's a long walk for Lowly. Do we have a cart in which we can transport him?"

"I can put something together," Judd said, "and the horse can pull him."

Daniel dipped his bread in some olive oil. "Shale, I'm going to take the scrolls to your father. Perhaps he might allow me to keep the book of Joel and the book of Daniel if I ask."

"You're still hopeful?"

Daniel cocked his head. "He might."

"Do you know who bought the farm?" I asked Judd.

"No, we don't know."

I glanced around the room. "I have one bit of unfinished business before we leave."

"What's that?" Daniel asked.

"I need to see Scylla."

"Why?"

"Closure."

Judd shrugged. "I tried talking to her about the King, but she didn't listen."

"She listened to me," Mari said, "although I don't think she believed what I said. She did listen."

Judd followed up on Mari's words. "She knows the truth, but once you're involved in the occult, the deception can be overwhelming."

Mari dropped her eyes. "Sometimes it takes time."

The conversation shifted to lighter subjects, but I lingered on what I needed to do. How would I feel when I saw Scylla again?

CHAPTER 44

THE NEXT DAY, Daniel and Judd packed up what they needed for the animals. Mari went through Scylla's stuff—silver cups, golden goblets, elegant utensils, clay pots, exquisite dishes, and handmade tablecloths. If anybody deserved beautiful home furnishings to start married life, Mari did.

I was also thankful to see significant changes in Judd. Was my father changed also? I was glad he was generous enough to give Mari and Judd everything they needed, but I wasn't sure if he'd let Daniel keep the books of the Bible he wanted.

Mari entered the bedroom. Teasing me, she asked, "Are you snooping around to see what secrets Scylla left behind?"

Many of Scylla's personal items remained—expensive diamond necklaces, golden rings, and pearl earrings. "Why do you think she left this stuff here? You think she would have taken them."

Mari sat on the bed, smoothing out the creases in the blanket. "I think Scylla was depressed." She leaned over and whispered, "The Romans violated her."

As much as I disliked Scylla, I felt sorry for her. No one should be treated that way. Sadly, her occult fascination blinded her to the King. I bit my lip, cringing at how horrible that day must have been.

Mari straightened back up as if embarrassed to say it. "Brutus' position in the Roman government probably prevented the Romans from stealing any personal belongings. They took nothing, except scattered the animals and destroyed some property. Really, all they wanted was Daniel. When the Romans left, Scylla was not the same. I don't think she cared about any of this stuff anymore. Maybe the memories were too painful."

I reflected. Even then the Romans were searching for Daniel. Thank goodness he wasn't here. I lifted several shawls from a large wooden trunk next to the bed. Colorful robes were stacked neatly at the bottom. "Where did she get these?"

"Your father brought them to her from Egypt. He loved her in the beginning."

I glanced at Shira who was watching. "Do you want to play dress-up?"

She jumped up and down, pointing to one of the robes. "Can I wear that one?"

"Sure."

I helped Shira slip on a purple robe. She made a valiant effort to model it, but it was too big. I put one of Scylla's diamond necklaces around her neck and a bracelet on her arm.

"Do I look like a princess?" she asked.

"Oh, yes," I replied.

Shira's face glowed.

I sat across from Mari on the bed. "I have an idea, but I need your help."

"What's that?"

"Can you dress me up as an old lady? I want to pay someone a visit."

Mari smiled. "Oh, you're going to visit Scylla?"

"Something like that." I turned to Shira. "Do you want to play a game of pretending?"

"Yes. How do we do that?"

"We'll pretend we're someone else. I'll be an old lady. You'll be my granddaughter. Mari can cut this toga down so you can wear it.

Does that sound like fun?"

Shira nodded. "Yes. Can we do it now?"

"As soon as Mari can work her magic."

"Should I stain the tunic to make it look old?" Mari asked.

I nodded. "We don't want Scylla to recognize me too soon. In the grand scheme, the clothes and jewelry have no value."

CHAPTER 45

MARI KNEW SCYLLA'S favorite adornments. She found them and put them in a bag, including a couple of pieces of clothing, an expensive diamond bracelet, and her favorite wine cup.

Daniel saw us leaving and hurried over to the gate. "I don't like you going alone."

"If you want to follow from a distance, that's fine, but I must do this."

Daniel nodded. "I understand."

The small village of Nazareth was an easy hike down the road. I'd visited Nazareth several times and knew the area well, although I would have to search among the shops for Scylla's new hangout.

The area residents were unrefined—bordering on uncouth, perhaps because there were so many Gentiles. Of course, that meant more worldly passions laced with spiritists, fortunetellers, and psychics. Gentiles living alongside Jews created tension under the best of circumstances.

Shira wore Scylla's purple toga and cap, which had been quite abused at the hands of Mari. I was dressed in a brown, stained robe.

The edges were shredded, and my hair was packed underneath my worn head covering. I looked like a hobo in any century.

We came to a line of shops along the busiest road in the village. The marketplace was stuffed with various goods that filled the bazaar. Local farmers, tanners, blacksmiths, artisans, and fishermen carved out their favorite den. A wide assortment of products, including fabric, soaps, wine, sandals, tents, and hand-carved tables were available for the right price—just make an offer. When I noticed some unsettling things, I turned Shira around and headed in a different direction.

Soon I saw a sign. "Spiritist's Readings for One Denarius."

Mari gave me a denarius if I needed it. I didn't want a reading, though. I wanted to try to make Scylla a captive listener.

I squatted down to eye level to talk to Shira. "Now, remember not to say anything, but in your heart, pray for me to say the right thing."

Shira nodded.

My heart pumped with anticipation. I counted to three and breathed in deeply. When we approached Scylla's tent, I recognized my stepmother. She was dressed in black. Heavy makeup plastered her cheeks set off by red lipstick and dark mascara. She seemed a shadow of her former self, having sunk into the dark world of occultism.

I noticed carved wooden figurines that appeared to be icons on display. Wretchedness pressed in on me as I drew near. I saw a fly land on the woman's forehead. Strange she didn't feel it crawling on her face.

Since Scylla left a lot of cosmetics at the house, I had many options. I'd applied the makeup liberally to my face so she wouldn't recognize me. I was at least three or four inches taller and almost four years older than when she knew me last. She couldn't possibly know who I was until I handed her the bag.

Judd found a cane stored in the cave that he gave me. Dressed like a homeless old woman with a very young granddaughter would not be what Scylla would expect if she was suspicious about my identity.

I called out to my stepmother. "Good afternoon."

Scylla twirled the tips of her hair with her smooth, pointed fingers. "Would you like a reading, my friend?"

Looking into her evil eyes made me uncomfortable. I counted to three again. "No, I don't need a reading. I need some advice. A friend encouraged me to see you."

I cleared my throat and looked away, trying to appear as pathetic as I knew how.

"It's the same price, one denarius," Scylla replied.

I gave Shira the money to make her feel important. "Sweetie, would you like to pay the lady for me?"

Once Scylla received her fee, she motioned for us to come inside her tent. As we entered, I noticed more images and carvings hewn out of wood and stone.

She waved her hand. "Have a seat."

I found a wooden chair past its prime and set my cane against it. Shira preferred to sit in my lap. Scylla's eyes bore into me. She couldn't know who I was, but she would figure it out.

Scylla's eyes went to Shira. My princess shot her a smile but didn't say anything.

"So, what is it you need advice about, my friend?"

I gulped in air to calm my nerves and kept my eyes focused on the ground. "I've done some things I regret. It's a long story, but the short version is I want to tell my stepmother I'm sorry, but I don't think she'll listen to me. How do you get someone to listen to you?"

"I could do a reading and tell you what you should do," Scylla replied.

I shook my head. "Oh, no, I couldn't do a reading. I just wanted someone to talk to."

"Can you tell me more—if I don't do a reading, I need information about this person."

Part of me wanted a reading so I could prove she was a quack, taking people's money and filling their ears with garbage. Once I handed her the bag with her clothes and personal items, she would be exposed for what she was, ripping off so-called clients, but that wasn't why I came. To fall prey to my human side of wanting justice would be displeasing to God.

Besides, I wanted to prove I'd changed and my faith was genuine.

She had already been victimized by the Romans and my father. No woman should be subjected to having to compete with another wife for affection.

I spoke slowly to enunciate my words. "Many years ago, when I was young, I treated my stepmother unkindly and made her life miserable. I want to tell her I'm sorry, but she disdains me. I don't think she would listen. What should I do?"

I didn't look at Scylla but instead stared at the ground.

"Well," Scylla said thoughtfully, "it shouldn't be that hard. Go to your stepmother and tell her what you've said to me. I'm sure she'll accept your apology."

"You think so?"

"Yes. I don't see why not."

I pointed to myself. "The reason why I want to apologize is the King changed my heart. When Jesus died on the cross, he died for my sins. Now I need to make things right with the people I've offended."

When I said Jesus' name, she flipped her hand, as if to say, "Oh, another one of those types."

I pressed in harder. "What do you think of the King?"

Scylla squirmed. "I worship a different god, but this isn't about me. This is about your stepmother."

"Well, if my stepmother worships a different god like you, do you think she can forgive me?"

"If she wants to."

"Can I practice what I want to say with you? Would you mind?"

Scylla fingered her dress and re-crossed her exposed legs, "Go ahead. Two minutes, and then your time is up."

I bit my lip. "Here's what I want to say. I was a disrespectful young teen. Only when I met the King did I come to know that deep kind of love that touches your heart. I met the King, and he changed my life. Now I want to ask you to forgive me."

I looked straight into her eyes. "Will she listen to me if I say that?"

Slowly, Scylla nodded. "Yes. If you say it like that, I think she'll listen to you."

"Very good," I said. "I appreciate you listening to me."

She attempted a half smile.

I stood. "Shira, it's time to go, sweetie."

"You forgot the bag," Shira said.

I looked beside my chair. "Oh, yes, the bag." I picked up the bag and took it with me outside the tent before handing it to her. "Here, this is for you."

Before she could open it, I grabbed Shira's hand and quickly rushed off, forgetting my cane. When there was enough distance between us, I glanced back, but I didn't see her.

"Shale?"

I turned and saw Daniel. When I was closer, Daniel answered my question. "Scylla opened the bag and ran back into the tent."

"She did?"

Daniel picked up Shira and held her over his head. "And you did awesome, too."

I ran my finger along my cheek, and oodles of makeup covered my fingertip. "Ugh—I've got to get this stuff off my face."

CHAPTER 46

THE NEXT MORNING, Mari, Judd, Daniel, Shira, and I left for Caesarea. We took with us Baruch, Lowly, three horses, clothes, jewelry, cooking paraphernalia, and odds and ends with no real value except for Mari's sentimentalism.

Daniel packed Brutus' scrolls hoping to convince my father to gift him the books of Joel and Daniel. Dozens of scrolls filled my father's extensive library, not only Hebrew writings, but many antiquities from Egypt, Assyria, Persia, and Babylon.

Daniel also took a few personal letters my father wrote, hoping to earn his favor. Perhaps Brutus might allow him to keep the two Old Testament books.

I didn't remember specifically what the book of Joel was about, except the prophet wrote about the Day of the Lord, but it made sense why he wanted the book of Daniel—for his namesake.

Only when we were on the road to Caesarea did I think about my father. Would he be the same as before—distracted and preoccupied with his work for the Romans? Despite my ambivalence, I did look forward to seeing my half- brother.

I turned to more important matters. How could I convince my betrothed to get married in Caesarea? Then we could return to the twenty-first century. My longing increased with each passing day to see my mother and friends although the friendships here ran deep.

Jesus told us to marry quickly. We could have a double wedding with Judd and Mari, and Shira could be the flower girl. A double wedding would be the perfect way to celebrate. He called both Jews and Gentiles. The church was his bride, but the Jews were his people. Maybe showing Daniel the photograph of his great-grandmother would convince him.

Of course, the Jewish evangelists were virgins, according to the fourteenth chapter of the book of Revelation. How could we get married unless we didn't consummate the marriage? Then I remembered Joseph and Mary wed, but they didn't have relations until after the birth of Jesus. I knew Daniel would want to wait until the time was right. I found it hard not to be jealous of Mari, and it frustrated me I was battling feelings I didn't want.

Once we were on the road, however, my conflicted emotions evaporated as the countryside captivated me. I hadn't seen this part of Israel before. The sun shone brightly with rain clouds off in the distance. Hopefully, they would stay there until we arrived in Caesarea.

The narrow road on which we traveled passed rocky peaks overlooking deep ravines rich in fertile fruit. Sparrows hopped from tree to tree in search of seeds and grasses. The lilies glistened in the sun between fleeting clouds. Several watchtowers lined the narrow road overlooking vineyards soon to be harvested.

Daniel was anxious to get through this part of the trip—making the point the King's Highway was safer travel and a more fortified road. He seemed worried about rain, but those clouds were miles away.

Judd constructed Lowly a wooden crate to be pulled behind Daniel's horse. It was a rickety contraption, not very sturdy, but Judd assured us it would be safe for the short trip.

Lowly voiced his concern to me when we tried to get him to enter it. "Sh-shale, I don't know about this. It rocks back and forth. I think I might get sick."

There is nothing worse than a stubborn pig, but after much cajoling, Lowly finally entered the crate. I felt like it was my duty to make sure he arrived safely. I insisted that Daniel's horse be the one to pull him.

We passed some curious nomads and shepherds. I'm sure we didn't look like the everyday travelers they were used to seeing.

Daniel insisted we not stop to make sure we made it to Theophilus' house before sundown. I packed snacks to eat along the way. Shira fell asleep in my arms, so I didn't have to dig into our food supply.

Suddenly raindrops began to fall. It didn't take long for the dusty road to turn to mud and become almost impassable. The golf ball-size raindrops pitted the way into a raging river. I never saw so much rain in such a short amount of time.

Shira woke up, cold and crying. I did my best to shield her by putting a blanket over both of us.

"Hee-haw! This is not good," Baruch complained. "If this rain doesn't stop, we're in trouble."

The donkey's brays were alarming. "What do you mean, Baruch?" For the first time, fear seized me. The rain kept falling, and sheets of falling bullets blanketed the narrow road.

Before Baruch could respond, Daniel spooked me when he came up alongside us. He looked like a ghost. I didn't even see him dismount. Shira wailed, and I couldn't hear him over the torrent.

"What did you say?"

Daniel shook his head.

Then I heard Judd shouting and Mari screaming. I couldn't see up ahead, but something gave way around us. The road was collapsing. Between sheets of rain, I saw Lowly's crate was inches from careening off the cliff. Anything that fell into the ravine would perish. Somehow, in the chaos, I heard Lowly's frantic squeals.

I shouted, "Someone help Lowly!"

Daniel ran back to the pig, but the water was filling the container too quickly. Poor Lowly was trying to keep his nostrils above the rising tide. I feared within seconds, the water would pull him over. I cried out to God. "No!"

Daniel held on to the crate, but now I feared for Daniel. One small puff of wind could knock him over. I glanced at Judd who didn't seem eager to do anything. My anger soared. What a coward.

Mari dismounted her horse and found a rope. She threw it to Daniel who snatched it midair. He wrapped the rope around his body and Mari secured the line to her horse. It wouldn't help Lowly, but it would keep Daniel from falling into the ravine.

Then Judd dismounted his horse and rushed over to help. It took a woman to show him up. Of course, I couldn't do anything with Shira in my arms but pray.

The ground shook followed by hoof beats. Was someone coming to rescue us? I held my breath as time ticked too slowly. The rain stopped, but flooding covered the roadway. I began to cry as our rescuers came closer. When they were visible, I wasn't sure I saw who I wanted to see —Romans.

It didn't take them long to assess we were in trouble. The lead rider held up his hand. Even though the rain was stopped, the water was up to Baruch's knees and fetlocks. The tip of his snout poked out through the wooden panels. Daniel clung to the rope with one hand on the crate.

Judd walked over to the soldier, but the Roman guard, who I perceived to be the captain, held up his spear and stopped him. "Don't come any closer."

The captain waved for the others to rescue Daniel. "Forget the pig. Throw him over. I want to meet this Jewish fellow who is obsessed with swine."

How did they know Daniel was Jewish? Was it his beard?

Laughter bellowed from some of the Roman soldiers.

I shouted, "Please, no, save my pig, too."

I caught their attention immediately, and their eyes went from me to Mari. They weren't sure which woman spoke.

When I couldn't think of anything better to say. I blurted out, "It's our only food for our young daughter. We'll die of starvation if you don't save our pig."

When I said this, they stopped laughing.

The soldiers sloughed through the water, grabbed the rope, and pulled Daniel toward them. Once he was safe, he shouted, "Quick, we've got to rescue the pig."

The captain pointed his spear at my betrothed's chest. "Who are you, Jew?"

Daniel answered, "I'm Daniel Sperling, Son of Aviv."

Silence filled the air as the soldiers glanced at each other. Did they remember him? I shook uncontrollably, partly from fear and partly from cold. Shira cried even louder as she clung to me.

My feeble attempt to save Lowly paid off. The captain motioned to his cohorts. "Get the crate on safer ground."

He stared at Daniel. "I know who you are, son of Aviv. Don't do anything foolish."

Then he turned to Judd. "And who are you?"

Judd said his name, and the captain shook his head. "Don't know you," and quickly lost interest in him.

After several minutes, the Romans secured Lowly on the road, and enough of the water drained out that he didn't look like a drowned pig. However, he was still a pathetic sight.

The captain motioned for Judd to stand off to the side away from his horse, and he focused his attention on Daniel. "Thief," he said accusingly.

I knew we were in trouble.

CHAPTER 47

THE CAPTAIN STRUTTED up to Daniel and grabbed him savagely by the shoulder. "Did you kidnap the girl?"

Daniel shook his head and waved his dripping hand. "I'm helping Brutus Snyder, the Roman diplomat for international relations in Galilee, to move his animals and family to Caesarea. He sold his estate in Galilee. He's now living at his Caesarea residence full time."

The Roman captain snickered. "Nice try, chariot racer. If the girl had not convinced her father to drop the kidnapping charges, I'd arrest you now."

The captain spat in Daniel's face. "A Jew who rescues pigs isn't even faithful to his own people."

I stared, horrified, but Daniel did nothing, not even to wipe away the spittle. I held my breath.

Mari spoke up for Daniel before I could think of what to say. "With utmost respect, what Daniel said is true."

"Prove it," the Roman guard demanded. "Or I'm seizing all of you until I can check out his story. Mr. Sperling may be kidnapping you as he did the girl. I have no information that he has ever been involved with Mr. Snyder."

"Daniel is my brother and what I speak is the truth," Mari said.

I'd never seen Mari be this bold, but the captain didn't seem willing to take her word for it.

The guard pointed his spear at me. "Who are you?"

"I'm Shale Snyder, Brutus' daughter."

The captain immediately dropped the spear and stared into my eyes. He approached me slowly, and I matched his stare without blinking. Shira grabbed me tightly as the guard neared. I could feel her fear rising, and I covered her face with the wet blanket.

How dare this captain cause us such fear—especially with me holding a small child, but if Roman soldiers could kill all the two-year-old babies of Bethlehem, I knew they'd have no problem hurting a three-year-old—or any of us.

Then he stopped unexpectedly midstride. I continued to stare him back.

The captain snarled. "Shale Snyder?"

I nodded.

The guard returned to his comrades, and they walked a few feet away to engage in a private discussion.

I whispered to Daniel. "The documents, you brought some of my father's letters, you said?"

Daniel nodded. He edged over to his horse slowly so as not to alarm them and unpacked his miraculously dry bag.

The Roman captain returned to us. "I need you to prove what you're saying is true."

Daniel pulled out Brutus' letters and a couple of scrolls. "If you know Brutus Snyder, then you know his proclivity to collect ancient parchments. I'm delivering his papers to him in Caesarea—that is, unless you interfere. I'm sure you wouldn't want a bad report to get back to Pontius Pilate—would you, sir?"

The captain straightened and adjusted his military garb. "Let me see what you have."

Daniel handed him the documents and scrolls. The captain passed a couple of them to his cohorts to peruse. Several minutes of silence followed.

"Of course," Daniel continued, "When I meet Mr. Snyder, I'll be sure to put in a good word for you, how you saved his daughter's life, as well as his grandchild and son-in-law."

The captain looked up. "Shale Snyder is your wife?" He pointed to Shira. "She's your daughter?"

"Shale is my betrothed. We plan to marry in Caesarea."

At that proclamation, my heart went pitter-patter. Was Daniel going to marry me in Caesarea, after all my consternation?

The captain responded, "If Shale is Mr. Snyder's daughter, she shouldn't need a pig to feed Mr. Snyder's granddaughter, should she?"

Daniel gulped.

I didn't know what to say. Now we were trapped by our own words.

Judd broke in for the first time. "Lowly is a prize-winning pig, but Mr. Snyder is very humble about it—doesn't tell anyone, you know."

The captain burst out laughing. "Prize-winning pig." He slapped the precious documents into Daniel's chest. "I expect a glowing report about how I rescued Mr. Snyder's family, including his daughter and grandchild. Festus is my name."

He clutched Daniel on the shoulder one more time. "Another captain may not be so lenient. Your name is well known. Many hope to prove their worth to Pontius Pilate. You are an escaped slave—and there is plenty of room for thieves like you at the salt mines. My advice to you is to stay out of Caesarea. Even Brutus Snyder doesn't have the authority to overrule Pilate."

Daniel drew in a long breath, and relief filled my heart.

The captain gathered his band of soldiers. As they picked their way through the flooded-out road, he pointed to the collapsed area as they passed. "We'll need to get a repair crew to fix this ..." His voice trailed off as they continued toward Galilee.

Once they disappeared, Daniel hurried over to me. "How is Shira?"

"We're fine," I reassured him. "Just cold."

Daniel glanced up at the sky. "The sun will dry you out. Let's go a little farther, to the King's Highway. We can eat and rest there."

Daniel turned to Mari and Judd. "Does that sound like a good plan?"

They both nodded.

I clenched my eyes and bowed my head. "Thank you, Jesus, for saving us, even Lowly."

CHAPTER 48

EXHAUSTED, WE ARRIVED in Caesarea at sunset. The estate covered several acres, and it took a few minutes to reach the house on the private rock-laden driveway.

Daniel dismounted and came over to help Shira and me as Judd and Mari wandered off for what appeared to be a romantic walk.

"Mari and Judd are family, but what about us? Are they expecting guests?" I asked.

Daniel grabbed Shira, who rubbed her eyes, not having had her afternoon nap. He held her as I dismounted. "We'll let you nap as soon as we get settled in, sweetie."

Shira grunted, wrapping her arms around his neck, too tired to say anything.

Daniel quickly scanned the estate, admiringly. "Cynisca and I stayed overnight here when we left Caesarea. I think Mari's mother passed away a few years ago. I promised Theophilus I would come back and tell him about Yeshua."

Soon a servant approached, and Mari came over to make the introductions.

"I hope my father is here," Mari said.

"He'll be excited to see you," the servant replied.

Some other helpers arrived to take care of the animals.

Before they were taken to the barn, I walked over and spoke to Lowly. "How is my favorite pig doing?"

"Sh-shale, you aren't going to eat me, are you?"

"Eat you! Of course not."

"W-e-well—that's what you told that man."

I squatted down to his eye level and spoke to him through the wooden spokes. It was a miracle the ruined crate didn't collapse. "I wanted to save your life. Besides, I don't even like bacon."

"What's ba-bacon?" Lowly asked.

I sighed. "I don't eat pork."

Lowly wagged his tail. "Oh, thank goodness."

The sun peeked through the canopy of trees. I lifted up my eyes to the heavens thankful Baruch and Lowly had a beautiful place to call home. If God could save a lowly pig from death, how much more could he do if we only asked? "They will take good care of you, Lowly, I promise."

"Thank you, Sh-ale. You are the best friend any pig could have."

"They might want to bathe you, though, get some of that smell off you."

"Do I smell?" Lowly asked. He appeared embarrassed at this revelation.

"Anybody would smell if they were cooped up in that thing like you. Once you get in your new stall, you'll be fine."

The pig bowed his head. "Thank you, Sh-shale."

I stood, stretching my legs and back from the long journey. "Now I must get back to Daniel." When I returned, I heard Mari's parting words, "I can't wait another minute to see my father."

Words of love I wished I could utter to my dad.

Shira wanted to look at flowers, so she wandered around exploring.

Judd went to the back to check out the stable.

Since we had a private moment, I reached for Daniel's hand and embraced him. "You explained at your mother's house how you and Mari are half-brother and half-sister in this century. I know your mother confused Shira for Mari, but all you said was that your mother was depressed about her sin. Of course, when we met Mari in Galilee, it took me a minute to put it together, but what about in the twenty-first century? What do you think happened to her?"

Daniel wrapped his arm around my waist. "I think my mother must have had an affair while she was married to my father. Here in the first century, the baby was adopted by Theophilus and his wife."

The question begged for an answer. "What about in our dimension? Your mother and father never told you anything?"

Daniel stiffened.

I touched his chest gently with my finger. "Listen, if you don't want to talk about it..."

Daniel shook his head. "No, it's not that. I've thought about it."

"Could Mari have died in our dimension?"

Daniel stared silently at the ground.

"So no one ever said anything?"

Daniel stepped back. "As I told you before, I met Mari twice in the seventh dimension, in the garden. Maybe—she ended the pregnancy."

"You think your mother had an abortion?"

Daniel bit his lip. "She always suffered from depression, even before my father went missing. It was more than the holocaust that bothered her. I don't think she could forgive herself. I really believe if I had a sister who died, I would have known. There would have been a gravesite. Or if they placed her for adoption, they would've told me."

"Do you think your father would know something?"

Daniel's face was sad. "I don't know. What kind of person might Mari have been in our dimension?"

Daniel's words were sobering, and I wanted to encourage him. "In the end, God will redeem everything, even something as abominable as abortion."

"The seventh dimension makes you question a lot of things," Daniel said.

I brushed my hair back from my face. "In reality, everything is spiritual. I remember when you didn't want to talk about spiritual things."

Mari approached, waving her hand. "Please come," she called to us.

Daniel got Shira's attention, and she came running. Judd hurried to catch up as Mari escorted us inside.

A distinguished elderly gentleman greeted us. His eyes focused on Shira. "And who do we have here?"

Mari made the introductions. Theophilus reached out to shake my hand, and I knew, although I wasn't sure how, he was the one Dr. Luke addressed when he wrote the Gospel of Luke. A Roman official—I never would have imagined that Mari was raised in such wealth. She was so humble, so kind—not my image of someone who could have been spoiled by the fleeting glamour of riches.

Theophilus was a large man, but his reassuring face emanated kindness. "Daniel, I'm so glad you came back to visit. I can't wait to hear about the recent happenings in Israel concerning Yeshua and the Passover."

"I look forward to our discussion," Daniel said. "God is doing amazing things that I'd love to share with you."

CHAPTER 49

T HE NIGHT PASSED quickly as there was no lack of things to discuss. Mari and Judd's upcoming wedding took center stage. Theophilus was excited for his daughter, and he and Judd seemed to have hit it off well.

Despite Judd's flaws, and there were many, I could see God accomplishing a great work in him. God brought them together. Money would never be an issue for Mari, and for someone who lived such an ordinary life under the shadow of someone I considered a witch, I could see God's blessings over their future marriage.

Theophilus was also the father I never knew—kind, sensitive, and God-fearing. Of course, when Daniel and I married, I could claim him as my father-in-law. What an exciting prospect.

I put Shira to bed early after dinner and joined the rest at the table where Theophilus, Daniel, Mari, and Judd reclined finishing off the meal with Roman pastries. I drank some tea.

Theophilus took a sip of wine and focused on Daniel. "Doctor Luke shared with me the incredible events surrounding Passover—the riots, the crucifixion of Yeshua Hamashiach, and then he said something most amazing. He said people claimed they saw Yeshua alive in Galilee a short time later. Of course, I didn't believe Doctor Luke at first, and then I heard it from others. Apparently, hundreds have seen him alive since his crucifixion."

"It's quite amazing, isn't it," Daniel said.

Theophilus shook his head. "Can you imagine what it would mean if it were true? One or two people might see a phantom or a lookalike and make an outrageous claim of seeing a dead man come back to life, but hundreds? That would be impossible—unless it was true."

I chimed in. "Doctor Luke is the most honest person I know. And, as a doctor, his reputation is on the line. He, out of all people, wouldn't make a claim unless he believed it was true. I hear he's considering writing a book to document the events. Anything of this importance needs to be written down by an objective, unbiased person, and he's that kind of doctor."

Theophilus nodded. "I agree. Doctor Luke claimed some of the people who witnessed these proceedings are personal friends, including the mother of Jesus."

Theophilus turned to Daniel. "What do you make of these incredible events? Do you think it's possible Jesus is the Messiah?"

Daniel dipped his bread into a sauce. "I saw him alive also, Theophilus, following his crucifixion, along with about five hundred people, on the banks of the Sea of Galilee."

Theophilus' eyes bulged. "I had no idea. You mean you were among the eyewitnesses who saw him in Galilee?"

Daniel nodded. "I was."

Theophilus stared at Daniel. No one uttered a word for a long time, contemplating what it meant. While Daniel and I knew it historically to be accurate, based on the Scriptures and having seen God's miracles for the last two thousand years, this was scandalous news to people of the day.

What would skeptics think in the twenty-first century if Jesus' crucifixion was broadcast around the world and then cameras showed him a few days later preaching at the Sea of Galilee?

"So it must be, Daniel," Theophilus said. He stared off in space shaking his head before returning his gaze to us. "Are you absolutely sure it was the same person, that it was Yeshua?"

Daniel drew in a long breath. "I know without a doubt. In fact, I watched him die on the cross. I saw the guard stick a spear into his side. I saw what happened—the three hours of darkness that fell over Jerusalem, the earthquake that shook the ground, the renting of the veil at the Temple. I saw dead people come out of tombs."

Once Daniel started, he didn't want to stop. I'd never heard Daniel share what he saw that day in such vivid detail.

"In fact," Daniel continued, "do you know the earthquake obliterated the Chamber of Hewn Stone? That's where the religious leaders condemned Jesus to death—as if God judged the council for their heinous deed."

Daniel closed his eyes. "And then the people scattered—seized with fear. I could feel the wrath of God, something I'll never forget.

"Except for a few—Nicodemus, Joseph of Arimathea, Mary, the mother of Jesus, and a couple of her friends stayed. The Roman guard took down the body of Jesus and handed it to Joseph. They took him to be buried in a borrowed grave."

None of us stirred as we listened mesmerized by Daniel's words.

"I visited the tomb. I can tell you, without any doubt, it was empty three days later. Jesus' loincloth was draped awkwardly—as if somebody snatched him out of his clothes. Even the look on Peter's face exiting the burial chamber was one of utter astonishment."

Daniel shook his head. "I can't make this stuff up. It's too unbelievable. Nobody would believe it—unless it was true."

We remained silent, caught up in Daniel's recitation.

Daniel waved his cup and took a sip. "In a strange series of events, I ended up on the shores of Galilee after Jesus was killed. I witnessed him preaching to a crowd of listeners. Hundreds of people were gathered along the water as he spoke.

"There was one difference, however, from before. Yeshua's wrists were scarred. I could see they were healing from recent injuries. In an instant, I knew it was him. I recognized his voice, I knew his mannerisms, and his eyes were familiar to me.

"I concluded this man must be the Messiah. I believed he was who he claimed him to be, the Son of God, who died for my sins."

Theophilus rolled his eyes—not mockingly but in astonishment. "How can a man die and come back to life? How could anyone believe that? I must think about this. I must learn more, meet more eyewitnesses. I must discuss it more with Doctor Luke."

"You are very wise, Theophilus," Daniel said. "I don't think you're far from the kingdom of God."

Theophilus smiled. As if to lighten the air he clapped his hands. "So—what are your plans, Daniel, while you're in Caesarea?"

CHAPTER 50

DANIEL TOOK A bite of his dessert. "First, Theophilus, thank you for allowing us to bring Baruch and Lowly. Shale is very fond of them, and we're glad to know they'll be well taken care of."

Theophilus smiled at his daughter. "I think Mari is pretty attached to them also."

She nodded.

Daniel steepled his fingers. "As far as plans, I need to pay Cynisca's father a visit. Do you know his name?"

"Justinian," replied Theophilus as he studied Daniel, no doubt wondering where this would lead. "He's a high-ranking official. To get a hearing with him might be difficult."

Daniel shuffled his feet at this revelation.

Theophilus picked up his wine glass. "To be candid, if he knew you were in town, he might put you in jail for his financial losses. While I know you didn't kidnap his daughter or rob his horses, you still broke the contract with him. Under Roman law, you're an escaped slave."

"That's why I wanted to visit him," Daniel said.

Theophilus cautioned Daniel again. "If the Romans find you, you'll be sent to the salt mines—if they don't torture you first—unless you're fortunate. God better be on your side, or I'd leave Caesarea and go back to Jerusalem. As a Jew, they won't bother you there—too many other troublemakers to worry about."

My heart quickened. "Daniel, why do you want to meet with Cynisca's father? This is insane."

Daniel turned to me. "I owe him an apology like you wanted to apologize to Scylla."

His words stung. "Yeah, but it wasn't a matter of life and death for me."

Daniel ran his fingers through his hair. "If I can get a hearing with Justinian, I might be able to offer him some financial remedy. I also want to confront Tariq about stealing my money.

"More than that, I want to find out what Tariq knows about my father. He and Nidal aren't brothers, based on what Cynisca told me. Nidal might even be in town."

"Tariq is still racing," Theophilus said, "and winning every race, although we haven't seen Nidal in a few weeks."

I tapped on the table as panic filled my heart. "That must mean Nidal didn't return to Caesarea when he left Jerusalem. This is a terrible idea, Daniel."

Daniel glared at me disapprovingly, as if his obvious irritation would silence me, but my emotions were too raw. "Didn't Nidal tell you everything he knew? How could Tariq know more? Besides, you said you would never race again. You aren't thinking about doing that, are you? You've already had one run-in with that Roman captain. God has given you many warnings…"

Daniel interrupted me. "If the situation were reversed, what would you do? This is about my father. Why would I not try to talk to both men involved in his kidnapping? That's the main reason I wanted to come to Caesarea."

I stared at Daniel until he looked away. "Why do you need to race against Tariq to talk to him?"

Daniel cocked his head. "I never said I was going to race."

I glared. "I know that's what you have in mind. To race against

Tariq and give the money to Justinian to reimburse him for the hardships you've caused him."

Daniel's eyes narrowed. "If I didn't know any better, I'd say you were reading my mind."

I threw up my hands. "I'm not stupid, Daniel. I know you better than you think."

An awkward silence followed. We knew better than to have an outright argument in front of our hosts, particularly Theophilus. I already regretted what we'd said. But I was so terrified at the prospect of Daniel racing I couldn't hold back my fear.

Daniel seemed oblivious. "It will be a surprise to everyone—especially to Tariq. Otherwise, he could manipulate the Romans into arresting me."

"I don't like it, Daniel," I repeated.

Theophilus cut in, diffusing the tension. "Daniel, I could talk to Justinian on your behalf, but I have no idea what his reaction would be."

That wasn't what I wanted him to say. I wanted him to tell Daniel to forget this outrageous idea.

Daniel leaned over the table and narrowed his gaze on me. "When I raced before, Cynisca said Tariq's team put curse tablets in our stall. The ventriloquist followed me everywhere. She threatened Cynisca."

Daniel sat back again, and his eyes flitted about the room. "Caesarea is a godless place, a hangout for those who dabble in the occult. I don't want to give Tariq's team foreknowledge. I can show up for the race and surprise him. He won't be prepared to race me mentally, and he won't have time to reach out to his contacts.

"I win the race, give Cynisca's father the winnings, and I confront Tariq. If I lose, he'd probably use whatever means at his disposal to get the scroll. Maybe I'd give it to him to encourage him to tell me what he knows."

I knew I wasn't going to win this argument, however crazy it was. "If you talk to Justinian, you have to take me with you."

"What about Shira?" Daniel asked.

I stopped to think. "I'd have to make arrangements to leave her here."

Mari jumped into the conversation. "I could take care of Shira while Shale goes with you, Daniel."

I turned to Mari. "Could you?"

"Yes, I would be glad to."

"I know Shira would love to spend more time with Baruch and Lowly."

"No problem." Mari smiled, glancing at Judd. "Someday she'll have a little cousin."

Daniel said to no one in particular, "I wonder if Cynisca could help me, if I contacted her, to talk to her father."

Theophilus interjected. "Daniel, as I said, I'm good friends with Justinian. Since I'm familiar with the situation, perhaps I could put in a good word for you and make arrangements."

"Would you do that?"

Theophilus smiled. "Of course."

Soon the servants came to clear the table, and Theophilus stood. "Your rooms have been made ready. I have an early morning tomorrow, so I must get some sleep. I'll visit Justinian as soon as possible and tell you what he says."

Daniel tipped his head. "Thank you for your hospitality."

Theophilus walked to the doorway. "You're most welcome. Good night."

Judd and Mari left the room discussing wedding plans. I grabbed Daniel's hand and led him to an area out of everyone's hearing. I knew we said too much at the dinner table.

"This is a terrible idea, Daniel. After the confrontation with the Romans, I know how dangerous this is. Why risk fate? Why do this crazy thing?"

Daniel dropped my hand and turned his back to me. "Why make this harder, Shale. I can't leave Caesarea and go back to Dothan without making things right. And I need to find out what Tariq knows."

I put my hand on his arm. I could feel his muscles tensing up. "You can go to the Coliseum and meet Tariq. Give him the scroll. Who cares about it now? Even Jesus didn't want it."

Daniel's eyes bore into me. "It's more than that. It's about my father. It's about the financial losses Justinian has suffered. If we go back to our time and the world has been deceived by a godless religion, how are you going to feel?"

I countered Daniel's argument. "You can offer the scroll to Tariq for information about your father. You don't have to race him."

Silence filled the air between us.

I crossed my arms. "Daniel, are you sure you don't want revenge? To beat him in a race and knock him off his pedestal?"

Daniel glared at me. "How do you know that my anger isn't righteous? I saved Nidal's life."

"Well, even Nidal said Tariq was evil."

Daniel clasped his hands. "If Theophilus can set up the meeting, then let's take that as a sign from God this is his will."

I sighed. "Okay."

"Now let's get some sleep," Daniel said.

I lifted my face hoping he would kiss me, but then a servant entered. I quickly pulled away. I didn't want curious eyes to see.

"Good night, Daniel. See you in the morning."

I left the room without looking back. I wasn't sure I could sleep.

CHAPTER 51

T HE NEXT DAY gloomy skies reflected my growing fear. Raindrops painted an even grimmer picture. I walked into the dining room as Mari placed a bowl of fruits and grains in front of Shira. I kissed her on the forehead.

My princess showed me another white-colored stone she found that resembled the wooden bird Dr. Luke gave her. She imitated the bird. "Tweet-tweet."

I sat beside her. "What did she say?"

"She said she's hungry."

I smiled. "Now you have two birds. They can be friends."

Shira reached into her bag and pulled out her other stone bird and set them beside each other. "I wish I had the one Doctor Luke gave me."

I grabbed some figs and olives from the table. "Can I tell you a story?"

Shira's brown eyes focused on me. "Yes."

I took a couple of bites. "When I went to the garden the first time, I walked along a trail that went through a thick forest. After a while, we came to a small pond of crystal blue water. Golden rocks covered the bottom. I climbed onto a flat rock and dipped in my hands. My whole body tingled as if the pond possessed magical qualities. While I lay there, a small blue bird landed on my shoulder and whispered in my ear, 'You are a daughter of the King.' Then she flew away. Even though I never saw her again, I never forgot what she said to me."

Shira turned over one of the stone birds. "Am I a daughter of the King, too?"

"Of course."

I lifted Shira's dark brown hair away from her face. "Sometimes God puts people or animals in our lives for only a short time, like the dove. Once they have carried out God's will, God uses them somewhere else."

Shira stroked the stone bird's head. "How come we didn't see the pond when we were at the garden?"

"We didn't have time to go down that trail."

"You don't think my dove will come back?"

"He's probably feeding the beggars."

Shira's eyes lit up. "Maybe the beggars need him more than I do."

"Just think how God used you to set the dove free."

That brought a smile to Shira's face.

Mari placed a tray of tea and crackers on the table and sat across from us. "Daniel is at the stable with Judd. They are making some adjustments with the new animals."

We were still chitchatting when someone entered the front door. Mari arose to see who it was.

Theophilus' voice reached my ears. "Are Daniel and Shale here?"

"Shale is in the dining room. Come join us at the table."

"Where's Daniel?"

"He and Judd are cleaning up the stable."

"Save me some fruit. I want to talk to Daniel first, and then I'll be back."

I heard the door shut and Mari returned. "Maybe he has some news about Justinian."

My stomach soured. I hoped we wouldn't hear anything for a

couple of days. However, I knew wishful thinking would only postpone the inevitable.

A few minutes later, Daniel and Theophilus entered through the back door. I could hear them dipping their feet in the water bowl. The rain must have brought mud to the backyard. Soon they joined us in the dining room. As Theophilus sat at the table, Daniel motioned for me to follow him.

Once we were alone, Daniel spoke in a soft voice. "Theophilus inquired of Justinian about making a visit. He said the magistrate seemed surprised I was in town but welcomed the opportunity to see me. Theophilus said Justinian will be at the training facility later today. He encouraged me to stop by. Do you want to come with me if Mari takes care of Shira?"

"I didn't anticipate things would happen so fast. Today?"

"Yes."

"I want to come, but I didn't know it would be this soon."

Daniel lifted my face to his. "How about that kiss we didn't have last night?"

I closed my eyes as Daniel touched my lips. For a moment, my worries were forgotten. I opened my eyes and smiled.

Daniel asked again. "Do you want to come with me?"

I nodded. "Of course I want to come. Do you know where the training facility is?"

Daniel chuckled. "I better know where it is. I spent several months there."

"Do you think Justinian would mind if I came?"

"If he does, you can wait outside. It's a beautiful facility, and I imagine Dominus and Cynisca will be there."

"The part I don't like is you racing. You already told me how dangerous it is. You almost died."

Daniel took my hand reassuringly in his. "Nothing is decided."

I looked for any sign of hesitation. "Suppose this backfires and Dominus wants to keep you. How much more time do you owe him?"

Daniel cocked his head. "I'd have to think about it—three or four months."

"You promise me just one race?"

"One race."

"Suppose he won't agree to one race?"

"Let's take it one step at a time. You are assuming the worst."

I complied. "Let me see if Mari can take care of Shira."

CHAPTER 52

A MISTY RAIN fell making the road sludgy. "The training facility is on the south side of town, so we'll pass through the heart of the city. It's quite beautiful," Daniel said.

Even with the rain? I doubted it.

Daniel squeezed my hand. "You'll have an opportunity to see the harbor."

As we traveled along the main thoroughfare and entered Caesarea from the north, the coastal metropolis looked deserted.

We passed through the city gates and walked a short distance when Daniel pointed. "Your father lives in that cluster of dwellings along with most of the government officials. Even Pontius Pilate—at least the last time I was here."

"Are we going to pay my father a visit?"

"If we have time, depends on how long this takes."

I didn't want to see my father today. I was already concerned about Daniel. I could only deal with one problem at a time.

As we strolled through the town, the light misty rain fell harder, giving me goosebumps. "We should have brought something to cover us."

The fountains, fed by aqueducts, were overflowing from the rain. On a warm summer day, I imagined their beauty enchanting tourists like me. If things were different, I would have longed to see the city—enjoyed watching the seagulls nosedive for fish, admired the sun's rays rippling over the blue waters of the Mediterranean, esteemed the skilled fishermen as they hauled in their daily catch, and felt the vibrant pulse of the city. I could imagine merchants selling their local wares and shops brimming with international delicacies, but not today. Not as long as I was worried.

As we walked, Daniel pointed to another structure. "There's Caesar's Temple."

The Temple stood atop a citadel towering over the Mediterranean. An impressive statue of Caesar filled the courtyard. Surrounding the figure were dozens of smaller ones that represented a pantheon of Roman gods.

A short distance from the Temple was a palace, nestled in a rocky outcropping. It overlooked the beautiful seaport where ships were in the harbor because of the inclement weather.

Several water fountains decorated the cloister. An elaborate swimming pool took up most of the back lot facing the sea. Flowers lined the walkway that bordered the gardens.

Daniel reached for my hand. "Most of the city's residents, if they aren't Roman officials, are merchants and fishermen, or people from other places that have taken up residence here. It's like a seaside resort."

Now I understood why government officials made this their home. It was a stunning resort town, more Roman than Jewish.

Once we reached the southern edge of the city, the most imposing building in Caesarea came into view—the hippodrome. Daniel pointed. "That's where I raced chariots."

I tried to imagine what this place would look like on race day. No matter how hard I tried, I couldn't. I didn't want to know. I didn't want to imagine, and I didn't want to be here.

Daniel interrupted my musings. "The singers, dancers, and performers who entertain the racing patrons enter through those doors.

LORILYN ROBERTS

Families come from miles to see the parade. If you come, you'll experience that."

I took a deep breath as my stomach churned. I was still hoping it wouldn't happen. I couldn't even think about the possibility my betrothed would race.

"How much farther do we have to go?"

"Not much. It seems farther because you don't know where we're going, and the weather is bad."

We approached some beggars.

I glanced at Daniel. "Do you have any money?"

"Not really. I have some loose change from Nepal and one of the coins Doctor Luke gave me."

Daniel rummaged around in his bag and threw the change into a beggar's cup.

When the other beggars heard the coin clanging, one of them cried out, "Have mercy on the poor man."

We passed several beggars. I dropped my last coin into an empty hand leaving the rest disappointed. There were so many we couldn't help all of them.

"We're getting close," Daniel said. "A little farther down this road is the Equi Palmati Stables."

The rain stopped, and we came to a quaint cobblestone street. "This used to be a dirt road," Daniel said.

We followed the road until it came to an open field. A few horses were out to pasture.

Daniel directed me. "This way."

I pointed to a short circular track to the right. "Did you race here also?"

Daniel shook his head. "That's a practice field for training."

We passed some buildings, but no one was around—at least outside.

Daniel pointed to a door. "Let's go in there."

I caught Daniel on the arm. "Wait."

Daniel stopped. I could see impatience on his face. I knew I couldn't change his mind, but it didn't dissuade me from trying again.

232

"If you can make things right with Justinian short of racing, will you promise me you will do that?"

Daniel nodded.

"I can't tell you how fearful I am, imagining you in a chariot. Tariq would like nothing more than to humiliate you, even kill you. Promise me you won't race unless you have to."

Daniel lifted my hair away from my face. "I promise." He opened a heavy door and motioned for me to enter. The barn housed multiple stalls, and I saw a short man advanced in age grooming a horse. Recognition crossed his face when he saw Daniel.

My betrothed greeted the man warmly.

The groomer smiled. "I didn't know you were coming today. Is Justinian expecting you?"

Daniel placed his hand on the groomer's shoulder. "Yes, a mutual acquaintance made the arrangements. I want you to meet Shale, my betrothed. Shale, this is Dominus, the head trainer."

Dominus raised his eyebrow.

Daniel crossed his arms. "Dominus and Cynisca are in charge of Justinian's racing team."

I reached out and shook the man's hand, recognizing his name from previous conversations.

We exchanged a few pleasantries, and Daniel glanced around the barn. "Is Cynisca here?"

Dominus' eyes swept through the stable. "She may be with her father. I'll go check. Wait here."

Daniel tipped his head. "Thank you."

We waited quietly, not saying anything until Dominus returned. Accompanying him was an attractive young woman, a few years older than me, maybe twenty-one or twenty-two. Her physique would have made me envious if I were inclined that way. She was dressed in farm-type clothing with her hair pulled back in a ponytail.

Her eyes flitted to Daniel, to me, and then back to Daniel. She smiled as she walked over to us. "Daniel, I can't believe you're here, and this must be Shale."

After a brief hug, Daniel made the introductions again.

Cynisca eyed me curiously. "My father told me you were coming, but I didn't believe him."

"I hope I caught him on a good day."

A shadow crossed Cynisca's face. "We haven't won a single race since you left. No one can beat Tariq. His brother quit racing, but Tariq races on. I'm not sure what my father will do if he doesn't win soon."

"If you take me to him, I have a business proposition."

"Do you want to race again?" Cynisca asked.

"We'll see."

"So you don't want to clue me in, huh?" Cynisca chuckled. "Very well."

I wasn't sure if I should follow Daniel or not, but Dominus put up his hand. "Wait here. Cynisca will be back in a moment. Justinian will only want to talk to Daniel."

Worry consumed me, and I watched as the two men disappeared from view.

CHAPTER 53

DOMINUS WENT OUTSIDE to tend to some horses, and my anxiousness deepened. I shuffled my feet as I paced back and forth.

Cynisca returned, smiling. "My father is pleased to see Daniel. I wanted to stay and eavesdrop, but business matters are only discussed between men."

My heart relaxed. "I understand."

Cynisca furrowed her brow. "Did Daniel tell you what happened that led to the charges against him?"

I bit my lip. "He said you went to Galilee to stay for a few days at my father's. Your father never got that message, and so he didn't know where you were. He believed Daniel kidnapped the horses and you. That's how the Romans got involved."

Cynisca nodded. "I was too scared to stay in Caesarea. A woman followed me who seemed like a demon. I know it sounds strange. When I heard about the Roman soldiers searching for Daniel, I knew I needed to return.

"When I explained to my father how Daniel protected me, my father was thankful, even though my disappearance caused him great pain. Plus, runaway slaves are a problem for the Romans. They punish them severely. My father didn't want to see Daniel prosecuted, not even for breaking the contract."

"Hopefully your father will be kind," I said.

Cynisca studied me. "You're worried about Daniel racing, aren't you?"

I nodded. I was afraid if I said anything, I'd start crying.

Cynisca changed the subject. "Would you like to see the chariot horses?"

My heart lightened. "Sure."

"Usually they would be outside in the pasture, but since it's raining, we kept most of them in today."

I followed Cynisca to two stalls, and she closed the gate behind us.

While I'd been around horses at my father's farm, being so close to them in tight quarters made them seem even larger.

"This is Mosi, the lead horse, and the one in the stall next to him is Oni."

I gently touched Mosi on his nose, and the horse whinnied. "Oh, that feels delightful. Can you massage a little higher, please?"

"Up here?"

Cynisca eyed me curiously. "What?"

I glanced at her. "I was talking to the horse. Mosi likes being rubbed a little higher."

Cynisca didn't take me literally but laughed. "They are quite the talkers, especially when we bead their mane for the races. They like being fussed over, but when you don't win, it's disheartening even for them."

"Do you remember Daniel?" I asked Mosi. "He used to race you."

The horse perked up at Daniel's name. "Oh, Daniel, yes. I thought that was his voice, but it's been a while. Is he going to race again?"

I glanced at Cynisca. "Do you think you could bring me a cup of water?" I pretended to sneeze and rubbed my eyes. "The stuffiness is making my allergies act up."

"Oh, sure. Can I leave you with Mosi? He's very gentle."

"Yes, I love horses."

I waited till Cynisca left and whispered to Mosi. "Listen, fellow, I have a special gift. I can talk to animals. Daniel wants to help you win again. Do you know anything about the team that keeps beating you? Are they cheating?"

Mosi nudged me. "Daniel was kind. We wanted to win for him, but since he left, even though we try, they always beat us."

I couldn't accept there wasn't some reason. "You don't know why Tariq keeps beating you?"

Mosi shook his head. "No. Actually, though, there is one thing that seems strange."

"What's that?"

"We haven't seen Nidal in a while, but Tariq won most of the races even when Nidal was racing. Tariq smells funny, and he has super-human strength. He can take turns faster than any human without falling off the chariot."

I rubbed my nose. "Tariq smells funny? What do you mean?"

"Humans have a certain smell. Even though each human smells differently, they still smell human. Tariq doesn't smell like other humans."

My heart skipped. "What does he smell like?"

The horse shook his head. "I've never smelled another human that smells like him. He doesn't smell like a human or an animal."

I heard Cynisca returning. "I'll tell Daniel what you told me."

Cynisca opened the gate and handed me a mug of water.

"Thank you." I took a few sips. I was thirstier than I realized. "Can I say hi to Oni?"

"Of course," Cynisca said. "I wish I had an apple. He loves apples."

I dug into my bag. "I have one."

After Cynisca opened his gate, I offered it to him. Oni whinnied. "Thank you."

"You've made a friend for life," Cynisca chuckled.

I handed another one to Cynisca. "Let's give Mosi one, too."

I heard Mosi chomping it down. "Thank you," he said from the other stall.

Oni heard my conversation with Mosi. He added, quite sincerely, "We would win again if Daniel were our gladiator."

My heart fluttered. What could I say? I hoped his words weren't foretelling that Daniel would race, but if he did, the horses had full confidence in my betrothed. That was frightening and reassuring at the same time.

After a few minutes, Cynisca was ready to leave. "I will shut the gate. It can be hard to close sometimes."

When we reached the entrance to the barn, Daniel and Dominus were chatting.

"Did everything go well?" I asked.

Daniel smiled. "I'll explain on the way back." He held out his hand to Cynisca. "Theophilus sends his greetings."

"Please reply in kind to him. We need to pay him a visit."

Daniel put his hand on my shoulder. "Ready to go?"

I nodded. I couldn't wait to hear what happened.

CHAPTER 54

I WAITED UNTIL we were on the cobblestone road to pepper Daniel with questions. "What happened?"

Daniel clasped my hand. "It went better than I expected. I apologized to him for everything and told him I wanted to race once more…"

Horrified, I stopped on a pin and stared at Daniel. "You offered to race again? How could you do that, knowing how terrified I am, and you promised…"

Daniel stopped midstride as if fearing I might have a mental breakdown. "What did you expect me to do? He could turn me over to the Romans for breach of contract. He's lost a fortune. He invested heavily in my training. He thought his daughter was kidnapped, and he believed he lost two valuable horses—essentially his livelihood. Did you expect me to walk in there and say a few words of apology, walk out, and pretend that would make up for months of financial ruin?"

My heart was breaking. I couldn't believe Daniel volunteered. It was one thing to be forced to race, but to offer—Daniel betrayed me. How could I forgive him for this?

"Besides that," Daniel continued, "these are people I care about. It was more than a contract. I spent time with them, ate meals with them. It was my life for some time."

Tears flowed. "Daniel, you betrayed me. You said you wouldn't race unless you had to."

Daniel's shoulders drooped as if he realized for the first time he'd hurt me. He edged away after seeing my tears, but he could never grasp my grief.

There was a bench close by, and I ran over to it. Ripping my bag off my shoulder, I dropped it in the growing puddles. Then I collapsed on the bench, burying my face in my hands.

How could Daniel choose to race after my pleas? Tears rained down my cheeks like buckets from a monsoon.

The sun dipped behind some clouds, and a sudden gush of wind pelted me with more freezing rain. I imagined the whole sky unleashing its fury on me. I never wanted to go back to Theophilus' house. I was convinced Daniel would die at the hands of Tariq.

How could I look Daniel in the eye? I didn't want to face the future without him. How could I trust him? There was no way I had the strength—mentally, emotionally, or spiritually—to raise Shira on my own.

"Oh, God," I cried. "Where are you?"

Daniel stood several feet away in the drizzle, like a shadow. Something had come between us. Perhaps I should share with Daniel what Mosi told me. Was I spooked more than I realized?

My hands smothered my pleas. "God, this isn't fair. You've given Daniel impossible odds and me a burden I shouldn't have to bear."

I imagined the times Daniel beat Tariq and Nidal. I wanted to believe nothing was impossible. I wanted to trust God, to have the faith Daniel had. Now all I could see was defeat. The stakes were enormous, and I wasn't willing to risk it.

I couldn't stop the negative thoughts, the worry, or the fear. A few minutes passed, and I felt Daniel approaching. I heard his footsteps and felt the warmth of his body beside me. He laid his hand on my shoulder but didn't say anything.

I listened to his prayer but believed it to be useless. I was heartbroken, and no prayer could rescue me from my depression.

Still, Daniel prayed. After a while, I couldn't deny I appreciated the gentle touch of his hand.

Eventually, the rain stopped, but we were more wet than dry. As the sun's rays melted away the raindrops, I heard a rustling sound above us. I glanced up to see what it was.

Worldly Crow was circling overhead and dropped an object on the ground near us. As quickly as he appeared, he took off, leaving behind a cold chill.

I stood, and Daniel picked up the object. He wiped off the moisture with his robe and examined it.

"What is it?" I asked.

"It's a key."

"To what?"

"A hotel room key, an apartment key. It looks like the key to the rented room I stayed in when I raced."

Daniel handed it to me, and I flipped it over. "This is where you stayed before?"

Daniel nodded. "I think so. It has the same chariot inscription."

I felt God speaking to me. "Daniel, I need time alone—to pray, to read my Bible, to learn what God is showing me."

I picked at my tunic. "I almost hate to tell you this, but back there on the street, I was angry with you."

Daniel nodded. "I know because I let you down."

"I can't go back to Theophilus in this condition. I'm an emotional wreck. I need time with God before I ruin my relationship with you, and Shira, and everybody else."

I grabbed Daniel's robe and pulled him toward me. "One night, Daniel—can I have one night alone with God?"

Daniel nodded. "Sure. I can take care of Shira. You don't want to stay at your father's? That way you wouldn't be completely alone."

I shook my head. "God sent me a key—and I think this is what he wants me to do. I need to be alone to pray and to figure this out."

Daniel eyed me inquisitively, surprised by my strong reaction. "Just because a wicked crow gives you a key shouldn't be used to validate what God is showing you. Besides that, we have no money."

"He's hasn't always been wicked, Daniel. He only knows the ways of the world. Sometimes he's done good things, too, like the time he gave me the key when Scylla locked me up."

Daniel chuckled. "Worldly Crow must like keys. You're the one who told me not to trust him. It's not like I can talk to birds."

"I know, but if you stayed there before, I'm sure the manager would remember you and give you one night's credit. We can pay tomorrow."

I glanced up at the heavens where Worldly Crow disappeared. Would God use a bird to show me something? But then, did God ever do things in a way we could predict?

Daniel wrapped me in his arms. "I love you, Shale. Let's see if this is God's will."

A few minutes later, we arrived. I looked up at the sky wondering about the time.

Daniel pointed to the bench in front of the steps leading to the entrance. "Let's sit over there."

I fumbled with the key and dropped it. Daniel picked it up and handed it to me.

I clasped my fingers around it more securely. "Thanks."

Daniel peered into my eyes. "Maybe it's not a matter of spending the night but having a few hours to pray. You've been a saint through all of this. I mean, you've been a single parent to Shira. You've been faithful to me on this roller coaster ride to find out what happened to my father. You've even gone to the ends of the earth—to hell and back, and through it all, you've shown God's grace."

I stared at the ground, embarrassed by Daniel's praise. I didn't deserve it, not based on my vindictive feelings moments earlier.

Daniel continued to lift me up. "We know God's return is near, and we know the Day of the Lord is imminent. God has shown us time is an illusion. Either of us could be back in our own time in a heartbeat, but God has put us here for a reason."

I wrapped my robe around my hands, squeezing the cloth between my tired fingers. "I'm so emotionally drained." I rubbed my eyes, flipping the key over in my hand. "God must have meant for me to have a few hours to myself, if not the night. I want to pray. I must give this race to God because I have such fear."

Daniel squeezed my hand. "You know, there is a parable in the Bible about the Pearl of Great Price."

I hadn't thought about that parable in a long time. I remembered the merchant sold all his belongings to buy one valuable pearl. "Are you saying this is my Pearl of Great Price?"

Daniel shrugged. "I don't know about you, but it is my Pearl of Great Price. I must do this."

I leaned my head on his shoulder. "I must tell you what Mosi told me."

Daniel's eyes showed surprise. "You talked to Mosi?"

"I know why Tariq keeps winning."

"Why?"

"The horse told me he didn't smell like a human or an animal."

"Are you serious?"

"Daniel, Tariq isn't human."

He shook his head. "If he isn't human, what is he?"

"I think I know."

"What?"

"I had a dream. I know you don't like to hear about my dreams, like my dream that the ventriloquist came and told me you didn't love me. I mean, that was not from God but the evil one's attempt to get into my head. However, sometimes dreams mean something."

Daniel clarified. "It's not that I don't think dreams have meaning, but how do you know whether to believe them or how to interpret them?"

"Didn't Peter quote at Pentecost that God's sons and daughters would prophesy? Young men would see visions, and old men would dream dreams."

Daniel nodded.

"A while back, I dreamed Rachel and I were questioned by government officials in Atlanta, but they weren't human. They looked human, but they were different."

"You think Tariq is a robot?"

"Daniel, suppose he's a Nephilim or a transhuman? Remember, Jesus said, as it was in the days of Noah, so it would be at the coming of the Son of Man. We know the Day of the Lord is near."

"So part demon and part human?" Daniel asked.

I bit my lip. "Maybe he's not human at all. That's why I'm worried about you racing against him. You might be racing against a demonic human."

Daniel thought for a moment. "Nidal only said he was evil."

"Demons are evil, Daniel."

"You really think he's a Nephilim?"

I sighed. "I don't know."

"Well, whatever he is, I beat him before, and I can beat him again, even if no one else can."

I lowered my head. "Let me stay here a few hours, rest, and pray. I must come to terms with this, whether this is my Pearl of Great Price or just plain ole trusting God. I need my own faith. You have yours."

I stood, and Daniel took me in his arms, briefly kissing me on the lips. "I wouldn't race if I didn't think I could win with God helping me. I have a feeling Tariq knows more than Nidal. He was the person behind the kidnapping."

The rain began to fall again, and Daniel motioned me toward the entrance.

We entered the lobby, and I saw a young, dark-complexioned man on duty. Daniel took the key from me and handed it to the attendant. "Are we checked in?"

"Name, please?"

"Shale Snyder," I said.

The man nodded. "Yes, you are checked in. Your room was booked . and paid for by a man named Jacob Sperling."

Daniel and I exchanged glances.

The attendant pointed. "It's down the hall."

"Thank you," I said.

Daniel accompanied me to my room. "It hasn't changed since I was here."

"So many statues," I noted, "and most don't have enough clothes."

"That's Caesarea. Greek culture, Hellenistic."

"And it didn't bother you when you were here?"

"Yes," Daniel said. "It did bother me. God seared my conscience not to want those things. However, he really got my attention when I lost the money."

Daniel unlocked my door. The room was a standard motel room, with a bed, table, and chest of drawers. A purple rug covered the floor. I sat on my bed.

Daniel sat beside me. "I'll be back at dusk. Read your Bible, take a nap, and pray. Remember, God has your back. He hasn't abandoned you, and he hasn't abandoned me. We are in this together, no matter what happens."

I stared at the floor.

"Are you hearing me?" Daniel asked.

I looked into Daniel's eyes. "You have so much more faith than I."

Daniel reached for my hand and kissed it. "Don't leave the room. I'll come back before it gets dark."

I nodded.

Feeling exhausted, once Daniel left, and I closed and locked the door, I went back to my bed. I pulled out my Bible. Fortunately, the pages were still dry. I wanted to read the parable that Daniel mentioned, the Pearl of Great Price, but I wasn't sure where to find it. My pride pricked me. Now I would have to hunt for it.

I turned to the first book in the New Testament, the Gospel of Matthew, remembering the parables Matthew quoted of Jesus. The Gospel of Matthew began, "The book of the genealogy of Jesus Christ, the son of David, the son of Abraham..."

Soon I came to the Parable of the Sower. Many more parables followed, simple stories I hadn't read in a long time. But it was the Parable of Hidden Treasure that struck a nerve.

Jesus said, "The kingdom of heaven is like treasure hidden in a field, which a man found and hid, and for the joy over it, he went and sold all that he owned and bought that field."

I broke into tears. What was my treasure? Was Jesus my treasure? Or did I want to substitute my own? I knew if God chose, he could give me the desires of my heart.

"God," I cried, "you know that I love you. I want this road of fear to end."

I heard Jesus' voice, not audibly, but in a way I knew was supernatural.

"It's in your suffering you are refined. Your soul is more precious than all the gold and silver in the universe. Don't lose heart. Cling to your faith, and someday, I will wipe away your tears at the Fountains of Living Water.

"Let the dross fall away, let the impurities melt. Remember, I will never leave you or forsake you."

Tears covered my cheeks. I knew then, I needed to trust God for the race. Did I have that kind of faith?

I laid my Bible down, imagining what it would be like to have so much faith I never struggled, doubted, or questioned. I closed my eyes. "Help me to love you better, Jesus," and then I fell into a deep sleep.

CHAPTER 55

I WAS AWAKENED by banging on the door. I couldn't remember where I was. As I sat up, my memory returned.

Daniel spoke through the door. "Shale?"

I unlocked it, and Daniel followed me inside. "You slept the whole time, didn't you?"

I nodded. "I must have been tired. What time is it?"

Daniel shrugged. "I have no idea without a watch."

"Or iPhone."

Daniel quipped. "Mine only works when the ventriloquist wants to get a hold of me."

I waved my hand. "Don't even mention that wretched name."

"It's probably about six."

I sighed, folding my arms in front of me. "I'm hungry, too."

"Dinner is almost ready at the house."

"Listen," I said to Daniel. "God did speak to me before I fell asleep. He told me I have to let go of my fears."

"I do, too," Daniel replied. "We can't assume God is going to allow me to win, but what matters most is we give Yeshua the glory. I want to know I'm doing what he's called me to do."

I swept my hair back from my face. "I suppose martyrs give God the most glory, don't they?"

Daniel scooted closer to me. "There was something I never shared with you after God placed his seal on my forehead."

"What's that?"

"I was taken to the throne room of God. There I witnessed a great multitude that no one could number. The people came from all nations and tribes, and they wore white robes and held palm branches in their hands."

"They were martyrs from the Great Tribulation?" I asked.

"Yes. You know what happened next? It's in Revelation if you want to read it."

"I don't remember."

"King Yeshua promised the martyrs they would never hunger or thirst again. He told them the sun would not bear down on them and burn them, and he led them to the Fountains of Living Water. He personally wiped away every tear from their eyes."

Goosebumps covered me. "Daniel, I'd never heard of the Fountains of Living Water, but God spoke something similar to me. He said he would wipe away my tears at the Fountains of Living Water, too. Do you think that means we're going to die?"

"God has our back."

"It would be reassuring to know how everything turns out."

"Then how would we build our faith?"

I knew Daniel was right. Neither of us spoke for a minute. "I guess we should head back."

Daniel stood and crossed his arms. "The next few weeks will be hard. I'll be gone all day, building up my endurance and preparing my body. It's been a while, you know. I don't have the same body I had when I quit racing."

"I understand."

"Don't think I'm ignoring you if I seem distant or distracted, but I have to prepare in every way possible—physically, mentally, spiritually, and emotionally."

I stood and rested against Daniel. "I'll try to help you as much as I can. I mean, I don't know how I can…"

Daniel kissed me. "Pray for me. Pray for me morning, noon, and night."

I took a deep breath. "I promise you, I will."

"Are you ready to go back?"

I nodded. "I think so."

"Good, because I'm hungry."

I rubbed my stomach. "Me, too."

We left the inn as cold rain was falling. By the time we reached the city gates, I knew we would be drenched if we didn't run.

I shouted to Daniel. "Guess what? Your training starts now. I'll race you."

We made it back to Theophilus' house within a couple of minutes. Even though I was out of breath, I felt rejuvenated, but Daniel beat me. It took me a moment to catch my breath as we stood on the porch. "What do you do tomorrow for your training?"

Daniel squeezed my hand. "I'll make some practice runs, heavy physical conditioning. Hopefully, I'll be ready in a few weeks, if not sooner."

I wrapped my arm around him. "I'll be praying for your protection."

Daniel replied. "If it's any consolation, I'm thankful you're with me this time."

I laid my head on his shoulder. "Me, too."

CHAPTER 56

THE NEXT DAY Daniel left before sunrise. Each day was the same making the days seem long and lonely. I hardly saw him until he returned late in the evening. As the days passed, I found it hard not to be depressed.

One morning Shira tiptoed into my room. I was aware she was there, but I only wanted to sleep—sleep until the big day. Reading my Bible took too much energy. I couldn't get through more than a couple of paragraphs when I would stop from fatigue.

Shira ran her fingers along my arm. I opened my eyes and smiled.

"When are you getting up?" she asked.

"I don't know," I mumbled.

"Auntie," she said softly, "you always seem sad now when you used to be happy."

Her words jolted me. I knew I hadn't given her much attention since we arrived, but Mari was so much better than me at the parenting thing. She even included Shira in the festivities of their upcoming wedding.

Everybody had a job—Daniel with his training, Mari getting married, and me—I prayed faithfully, but that seemed like so little. I mean, who can pray eight hours a day? I still struggled with fear, no matter how often I took my concerns to God.

I needed to pull myself together. If this was my job, I failed miserably. I lifted Shira up on the bed and held her in my arms. "Shira, sweetie, I'm just tired. You know I love you."

She wrapped her arms around my neck, and I kissed her on the cheek. "Do you feel better now?"

"Uh-huh. Can you play with me?"

I smiled. "I've got a better idea," trying to add as much excitement to my voice as I could. "Let's go out to the barn and visit Lowly and Baruch."

Her eyes brightened at my suggestion. "Right now?"

"Yes, as soon as I get dressed."

A short time later, we walked outside as bright sunshine peeked through the canopy. Fresh flowers graced the fence, and a new crop of vegetables filled the garden. Baruch and Lowly were grazing a short distance away. When they saw us approaching, they came over to greet us.

"How are you doing today, Miss Shale?" Baruch asked.

I massaged the donkey on the top of his head, and contented brays showed his approval. "I'm doing well. And you?"

Baruch appeared to be smiling. "I'm the happiest donkey in the world, Miss Shale, thanks to you and Mari."

As Lowly joined us, I remembered how close we came to losing him.

"Can I do that, too?" Shira asked.

I picked Shira up and showed her how to use her fingers to rub his back. After a while she became too heavy. I praised her. "You are doing a great job, but I need to rest my arms."

After I set her down, she took off exploring. I filled Baruch and Lowly in on the news, sharing with them mostly about Daniel's upcoming race. "I still need to take my father's scrolls to him, but I've been so concerned about Daniel, I don't have the energy to visit."

"Sometimes," Lowly stuttered, "things can seem so dark, you lose hope, but that's when God intervenes. Just as Jesus gave us a new home, God will take care of Daniel. Here we get all the insect larvae, worms, fruits, and vegetables we want. Isn't that right, Baruch?"

Baruch grunted. "Leftovers and insects may taste good to pigs, but I prefer barley, hay, and nuts."

I chuckled at eating insects. "You're right, Baruch. Jesus provides for our needs. Yet it's hard for me to remember that. I mean, I can believe it easily enough, but living it out is another matter."

This time it took a donkey and a pig to give me perspective. I remembered a song I used to sing, "This is the day the Lord has made. We will rejoice and be glad in it." Humming the tune lifted my spirit and the darkness of my heart fled.

Delightful animal sounds followed me as I went to chase down Shira, but instead, she ran back to me. "Keep singing, Auntie, I want you to hear the flowers."

She took my hand and led me to the blooming garden as I sang.

"Auntie, isn't it beautiful?"

"My singing?"

"No, the flowers are singing. They are singing with you."

I sang some more, hoping to hear what she heard, but I could only hear my voice.

Joy crossed Shira's face. "You must sing more often. You bring joy to the world every time you sing."

After we went back into the house, I shared with Mari my intentions to visit my dad.

"Send him my love," she said. "He was always kind to me." She handed me a sealed envelope.

"What's this?"

Mari smiled. "An invitation to our wedding."

I lamented. If only Daniel and I could have a double wedding with Mari and Judd. What if I asked one more time?

CHAPTER 57

ONE EVENING DURING dinner, Daniel appeared unusually tired. He didn't eat much, and that concerned me. How could my betrothed build muscle if he wasn't eating protein? Mari made it a point to buy extra portions of fish, but tonight Daniel didn't touch it. He left the table before the meal was over and went to his room.

Following dinner, I cleaned Shira up and tucked her into bed. After saying her prayers, I kissed her on the forehead. She soon fell asleep, and I went to Daniel's room. After pulling up a chair, I sat beside him as he lay on his bed. "Is everything all right?"

"I'm exhausted and sore."

I pressed my fingers into his shoulder muscles as hard as I could. He moaned.

"Am I hurting you?"

"No, keep doing that. Your fingers are better than any muscle relaxers."

I massaged his shoulders and arms as he directed me. "A little higher, a little lower, yeah, that's good."

For the first time in almost three weeks, I had a purpose besides praying. Not that that wasn't important, but Daniel needed me.

For more than thirty minutes, I worked my fingers to the grind, massaging muscles that felt like rocks. I wished I'd thought about doing this before. We were approaching three weeks of training, and Daniel hadn't mentioned when the race would be.

When my hands were about to give out, Daniel reached over and clasped my hand. "Thank you. You never told me you had that gift."

I smiled. "I've longed to do something for you."

He returned my smile. "You've done a lot."

I hadn't shared my experience in the garden as I was waiting for the right opportunity. "I have something to show you. I'll be right back."

He mumbled under his breath, "I'm not going anywhere."

I returned a few minutes later. "Do you recognize this photo?"

Daniel opened his eyes but couldn't see what I was showing him, so he sat up. I handed it to him.

His face turned ashen. "Where did you get this?"

"I found it in a house in the garden when you went to the castle."

Daniel shook his head. "This is the same one by my mother's bed. You didn't take hers, did you?"

"Of course not. You know I wouldn't do that."

"Where in the garden?"

"When you went to the castle, Cherios took Shira and me to the spot in the garden where I met the rabbit on my first adventure. Remember, I followed Much-Afraid through the door. I interrupted Cherios's picnic with the donkey under the apple tree.

"Not far from that spot, a stone's throw away, a brand-new house is being built. We went inside, and Shira found the photograph and brought it to me."

Daniel held it up to the light from the candle. "You found this photo in a house in the garden?"

I nodded. "What do you think it means?"

Daniel examined it more closely. "It looks like the exact one by my mother's bed."

"Daniel, it is the same photo. It's your great-grandmother as a young girl wearing the Star of David. It's the same girl we met on the train."

Daniel shook his head. "This is a mystery. I wouldn't be here if God didn't save her life."

I leaned in closer. "And you returned the girl's necklace to her."

We remained silent for a minute unable to solve the paradox. However, seeing the photo in the garden gave me hope that we would marry. "Perhaps we'll live in the garden," I said. "Maybe that's our house."

Daniel chuckled. "A house made by the grand carpenter." He kissed me on the forehead.

I wanted him to kiss me again, but he lay down. "Did you see anything else in the garden while I was gone?"

I leaned over and whispered, "Daniel, many houses are being built, perhaps thousands."

Daniel closed his eyes. "There would be millions. Jesus told his disciples, 'In my father's house are many mansions. If it were not so, I would have told you. I go to prepare a place for you.'"

I smiled. "Yes, that's one of my favorite verses. You know what's strange?"

"What?"

"You would think there would be many people in the garden, but there was just us."

"Remember," Daniel said, "you saw sheep and goats."

I sat up straighter. Now that I understand more, I wish I could go back. I put my hand on Daniel's. "Do you have any idea when we can get married?"

Daniel propped himself up on his side. "When God makes it clear."

I scooted closer. "Mari is getting so excited about her wedding. I was thinking…"

Daniel squeezed my hand. "Shale, we can't have a double wedding. I mean, I can't think about it until after the race. I need to focus on my training. Mostly, I need your prayers. I'm racing against powers of darkness, against spiritual wickedness in high places. Yes, I'm racing for my father, for Cynisca, Dominus, and Justinian, but ultimately, I'm racing for God."

Daniel peered into my eyes. "I don't know if I ever told you, but the last race ended strangely. I lost my contacts—remember I used to wear them. After the race, they were gone, and I saw better without them. In fact, I witnessed the heavens open."

Daniel peered at the ceiling. "God showed me the race is about more than making things right with Justinian, or finding out what Tariq knows about my father. It's about defeating evil through the power of Yeshua. It's about joy and love in difficult circumstances. It's about trusting God when the outcome is uncertain."

"I'm praying for you, Daniel."

"And you'll never know how much that means to me."

"Where do you think Nidal went since he didn't return here?"

Daniel shook his head. "I don't know. He wanted to stay here, race, and make money." He sighed. "I need to get some sleep and so do you."

I nodded. "One last thing."

"What's that?"

"We didn't visit my father as planned because of the bad weather."

"I almost forgot," Daniel said. "Do you think you could go without me?"

"You don't want to go?"

"Not until after the race. Perhaps you could go now, and I could visit later."

"I'd like to see how Nathan is doing, too," I added.

"Don't forget to take the scrolls, and ask your father if I could have the books of Joel and Daniel."

"Can I tell him you'll come and visit?"

"Sure." Daniel closed his eyes, and I trudged back to my room.

"God, give me patience," I prayed.

CHAPTER 58

T HE NEXT DAY, after putting Shira down for a nap, I studied Daniel's directions. My father's house didn't seem that difficult to find. While I didn't care about meeting Brutus again, I couldn't wait to see Nathan. Fond memories returned of the day Jesus healed him from being tongue-tied.

Mari hugged me. "I'll be praying."

I closed my eyes. "Thank you."

She walked me to the front door, and I set off, following the same road Daniel and I traveled three weeks earlier. Once I reached Caesarea, I came to the area where the wealthy lived, and I searched for the two-story villa that matched Daniel's description. I walked down the cobblestone street lined with flowers, water fountains, and statues. When I found it, I climbed the steps and knocked, still not sure what I would say.

When the door opened, Nathan greeted me. "Shale!"

He recognized me immediately. I reached out to hug my half-brother, noting what a handsome young man he was.

"Come in, sis, come in."

Nathan never called me sis before—of course, most of the time we lived in Galilee, he couldn't talk. He took me to the living room that was pleasantly decorated and pointed, "Have a seat on the sofa, and I'll get Dad. He'll be delighted to see you."

I hoped he was right. I double-clutched my bag and looked around. The décor reminded me of his estate in Galilee, but was more lavish in appearance.

I heard my father approaching. When he entered the room, the resemblance to his twenty-first-century counterpart was striking. He looked no different in the first century from four years earlier. In fact, the toga suited him well.

His voice boomed through the room. "Shale, what brings you to Caesarea?"

He embraced me warmly, and I showed him the bag. "I brought you something."

"Did you bring my scrolls?"

"Yes, I did."

"Bless you, Shale. You are an angel. I wasn't sure how I would get back to retrieve them."

I handed him the bag, and he laid the contents out on the table. There must have been thirty parchments. He pulled one out and opened it. Then he put it back. His eyes turned to me. "Thank you for bringing these."

"You're welcome."

He continued to peruse the ancient books, some more than others as if taking a trip down memory lane.

"I wanted to ask if Daniel could have two of them. He became quite fond of the books of Joel and Daniel."

"Yes, of course. I'd be delighted for Daniel to keep those two." After a brief search, he handed them to me. "Did he come with you to Caesarea?"

"Yes. As well as Mari and Judd—oh, before I forget, I have something else to give you." I retrieved the wedding invitation from the bag and handed it to him.

He opened it and smiled. "I always thought that might be a possibility." He closed the invitation and set it on the table. "Let them know

I'm looking forward to attending."

"I will," I promised.

"And Daniel, what is he doing?"

"Tending to business—he's a hard-working man." I wouldn't tell him about the chariot race.

"And how are you doing?"

I noticed Nathan was listening. "Well, I'm taking care of a young child who lost her family. Daniel and I are betrothed, but we haven't set a wedding date yet."

"Wonderful," my father said.

An awkward silence followed. "Make sure you give those scrolls to Daniel—it's a wedding gift."

"Have you read them?"

My father smiled. "Not enough time."

I changed the subject. "Did you ever get a chance to meet Jesus on one of your trips to Jerusalem?"

"I go to Jerusalem a couple of times each month, but I never got to meet the rabbi. I should have made the time. Now it's too late."

I nodded. "Of course, I've heard reports that Yeshua has been seen alive since the crucifixion."

My father laughed. "Yes, I've heard that, too, but the reports don't come from reliable sources."

I couldn't resist stating my opinion even at the risk of getting into an argument. "So you discount the five hundred eyewitness reports out of Galilee."

Brutus cocked his head. "That's unofficial."

I bit my lip. "What would make it official?"

"I'd like to talk to someone who was there."

"When Daniel visits, you can speak to him."

"Daniel heard him?"

I nodded.

My father crossed his arms over his chest as if surprised. "That's quite remarkable." Then he quickly changed the subject. "Shale, it's wonderful seeing you. You've grown into a beautiful young woman. I wish I could visit with you longer, but I have an important meeting. How long are you going to be in town?"

I tucked a lock of hair behind my ear. How should I respond? "Daniel said he would get by to visit you soon, but I don't know when."

"I would love that. Then we'll have more time to talk about these things. My wife, Lydia, is an excellent cook. We could have you over for dinner."

I still found it hard to believe he had a secret wife in Caesarea when he was married to Scylla. "I look forward to that."

His eyes darted about the room. "Well, I must be going, as much as I would like to stay and talk."

"One other question."

"What's that, Shale?"

"Who bought the estate in Galilee?"

"Oh, I don't know. Someone took care of that for me."

"I see," I said.

Brutus gathered the scrolls together and put them back in the bag. "I must be going. Why don't you stay and visit with Nathan."

I smiled. "I can stay a little while."

My father hugged me again and took the scrolls to another room.

"Where are you staying?" he asked when he returned.

"With Theophilus."

"Oh, excellent. Glad to hear you're acquaintances."

"Yes."

Brutus headed to the door and paused briefly. "It's good to see you, Shale. Come back and visit anytime."

I watched through the window as he walked down the street. He hadn't changed a bit.

I turned my attention to Nathan. "Have you shared with our father about Jesus?"

"Oh, yes. Many times. Dad listens, but that's it."

We talked for the better part of an hour, reminiscing about our time together in Galilee, meeting Jesus at the Decapolis, and the miracle the King performed on Nathan. My half-brother would still be tongue-tied if Daniel and I had not snuck Nathan out of the house in the middle of the night.

As I left, I was assured of Nathan's love for Jesus. That made the trip worthwhile, but his words rang in my ears all the way back to Theophilus' house. "Dad listens, but that's it." What would it take for my father to really listen?

CHAPTER 59

T WO WEEKS LATER

THE DAY arrived—the day I hoped would never come. I arose early and prepared Daniel a light breakfast, one of his favorites—home-made bread with hummus, figs, olives, and dates, as well as a fresh filet of fish from the Mediterranean, topped off with pure grape juice.

Daniel sat across the table from me. No one else was awake. His appearance was so different from when we left Jerusalem. His beard was full, and after five weeks of training, his body tone and muscle gain amazed me.

He was more quiet than usual, and I was afraid to say too much. I didn't want to take away his focus for the race.

"Can I say the blessing?" I asked.

Daniel smiled. "That would be great."

We bowed our heads. "Thank you, Jesus, for the blessings you give us. Help Daniel to win this race for your glory. I pray the prize money could help Cynisca's father to pay off outstanding debts as a result of Daniel's actions and compensate Justinian.

"Lord, I pray for Daniel's protection. I pray that it will be a clean race. Help me to trust you for his safety. Also, please help Daniel to learn about his father. Thank you for this food that you've given to us in abundance. Amen."

I watched as Daniel poured enough servings on his plate for three people—enough to feed a giraffe. I'd never seen him eat so much as he had eaten since he began training.

He was wearing his usual toga. I wanted to see him in his racing attire, whatever that was. I'd have to wait until the race.

"Will you change before you get to the hippodrome?"

Daniel laughed. "I won't change until the very last minute. Remember, it's a surprise. No one knows I'm racing, and we don't want to give a hint.

"Tariq has no idea, and we don't want to risk the Romans coming after me. It's not that I think they would, but I have a sense of uneasiness with them. Once the Romans see how excited the spectators are, they won't want to capture me until afterward."

"What about after the race?"

Daniel reassured me. "Justinian dropped the charges. All I'm concerned about is winning the race."

What would happen if Daniel lost? I couldn't go there. He had to win. God was with him, and I needed to trust God.

Daniel finished his meal, and I walked over and wrapped my arms around him.

"Daniel, I have faith God will help you to win. May he be with you and give you strength."

Daniel lifted my face to his and kissed me. "Do you remember where I told you to sit? Two seats, one for you and one for Shira, have been reserved."

"Shira and I will be there, but I haven't convinced Mari and Judd to join us."

Daniel shrugged. "I wouldn't expect them to come. They're

working on their wedding plans. It's not important to them. Don't take it personally."

I clasped my hands. "I know, but it would have been nice to have their support."

Daniel stepped back. "I must be going."

I walked him to the door, trying not to be clingy. I hoped for another embrace, but he stepped outside and kept going. "Shalom, my darling," he said as he walked away.

"Goodbye," I whispered under my breath. My betrothed never said that to me before. I loved the way it sounded.

CHAPTER 60

A FTER BREAKFAST, I dressed Shira in a new blue toga Mari made for her, and we headed into town—along with thousands of others.

Shira pointed. "Auntie, look at all the people."

We had a long walk since the hippodrome was on the south side. Walking with a three-year-old among such a mob scared me. I held Shira's hand tightly and warned her. "You must hold my hand. I don't want to lose you."

We passed through the downtown gates as hordes descended upon the heart of the city. The festive air reminded me of attending my high school football games, but they were always dull.

Soon we came to a bazaar that lined the façade along the harbor. The sun streamed through the clouds casting light and dark shadows over the Mediterranean. Several fishing boats anchored along the shore attracted birds hoping for an easy meal. Many fishermen had secured their prize spot to sell the "fresh catch of the day."

Shira pointed to several children gathered around a booth. "Can we go over there?"

As we approached, I saw an extensive collection of children's chariots, horses, and dolphins. Clothing was also on sale that I assumed were replicas of the charioteers' team outfits.

Shira pulled on my hand. "Can you get me something?"

"Maybe one small thing."

Shira's eyes fell on the dolphins. She leaned over to examine them. I picked one out. "Do you know what it is?"

"No"

"It's a dolphin. It swims in the ocean."

"Oh."

"But I don't think we should get it."

Shira looked disappointed. "Why not?"

"What if you drop it? It's breakable. Why don't we get something that's made out of wood, like one of the horses?"

We edged over to where they were, and she pointed at a baby horse. "I like that one."

I picked up the wooden horse and placed it in her hand. She turned it over. "Is it a girl?"

I chuckled. "Yes, it's a girl."

Satisfied, she handed it back to me. "Can you get it?"

"Sure." I only had a small amount of money Mari gave me for the day, but enough for one purchase. After paying, we joined the growing sea of people. Daniel's race would be one of the first ones since he was racing with only two horses.

I heard music coming from somewhere and looked around. A parade was approaching the forum, slowly making its way along the cobblestone road. At the head of the ceremony was a dignitary, followed by charioteers. They looked like the teams as they wore colored tunics with sleeves that were red, white, blue, and green.

Shira leaned on my arm. "There's Daniel."

I squinted to see. How did Shira spot him so quickly? Was that him? He was shaved. I didn't think he saw us, even though we both waved. His attention was diverted elsewhere.

Singers, musicians, clowns, mimes, tumblers, belly dancers, and people dressed in strange costumes followed the teams.

Daniel didn't tell me this was such a celebration. I found myself getting caught up in the excitement—enough that I could put thoughts of defeat or death out of my mind temporarily.

The patrons entered through a different gate than the participants, so we watched as the parade disappeared into the hippodrome. I was anxious to get inside.

Shira jumped up and down. "I can't wait to see Daniel."

The trumpet sounded, and my heart skipped. I panicked that if Daniel raced first, we might not make it inside in time.

At last, the line started moving, and we made progress. Once inside, the interior took my breath away. The roar was deafening, followed by the blowing of the trumpet.

I didn't know what to expect, but part of the fanfare leading up to the first race included the charioteers and horses taking a lap around the track. That way the patrons could see the teams before the races started. I was glad since that would give us a chance to find our seats.

I saw in front of the track at ground level the box seats for high-ranking officials. Daniel said there were a few seats reserved for friends and relatives of the racers behind the bureaucrats. As the charioteers progressed ceremonially around the track, the noise ramped up louder.

I pulled Shira along. "Hurry. The races will be starting soon."

We stumbled, and a disgruntled man shouted profanities at us, but I ignored him. I finally carried Shira thinking it would be easier. She clasped her hands around my neck, digging her toy horse into my back.

It took me half a second to find Daniel in the ceremonial procession. Most of the gladiators were racing with four horses, but some had two. I didn't know Tariq's team colors. I should have asked.

Horses draped with banners led the full complement of teams. The trumpet blew louder as the oval dirt track baked in the sun. Fortunately, a fresh, salty breeze from the ocean made it tolerable.

The team competitors looked fierce, hardened, and determined. I was too biased to think they were more intimidating than Daniel. He'd trained hard for five weeks and won many races previously. I prayed, nonetheless. "Please, God, help Daniel to win."

Several of the charioteers waved at the fans, and the crowd roared back. When I glanced at the other end of the hippodrome, I could see men gesturing with their hands as they stood in front of overcrowded tables. Transactions were being carried out at a frenzied pace. Something told me they must be placing bets.

I focused on finding our seats knowing the first race would start shortly. A few magistrates were still arriving, and I figured the festivities wouldn't begin until the VIPs were seated. The dignitaries were dressed in exquisite togas. I was surprised that as many women filled the seats as men.

Behind the upper echelon stood at least a dozen soldiers decked out in Roman accouterments. Helmets with red fans on top, spears pointed at the sky, and colorful red and white skirts that reached their knees spoke of authority. Their appearance was enough to intimidate anyone bold enough to confront them. Fear crept into my thoughts...what if?

We made it to the area reserved for guests of participants. I set Shira in the chair beside me. The dignitaries were below us. To our right was the entrance for top officials. A man in a purple robe wearing a crown descended the steps and sat on the throne. Those around bid him the utmost respect.

That must be Pontius Pilate. The spectacle was stunning, but I would have preferred that it was only a movie. At last, the horses finished their final turn on the track and cantered to the starting line.

In the center of the forum were dozens of marble statues. One tall figure must have been of Caesar. His statue seemed to be on every street corner. Next to him mounted high on two poles were a row of dolphins. I didn't know their purpose.

The horses, chariots, and drivers disappeared through a large gate at the far end of the hippodrome. The trumpet sounded again. The racing fans leaped from their seats waving handkerchiefs.

Over the clamor, a man on a loudspeaker announced names and teams. "Our first charioteer is Tariq Naser of the Green Team. He has won twenty-nine straight races."

He came out and took a bow, and the multitude roared.

After a respectable pause to allow the fans to settle back into their seats, the announcer said the second name. "Welcome back, Daniel Sperling, charioteer for the White Team."

A stunned silence followed. Slowly, a few started clapping. Soon the whole hippodrome erupted in cheers and applause.

Since I was sitting so close to the dignitaries, I saw concern cross some of their faces. A barrage of activity followed. Several guards ran over to question their superiors.

I turned my attention to Daniel who took a bow, waved at the fans, and then walked back through the gate.

His appearance created a stir among the Romans. Several approached the man sitting in the currilis, who I presumed to be Pontius Pilate, but he waved them off. Oh, if only I could have heard that conversation.

Whispers abounded. "That's the Jew, isn't it? I thought he died in his last race."

More voices gossiped. "Is it really Daniel? He doesn't look like a Jew. He looks like a Roman. That can't be him."

I heard a man's voice. "Looks like Pontius Pilate is going to let him race."

So the man on the throne dressed in purple was Pontius Pilate.

"Who is he racing against?" someone asked. "I hope it's Tariq Naser. He's won too many races. Someone needs to beat him."

The banter continued, and I sat frozen, unable to look at who was talking. My throat was so dry, I couldn't speak.

More names were announced until all the names of the charioteers and their teams were recognized. I followed everyone's gaze to the entrance. Two riders on horses carrying banners led two chariot teams. One was the White Team, and the other was the Green Team. I recognized Daniel. Tariq was racing for the Green Team. This was it—at least we would get it over with without having to wait.

Suddenly people began to chant. "Daniel, Daniel, Daniel."

Pontius Pilate stood holding a handkerchief in his right hand. The designated person lined the horses up to start. Tariq was on the inside, and Daniel was on the outside. The trumpet sounded again.

LORILYN ROBERTS

Pilate dropped the handkerchief, and the chariots took off in blazing speed leaving behind a wake of dust.

CHAPTER 61

THE ROARING CROWD and horses' hooves pounding the dirt track shook the stadium. Tariq viscously whipped his horses. It didn't take long for disgust to settle in my stomach.

The overwhelming truth consumed me that the guy was a cheater—a Nephilim from the future. He came here and made a mockery of the races.

What had he done to Daniel's father? He was a hybrid without a conscience, without a soul. I felt stomach contents threatening to disgorge. I slumped over pressing my arms into my midriff.

The two chariots sped down the track neck and neck into the first turn. Daniel lost ground on the outside, and Tariq took the lead. Daniel thrust his reins.

Tariq glanced behind him. Seeing Daniel gaining, the Nephilim whipped his horses, and I heard their cries. The animals were at the mercy of a demonic tyrant.

Daniel caught Tariq at the turn, but Tariq wouldn't let him pass on the inside. Daniel tried to go around him on the outside, and he lost ground.

Tariq cut the turn sharper. Daniel dropped back. He'd have to find a way to get around Tariq on the inside.

The first metal cut-out dolphin fell.

Shira grabbed my arm. "Auntie, look."

"Yes, I see." My voice shook.

She noticed. "Are you all right?"

I nodded. I couldn't speak.

Daniel charged ahead. The chariots zoomed around the turn at the far end. Daniel trailed. Could he sneak up on the next straightaway?

One of Tariq's horses took a misstep. Daniel seized the moment. He plunged ahead of Tariq on the inside.

When Tariq caught up, he hurled his whip at Daniel. The unexpected attack left Daniel wobbling. He struggled to regain control. The chariot lurched sideways.

I held my breath. When my betrothed recovered, he whipped the reins once more. His horses swooped forward, but Tariq passed him. Daniel maneuvered around the turn tighter this time. Could he catch Tariq? I couldn't watch.

The spectators chanted, "Daniel!"

Daniel exited the turn behind Tariq but inched closer. Perspiration beaded on my forehead, and I felt faint, leaned over, and vomited on the stone pavement. Shira looked away, disgusted. No one else noticed —they were too busy watching the race.

Tariq pulled ahead going into the next turn.

A second dolphin fell. Five more laps.

Daniel crept up on the outside. Again, the hybrid creature slashed his whip on Daniel's back. How was Daniel going to get around him without being attacked? That couldn't be legal. I covered my eyes. Five more laps to go.

"Is Daniel going to lose?" Shira asked.

"Pray," I urged.

The gladiators hurtled down the track, but Daniel still trailed. I shook my head. The Nephilim was demonic. Making the turns so fast, one would think the centrifugal force would sling him through the air.

Daniel kept losing ground on the turns. Then he would have to make up the distance on the straightaway. If Daniel could pass Tariq on the inside, he could win. Daniel's horses were faster.

The excitement reached a fever pitch. Most of the fans stood at their seats and waved banners and hankies. Fortunately, we were in the front, or unfortunately. If something happened, I'd see it.

Daniel and Tariq rounded the turn and entered the straightaway. Daniel once again came within a horse's head but couldn't pass. They galloped into the next corner.

A third dolphin fell. Four more laps to go.

The thunderous roar shook the stadium. The two chariots passed us. I shouted, "Go, Daniel."

Daniel was pushing the limits of the horses. Unexpectedly, he slipped past Tariq. Could he maintain it through the next turn? Daniel went low so Tariq couldn't overtake him on the inside. Tariq almost careened into Daniel. I held my breath. Both chariots wobbled, but Daniel charged ahead.

The crowd roared, "Daniel, Daniel!"

Tariq lashed the whip on the horses. Again, I heard their cries. They ran harder. Tariq shot even with Daniel.

"No," I cried. "Don't pass him."

The Nephilim struck Daniel with the whip. He jerked, swaying back and forth.

"No," I shouted. I raised my fists in the air. "No, you"—I stopped when Shira looked up at me. "God, please help Daniel," I prayed.

The hybrid creature whacked the whip again at Daniel, and the belt wrapped around Daniel's neck. Gasps came from the spectators.

The trumpet sounded. Was it over? Daniel struggled to extricate himself. He managed to get the whip off before entering the next turn.

Tariq, enraged, pursued him.

"God," I cried.

The fourth dolphin fell. Three more laps to go.

Daniel regained control pivoting into the turn. Tariq smacked the whip hard. Instead of hitting Daniel, the cord got stuck between the spokes. Tariq jerked forward, almost falling. Daniel surged ahead.

I waved my hands. "Go!"

Then I noticed Tariq's whip was on the ground. "Thank you, Jesus."

The fifth dolphin fell. Two more laps to go. If only this were the last lap. If only.

Daniel plunged forward, flashing the reins. Tariq thrust ahead nipping at Daniel's back wheels. They sped into the next turn, and Daniel cut sharply. Any sharper, he would have overturned.

Daniel's opponent again tried to plow into Daniel's biga. They came out of the corner and hit the straightaway. Daniel's chariot seesawed before leveling out. They entered the final turn with Daniel in front. Tariq was a hands-breadth behind.

The sixth dolphin fell. One more lap to go.

Tariq snuck up from behind. His front chariot wheel was even with the back of Daniel's. Then I saw what Tariq was doing. There was a sharp spike on his wheel. Could he saw off the spoke of Daniel's biga?

They entered the corner with Daniel leading. Tariq bore down. A horse's head separated them. Daniel pulled out in front. The distance widened, but as my beloved neared the next turn, Tariq gained ground.

"Please, God," I cried, "protect Daniel's wheel."

They passed in front. Too much dust hampered my view as the horses went into the far turn. Daniel stayed tight. Tariq was desperate. Thankfully he didn't have the whip.

They came out onto the straightaway. Tariq pressed even harder, but his horses were tiring. He couldn't torture them anymore. Daniel blazed forward into the final corner, and I held my breath. The spectators stood on their feet waving their hands and shouting, "Daniel!"

The racers pounded the track, and the horses stormed toward the finish line. Tariq made one last attempt to catch Daniel, but his efforts were futile.

The last dolphin fell, and I joined in the cheers. My hero won.

Then, momentarily, I didn't see either chariot. Seconds later, they were back. I saw the chariots and the horses, but where was Daniel? I glanced at Tariq's chariot. Where was the wicked one?

The riotous crowd seemed to notice something was amiss. A hush fell over the hippodrome. I peered through the settling dirt on the turn and straightaway. Where were they? Had they gone into the center island? My heart pounded.

"Where is Daniel?" Shira asked.

I stared at the unmanned chariots. "I don't know."

Shira pointed. "Look, Auntie."

Distracted and upset, I didn't want Shira bothering me. I ignored her, straining to see down the far side of the track. I glanced at the Roman socialites—some stood, gazing at the chariots.

Shira shook my arm. "Auntie, look. There's a dog."

I peeled my eyes away from the track to see what Shira was pointing at. "My God," I cried. I touched my hand to my heart. "Much-Afraid, is that you?"

She ran toward me, wagging her tail, avoiding where I threw up. "Shale, you've left such a mess."

"It is you!"

CHAPTER 62

From *Seventh Dimension – The Howling, Book 6*

My horses, Mosi and Oni, took the lead. I could taste victory—sweet victory. They could run like gazelles when I let them. Just one more lap. I heard the roaring crowd chanting my name.

"Run!" I shouted. We passed Tariq, and a scowl covered his brow. He slapped the reins at me in a last-ditch attempt to yank me off the chariot, but I was a seasoned racer now. No chance of that happening.

We rounded the first turn, and I kept my distance. I didn't want any more trickery or sleight of hand—like Tariq sawing off my wheel. The other racers had been knocked out or given up. Only Tariq was left but dropping farther behind. The finish line called my name.

Less than a minute later, I threw up my hands triumphantly. I flicked the reins to slow the horses, and the crowd drummed their feet in the stands. Celebratory flowers littered the hippodrome as the fickleness of the spectators never ceased to amaze me. The Romans believed I was a criminal, and a Jewish one at that. Now that I was the winner—

making risky gamblers wealthy— the crowd was on my side. Besides, everybody loved an underdog.

I relaxed for a moment in all the accolades. The Roman authorities wouldn't dare arrest me in front of the fans. The last thing Pontius Pilate wanted was a riot on his hands and be called back to Rome.

Now was my turn for sweet revenge. What had Tariq done to my father? And that time traveler who terrified Shale at the inn, Tariq must know who sent him.

I searched for my betrothed and Shira behind Pontius Pilate and his entourage, but I couldn't find them. Out of nowhere, I saw Much-Afraid scurrying across the racetrack. What was Shale's dog doing here? Horses and chariots were everywhere. Fear that she might get trampled made me panic.

As I was scheming how to help her, a mysterious cloud settled over the racetrack. Amid the fanfare, I heard someone whisper, "Daniel, the race isn't over."

Of course, the race was over. I looked around. Who said that, but I couldn't see anyone in the fog.

The noise of squeaking wheels and cheering crowds began to fade into the distance. When the haze lifted, I saw an open scroll, and Tariq and I were racing again—this time among the stars.

I head a familiar, angry voice. "Michael, he's finished the race."

"Not so fast," the authoritarian voice replied.

The forgotten event happened on my way from Hurva Square to the first century—the argument between these two invisible creatures. I arrived at the inn with an injury to my forehead and couldn't remember how it happened. Dr. Luke bandaged it—the first time I met the impressive doctor.

"Time is an illusion until God's appointed times," Michael replied.

The angry voice retorted, "I'm outnumbered two to one. Isn't that like God, to stack the odds in his favor?"

"The Lord rebuke you. No one is taken until God's appointed

time." Michael's answer seemed to settle the matter, and an uneasy silence followed.

Suddenly, my biga became unstable as Tariq appeared beside me in his chariot. He smiled, flipped his reins, and took off ahead of me.

"The race is over," I shouted to Tariq. The race had to be over. I won, despite what Michael said. The powerful angel must be referring to something else. I tried to catch Tariq, but everything was a blur until the earth came into view. A man appeared galloping on a white horse across the planet. While he was far away, he was also near. As the horse cantered, the rider's hair rippled around his smooth face. His narrow brown eyes matched his skin tone. Handsome, charismatic, and mysterious, he held a bow with no arrow. He was poised and self-assured. I continued to watch as reptilian-like hands placed a crown on his head. The rider turned his eyes toward me. He mouthed, "Mine," and galloped across the Middle East.

A second man riding a red horse appeared. I recognized him when I saw his face. He had become more powerful, more famous, and more profane. He held a sword in his hand and seized control of the king-doms of the world. He took great delight waving the weapon as he galloped across Europe.

A third horse followed. The black stallion's rider held a pair of balances, and cries of mourning reached into the heavens. Burning grasslands crisscrossed the former breadbaskets of the world as the black horse turned into death. The rider had grown into a monster—deceptive, cunning, and evil.

Soon a green horse appeared. Whoever rode him was longer human. He was possessed, and wretched creatures followed him. The earth, wounded, hung limply in space. Death lingered over the planet and clung to me like poison.

I saw killers roaming the earth in the guise of beasts, plagues, wars, and famine. After much sadness from seeing so much suffering, I turned my eyes toward the heavens and saw an open door among the stars.

Through the door, I saw an altar. Under the platform were souls without heads wearing white robes. A heavenly counter was counting upwards with a number so significant I didn't know how to read it.

I heard in the seventh dimension one of the headless souls ask, "How much longer?"

"Rest a little longer," an angel said.

A holy quietness followed until a tsunami-like wave exploded. Shockwaves battered the solar system, and a blood-stained moon cast shadows over the earth's surface. The sun became blackened, and a cold wave of icicles clung to my bare skin.

Balls of fire fell upon the earth. The mountains shook, the islands split, and the seas roared. The earth reeled like a drunkard. Terrified earth-dwellers cried out to the rocks and mountains, "Fall on us. Hide us from the face of him who sits on the throne and from his wrath."

As quickly as it all began, the open door closed and a seal was stamped on the scroll so it couldn't be opened again except by the King.

A scarred hand touched my forehead. "Remember."

NEXT BOOK IN SEVENTH DIMENSION SERIES

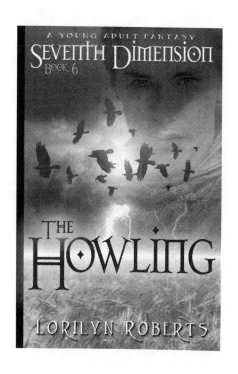

ALSO BY LORILYN ROBERTS

LorilynRoberts.com

Children of Dreams

As an Audiobook

Tails and Purrs for the Heart and Soul

As an Audiobook

THE DONKEY AND THE KING
(A Story of Redemption)

Lorilyn Roberts
Illustrated by Linda S. DiFranco

Look for the hidden word "good" on every page.

The Donkey and the King: A Story of Redemption

"Wonderful story with positive Christian values. Loved the illustrations. It's a hit with my kids!"

—"Goodreads" reader

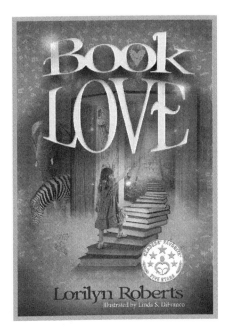

Young readers become world leaders.

Book Love

"Book Love is beautiful inside and out. Roberts uses a child to teach children the love of books and it works beautifully. This book is a must for elementary classrooms and libraries. I highly recommend Book Love by Lorilyn Roberts if you have a child wanting to learn to read."

—Joy Hannabass, Readers' Favorite Reviewer

SEVENTH DIMENSION SERIES

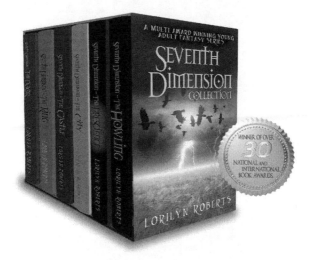

LorilynRoberts.com

Seventh Dimension - The Door, Book 1

As an Audiobook

Seventh Dimension - The King, Book 2

As an Audiobook

Seventh Dimension - The Castle, Book 3

As an Audiobook

Seventh Dimension - The City, Book 4

As an Audiobook

Seventh Dimension - The Prescience, Book 5

Audiobook coming

Seventh Dimension - The Howling, Book 6

As an Audiobook

ADDITIONAL BOOKS

LorilynRoberts.com

Food for Thought Cookbook

Seventh Dimension Devotional Series: Am I Okay,God?

Born-Again Jews - companion book to *Seventh Dimension - The King* - coming

ABOUT THE AUTHOR

 When not writing books, Lorilyn provides closed captioning for television. She adopted her two daughters from Nepal and Vietnam as a single mother and lives in Florida with many rescued cats and a dog.

Lorilyn has won over thirty-five awards for the *Seventh Dimension Series*. She graduated Magna Cum Laude from the University of Alabama with a bachelor's degree in social sciences/humanities that included an emphasis in Biblical history and on-site study in Jerusalem. She received her Master of Arts in Creative Writing from Perelandra College. In her spare time, she is also a ham radio operator. KO4LBS.

Visit Lorilyn's website at LorilynRoberts.com to learn more about her books.

If you enjoyed *Seventh Dimension - The Prescience, Book 5*, please consider posting a short review on your favorite book website. Reviews help authors a great deal, and they are the best way to spread the news about a book. Thank you for your interest and support.